TIME
IN MY
POCKET

GINA DEWINK

Copyright ©2017 by Gina Dewink
All rights reserved. Published in the United States.
ISBN 978-0-9989877-1-2 (paperback)
ISBN 978-0-9989877-0-5 (ebook)

Library of Congress 2017910963

www.ginadewink.com

Book cover design by Alchemy Book Covers
www.alchemybookcovers.com

Book layout and formatting by Gessert Books
www.gessertbooks.com

For Mom, my best friend and moral advisor

ACKNOWLEDGMENTS

Making up stories has been a part of my life since the early days of traveling across the Midwest in a station wagon driven by my dad. So first, I must thank my parents, Paul and Mary Depuydt, for forcing boredom upon us, as well as my five siblings for being my first (captive) audience. Among my siblings, special thanks go to my oldest sister, LaVonne, for being my first reader, supporter, researcher and adviser through the process of self-publishing. As well as Sondra and Nicole for giving me and my project invaluable time and connections.

Special thanks, obviously, must go to my partner and best friend, Craig. He is the love of my life and the terrific father of our two zany children, Lenora and Calvin. Without their inspiration, this book would not be.

My team of readers, proofreaders, editors and supporters also deserves a huge thank you. Vicki Snyder, Brent Hilgart and Rebecca Hoffman, thank you for responding to all my random texts and brainstorms! Your input made this a better book. Tracy Loberg, you are literally in the book. Because you were there for it all, and I can't imagine it any other way. Kathleen May and Sandra Pysher, without your edits, I would be embarrassed my words were out in the world. You made my story go from Word doc to novel. Thank you.

Additional thanks to my cover designer, Keri Knutson of Alchemy Book Covers, for enduring my hundreds of edits, and coming up with a brilliant design, and to Phillip Gessert, for the beautiful book interior. I thank Amanda Meidl for being the voice of my audio book, as well as for working with James Malouf tireless hours in the recording booth. Thank you for bringing my words to life!

*Is all that we see or seem
But a dream within a dream?*
EDGAR ALLAN POE

CHAPTER 1

THE RHEUMATOID RUSSIAN

GRAMPS STABBED HIS fork into the rye bread and sawed with a steak knife, his hand trembling. I'd come to learn he always ate his sandwich with a fork and knife. Eighty-three years and he still had his faculties intact. I was banking on that meaning good genes passed on to me.

A white blob formed in the corner of his wrinkled mouth. When he lifted his fork, he looked me in the eye. I looked away, glancing around the home. There was a smell—unidentifiable. There was a sadness—like everyone here knew the end was near. I read a sign hanging in the hallway: *Sunny Ridge, Where Life Can Sunset Peacefully*. I looked back at Gramps. I still wasn't sure he belonged here. His cloudy eyes were inspecting my face. The traces of a thick head of black hair were apparent in a horseshoe around his head.

I adjusted Jakey in my lap, his chubby toddler limbs limp from sleep.

Gramps finished chewing and continued, "When I wake up in the morning, my mind is an enormous gymnasium with shining floors." He stretched his hand out in front of him. It was still clutching his fork. "This gymnasium is just being swept and mopped up for the new day's activities to begin. And as the sunlight filters in…" He paused to jeer at his own words and look up. "…a trickle of ping pong balls is dropped from a single hole in the ceiling. Those sons a bitches bounce and jag and ricochet offa each other. And as my consciousness takes hold, millions are dropped. The noise is deafening." He set his fork and knife down with a clank. "Each ping pong ball is *one thought* in my giant, gymnasium of a mind." He finished, holding up his pointer finger. Letting his hand drop, he took a drink of water, fizzing from Alka-Seltzer. "With this part-blessing-part-curse, comes a strange knowledge—the ability to know when others *also* live with this condition."

Looking away from his stare, I frowned when my eyes met an elderly woman shuffling across the linoleum floor. I recognized my daughter's light brown hair bobbing behind the communal sofa and, with my mom-radar quieted, tried to focus on Gramps again.

"When I first heard about you," he said, "your off sense of humor and your hippie job, I jumped to the conclusion that you weren't one of us. But behold! I saw that cluster behind your eyes. I believe you refer to it as being an *intellectual*... But I just call it too many damn balls." He appeared amused with his own words.

I knew he wanted a smile, but I couldn't muster one. "I've always just called that being a woman."

He snickered. "Well, I certainly ain't no woman." He picked up his fork and knife again, severing off another bite of his lunch.

I had known Gramps for the past few years, and he had made it well-known that he was someone worth knowing. He was always more than happy to list the reasons he was, and I quote, *remarkable*. Because of some big family disagreement back in the eighties, my mother had removed us from his life. I grew up not knowing who my grandparents were. Later in life and pregnant with my first, I'd felt the need to reconnect with the part of our family my mother had taken away. Strange how being pregnant had made all of my normal emotions radioactive. The need to connect had been strong and backed by no reasoning whatsoever. But years later, with the every-other-week commitment I'd made to visit Gramps, I was questioning those strong emotions that had landed me here.

Especially since the divorce that had left me with partial custody of two kids under age four, and a last name forever linking me to my stupid ex-husband, Doug Anderson.

A murmur of activity made its way over to our table. I saw my Jules running at us, singing so loud it was more of a shout than music, "Have I not commanded you be strong and courageous! Do not be terrified! For the word of God will be with you for-ever, for-ever, wherever you may go. Hey! Hey! Hey!"

Gramps chuckled. "Who put a quarter in her today?"

Jules was still yell-singing the verse over and over as we attempted to continue talking so I just shrugged.

"I thought you weren't religious?" he yelled.

"We're not," I said in a flat tone. "But apparently Doug is now."

"Forever, forever, wherever you may go! Hey, hey, hey!" she finished again.

"That's enough now." I heard my tone's annoyance. So did Gramps.

He stooped in his chair to look into her angelic, three-year-old face. "Where'd you learn that song, little one?"

Jules had gotten her hair in a messy knot and I saw the shine of snot under her nose as she answered. "It's a church song, Gramps. Do you go to church?" She started picking at the top button on his collared shirt.

He opened his mouth to launch into a long history of the Jewish religion, I presumed, but Jules declared, "I want a popsicle!" Kids had a way of speaking their minds that always seemed to catch adults off guard. And at that, Jules was a pro.

Gramps chuckled, shook his head and smiled. Using the table and back of the chair, he hoisted himself up and groaned as he stood. "I'll take her to the cafeteria."

"Yay!" Jules yelped, hopping up and down.

He looked back at me. "You should go see Valentina now."

I knew his words were not just a suggestion. "Is she having a good day?"

Gramps nodded and took Jules by the hand. "I believe she even has something for you."

I thought I caught a glimpse of concern in his eye. "For me?" I didn't hide my shock.

Gramps was already being pulled along by my rambunctious preschooler, and neither heard nor cared about my rhetorical question.

Heaving Jakey further up on my shoulder, I silently thanked him for taking his nap in my arms and not running around like a hyper ferret per usual. I followed the signs hanging above my head in the hallway to the room I knew to be Valentina's. I passed a flyer proclaiming, *2011 Sunny Ridge Dance: Tonight's Gonna Be a Good, Good Night!* My cynicism was showing as I pondered which was a worse offense—the nursing home trying to be trendy by using a Black Eyed Peas song, or the nursing home being an entire year too late to jump on that bandwagon.

A nurse saw me peek into the empty room. The smell was stronger in there. All of Valentina's things were gone.

"Looking for Ms. Ivanov?" the young nurse asked.

I nodded, adjusting my backpack and heavy toddler.

"I'm sorry to be the one to tell you, but they moved her to hospice yesterday," she said, pointing in the direction I should go.

Hospice. Yikes.

I glanced back the way I had come, wondering how long Gramps would be able to handle Jules. Hoping a popsicle was really happening, I made my way to Valentina's new room.

Jules referred to Valentina as the "saggy ol' lady who talked funny." She had once asked me if Valentina was her grandma. But I'd been too late in reconnecting with Gramps to ever meet Grammy. Judging from Gramps and his enormous ego, Valentina would have never been his type. But she was just kooky enough to keep him entertained. I'd been told they'd been friends since his first day at Sunny Ridge.

I walked in and was surprised to see Valentina propped up in her chair, facing the door, looking anxious.

"You found me!" she bellowed, electrified by my appearance.

"You really were expecting me?"

"Of course. Sit down." She gestured toward the bed the best she could with minimal muscle mass left. "We don't have much time before nurse comes back."

I did as she instructed, careful not to disturb the floppy sleeper in my arms. I couldn't hide my skepticism...or curiosity. "It's so nice to talk to you again. Gramps and I came to chat with you last week, but the nurse said you weren't up to having visitors." My mind delivered images of Valentina thrashing around in her hospital bed, semi-conscious just a week earlier when I'd stopped in. I wondered if her seizures had been the reason she had ended up in hospice.

She strained to lift her fingers in a shushing fashion. "I wanted to go back to Russia. That's all I wanted." Her *w*'s came out sounding like *v*'s, even after so many years in the States. She had once told me how she had come to America when she was eighteen to live with her mother, who had divorced her father. That was long before I was born.

"You wanted to go to Russia when you woke up from your coma?"

"No. Listen. I thought that if I looked in and it worked, that I could go back to Russia and see things. Learn things. I was so lonely here in America." She finally rested her arm.

I tried to understand what she was saying to me, but I was already looking toward the door for the nurse. It seemed like she was having another confused day.

"My neighbor died. That is when this all started. She died and left me *awful*, gray sweater."

I nodded. My forehead scrunched in pity for this aging—and apparently dying—woman in front of me. "Valentina, are you sure you wanted to see me? It's me. Liza Anderson. Joseph Greensburg is my grandfather."

Valentina agreed with violent nods. "Yes! I know that! I'm trying to tell you something very important. Something that will change your life forever."

Her loud voice caused Jakey to stir. I brushed the baby curls off of his forehead. I looked back to the old woman in front of me. "I'm sorry. I'm listening."

"In 1977, I turned forty..."

I cut her off, "Hey, I was born in 1977!"

She winced at my interruption but kept talking. "I had lived a long, sad life already. I was a childless spinster..." she stole a glance at the one-year-old boy in my arms. "Next to me in apartment lived an old Jewish woman. A few days before she was to turn eighty, she knocked on my door. This was odd because though we had talked before, we were not friends." She pointed at me. "Much like you and I."

I squirmed in my spot on her hospital bed.

"I knew her to be named Zizi. She did not look good that day at my door. She handed me a wool sweater and told me she wanted me to have it in case anything should happen to her. I told her I would see her at her birthday party, and she nodded sadly. I think she knew she was going to die."

I furrowed my brow at Valentina.

"But she did not warn me!" She threw her head back in anger. "I spent so many years *hating* Zizi! I do not know if she thought I would be able to figure things out or maybe that I wouldn't even be able to see past myself... I don't know, I don't know, I don't know..." She trailed off, shaking her head with a crazed, pondering look on her face. She snapped back to me. "But it won't be like that with you, Liza. I feel sure you will be able to see past yourself. And I will guide you. You will not be left to die a confused old woman like me."

I set my hand on top of hers. It was bony and cold. "Valentina, I'm sorry, but I'm not sure what you're trying to tell me. I can tell it's important to you."

She jutted out her chin. "I am leaving locket with you when I die. I have chosen you."

There was a long pause. I wasn't sure what she wanted me to say. "You...want to give me a locket?"

"Yes. Zizi left it in the pocket of that damned sweater with only the words of "time travel." I opened it, I looked inside and...and...I lived another life while my body sat here. Rotting. For twenty-nine *megillah* years!" Her foreign pronunciation was so sharp, she had spit.

I shook my head as I thought aloud. "Are you talking about the years you were in a coma?"

"Basi-cally," she said, dragging the word out into four syllables. "I was not here. I was gone...Living in New York. Living as a ten-year-old boy." Her eyes were closed, and she was nodding.

I balked. Leaning forward to see out the door for the nurse, my eyebrow arched to maximum capacity. Shouldn't someone be checking on her? Her breathing was quick and raspy.

When I looked back, Valentina's face held an intense and almost angry stare. "You do not believe me, this I can see. But it does not matter whether you believe or not. It does not matter if you think I am crazy. It does not even matter if you know anything about it...If you can see past yourself, you will just fall into another time."

She put her hand into her pocket. I half expected her to pull out a locket. Instead, she pulled out a note. "This is all I was able to write for you. When I first came back here, I tried to tell everyone what happened, but doctors said it was just a dream. My old, tired mind playing tricks on me. But it was not a dream, Liza...I left." She pointed to a note on her lap. "And now I cannot remember details like before."

Jakey started whining even though his eyes weren't even open yet. I took the note from her and stood.

"Read it," she commanded. "Return here tomorrow with your answer. I do not want it to happen like it did with me. You have children to think about. I am not even giving you locket now because I am afraid you will leave before you know enough."

Jakey was awake. He turned his head and waved at Valentina in a half-asleep daze. Instead of cooing to him or waving back like everyone else, she winced. "Read it and come back tomorrow. If you don't…"

"I'll read it, Valentina. I will." I stuffed the note into my backpack just as the nurse came in.

"And how are we feeling today, V?" she asked Valentina.

"Worried. Very worried."

The nurse was hoisting her out of the chair when I heard the familiar slapping of tiny feet running down the hallway.

"Mom! Maaa-aam!"

"In here!" I called back, poking my head out the door.

In trounced my precocious, exhausting girl. I didn't want her to see or hear Valentina in this state. "I was just saying goodbye," I told her, as she watched the nurse lower Valentina onto her bed. I could hear the crunching of her adult diaper. There was no dignity in aging.

When I stepped over to Valentina, Jakey wriggled to get down out of my arms. "I'm glad we were able to talk today. I promise I will read the note as soon as I get the chance tonight."

Valentina groaned and wrapped her skinny fingers around my wrist. "And you will come back tomorrow. I need to give *it* to you." She gave a sideways glance to the nurse.

"I'll see what I can do. I have patients to meet with tomorrow morning." I leaned in to let Jakey give her a sloppy kiss. At last, she smiled when he open-mouthed her hollow cheek.

"I do hate that it will take you away from these angels…" She was nodding again.

"Oh, they're not always angels," I said, aware Jules was flipping the television on and off over and over behind us.

"Trust me. Blessings. Healthy children are the only blessing in this life."

I couldn't help but pity her once again. I grabbed Jules by the hand and hiked Jakey up on my hip again. "Say goodbye, kids," I told them in my mom voice.

They both waved. Jakey even blew another kiss, the little flirt. But Valentina just looked apprehensive.

In the hall, I saw a nurse standing at a computer station. I stopped, despite the impending meltdown both my children were about to have. "Excuse me. Can you please have an NP or someone check in on her? She seems confused again. She wasn't really making sense." Jules was trying her best to drag me down the hall, yanking my arm and springing back to my body.

The nurse visibly put on her working face. "I think she knows her days are numbered. It's very common for people to exit their coma with a myriad of psychological and physical concerns. Valentina has received personalized care since arriving here. There are very few documented cases of anyone ever recovering this much cognitive and physical strength after so many years in a coma. We know she needs special attention."

Jules pulled my arm harder, and Jakey was attempting to scramble over my shoulder. "Okay...thank you."

I managed to wiggle my cell phone out of my pocket and check the time. "Crap," I mumbled.

"Crap!" Jules repeated. But I didn't even have time to care.

"We have to get going or mommy will be late again."

I REALIZED THE note from Valentina was still in the backpack hours later. Through the kids' chaos, traffic and in and out of those damned car seats, I hadn't even had a chance to open it. Valentina's words echoed in my mind most of the evening. But between fighting the kids to eat and getting them to go to bed, it was no more than fleeting curiosity.

As I went for the note, I heard my cell vibrating.

Damn. It was Doug. "Hi," I said, my annoyed tone already in place.

"Hey," he replied. "So, I need to change things around for to-morrow."

"Do-ug," I whined. "We just got this schedule sorted out."

"Come on, Liza. This is so hard for me. I'm just not used to it all yet."

My mind started reeling through the thousands of times I had been with the kids for fourteen hours straight while Doug was home for a mere three hours after work and before bedtime. "What time should I drop them off then?"

"I just need another hour. God, they take up every minute. I just have to make a few calls before they get here and I suddenly don't get the chance to check my phone for the next *five* hours," he exaggerated. "I can't even sit down and have a cup of coffee with Jakey running loose! Uh, but I know you know that."

Button pushed. Rage achieved. "This shared custody agree-ment has me so torn up! It's more complicated than you'll ever understand to go from a stay-at-home mom to a part-time mom. I still relish every free moment away from them, and it's been a month! Then I am filled to my eyes with guilt for not missing them more when they're with you. Once we get this all settled, I'm sure I'll miss them more." He didn't interject to reassure me. "I just can't believe we fight over who *has* to take them. What's wrong with us? Shouldn't we be arguing about who *gets* to take them?"

Doug was quiet for a moment. "Are we totally fucking them up, Liza?"

I sighed, hating that he was still my friend. "I don't know. But we both love them. So we should both care for them." I thought a moment. "You're a good dad, Doug." He was quiet again. "So

Jules would *not* stop singing this weird church song today. What is that all about?"

Doug startled me with a chuckle. "Um...she was in vacation bible school last week."

"What!" I didn't even try to hide my astonishment.

"Hey, the neighbor girl was going, and her mom offered to take Jules, too! Free childcare."

I just sighed. Again. "Okay, well, thanks for checking with me first," I jabbed. "I'll be there tomorrow at nine. Enjoy your sleep, you jerk." I could feel him smiling. We both knew Jakey would be awake at 5:30 in the morning at my place.

I hung up the phone and grabbed the backpack. With the kids tucked away in bed, I was finally able to sit down with the glass of red wine I had poured exactly two minutes after their bedroom doors were shut. Digging past the baggie of Cheerios, a lone sock, and some diapers, I felt the piece of notebook paper from Valentina. I took a gulp of red and tossed the backpack to the floor.

For Liza, it said at the top. The handwriting was dark and squiggly. Very intentional. Hard to make out. Amazing, though, that a woman who had lived for nearly thirty years in a coma had even been able to write again. I read on:

> *In the year 1898, I hid a diary in our store in lower east side. It is now mens suit store on Orchard Street called Hals. Diary is in cigar box in vent of mens bathroom. If you travel to a time later than 1898, you can read more than I can remember. Please take locket. You are a seer. You should see what you need to see.*

I sucked in a deep breath. Then another gulp. I still wasn't sure how lucid Valentina was. This was nuts. *If I travel in time?*

I grabbed my laptop. Once I saw the familiar search engine, I typed in *Hal's Orchard Street Manhattan*. And in an instant, there it was. It was indeed a real place in New York.

I clicked on the "About" tab and scanned the store's history. Built in 1860, now owned by Orthodox Jews. There was a grainy photo on the page of the original owners. The caption said, "Zeyer family in 1890." The photo was a mother, father and three children. One of the boys looked to be about age ten.

I got goosebumps…then slammed the rest of my red.

I heard Jakey whining through the monitor. And though it made me grumble, I got up. Maybe it was the wine or maybe it was the weird feeling I'd just gotten, but I longed to be close to someone. Tossing the laptop onto my saggy couch, I hurried to his door.

"Hushhh," I whispered, entering his dark room. "Mama's here."

I reached down in the darkness and pulled him up from his crib like I had a thousand times before. He was so big. So heavy.

But here in the dark, he was still just my baby.

He wrapped his pudgy arms around my neck, the best feeling in the world. I backed into the glider without looking and began rocking him.

I took the moment of quiet to just hold him. To nuzzle his forehead. To kiss the top of his head like I had when he was a helpless newborn. There we sat, rocking back and forth for a long time. With him half asleep, I was able to feel my full love for him. When the distractions of his naughty nature and conniving spirit were at rest.

Then Valentina's words came back to me. She didn't want me to leave my angels. Had she meant through time travel?

I shook my head at my own thoughts. I noticed the proverbial lump in my throat at the thought of it being the very last time I ever rocked my baby.

And just like that, Jakey whined and pushed me away. Already such a big boy. He might as well have spoken, "No more cuddling, Mommy."

I laid him back in the crib without a sound.

THE NEXT MORNING, he was right on cue. Just after 5:30, and he was crying for me.

I growled and got up. After pushing his door open, there he was—standing in his crib, reaching for me.

We went into the kitchen to start breakfast and wait for Jules to wake up. I realized I hadn't taken a shower before bed. Jakey was still into everything, and a shower with him awake was not an option without trapping him and listening to him scream the whole time. So I was going to work looking like a hobo again.

Jakey played with rogue toys he'd left on the kitchen floor, as I measured out scoops of my most treasured addiction: coffee. Today seemed like an extra scoop kind of day. The tiny grounds scattered all over the counter. I grumbled but didn't wipe them up.

Jakey was pulling at my pant leg, trying to show me a playing card he ripped in two. I nudged him back so I could pour the water into my stained, silver pot. Content the kids would be Doug's problem for the next two days, I had decided to head to Sunny Ridge before work. I needed to talk to Valentina. After all, it seemed like it was a dying woman's delusional wish to fork over a locket. I could just accept it, throw it into a drawer and be done with the whole thing.

As the coffee pot rumbled to life, I swept up my boy and went to the couch.

"Moo-moo! Moo-moo!" Jakey urged in a masculine pitch, pointing at the television.

Bad habits had been formed. Every morning he wanted to watch a stupid animal show. The abundance of cows in the parade of animals had forever dubbed his favorite show "moo-moo."

I started his show and grabbed my smartphone. Scrolling through emails, I saw one from the receptionist at the Birth Center. "The new patient tour scheduled for this morning has been rescheduled for next week."

Jakey was swiping the remotes off of the coffee table. I grabbed his arm and told him "no no" without even looking up from my phone.

I had forgotten all about the new patient tour. Thank goodness it was canceled or the kids would have had to come in with me again. Last time I had to bring them in, Jules tripped up the grand staircase spilling milk all over, and Jakey had crawled into an exam room during an ultrasound. The Birth Center encouraged children to join their expecting mothers with toys and books available, but the building was regal, old and not childproof. The day I was interviewing for the birthing assistant position, I had driven past two times before realizing I was in the right place. Pillars, brick, dignified bushes in the front—the whole bit.

I opened my calendar to see the day's lineup. A first-time mom was coming in for her consultation at ten o'clock, followed by an eleven o'clock wellness check with a mama planning her third birth at the Center (she didn't even have time to think about what's going on in there), and a lunch interview with the local television station.

"Moo-moo!" Jakey bellowed.

I looked up to catch a glimpse of an enormous cow before the show moved on to other barnyard animals. "Good job, honey. That was a cow. Moo!"

My fingers were already searching the Internet for more information on the reporter I was meeting with. Communications were my bread and butter. Back in school, I never would have imagined birthing babies in bedrooms that looked straight out of a Marriott. I'd majored in mass communications. A major as common as it sounded. Everyone and their brother had graduated with the same degree. And what had we studied? Pop culture, basically. The history of commercials. How to market in an increasingly digital world—though back in 2000 when I graduated, they were only guessing at what that might be. At that time, I still knew people who majored in print journalism. I bet they were really raking it in these days.

After a major life redirect (i.e. being unemployed for over a year), I'd watched a documentary that changed my life's focus. It was called *The Business of Being Born* and featured Ricki Lake. (Yes, as in Ricki Lake from daytime television. And in the film she is naked. Like birthing babies naked.) And it had gotten me all hopped up and passionate about the rise and demise of obstetric hospital care. Bewildered by all the new information, I decided my generation of women should get back to the basics. But in searching around, I realized I was almost late to the party. Thousands of women my age were choosing birthing centers and non-medicated, natural births. We were all getting back to our inner hippie chick, I guess.

And then there I was. Just days after first writing *Certified Birthing Assistant* after my name, interviewing at a mansion-turned-birth center.

"Morning, Mama," Jules said, dragging her blankie along behind her. She sauntered with such a grown-up grace about her. She was an old soul.

"Morning, sweetie," I called, closing the browser windows and grabbing her as she walked past. I forced a hug on her, inciting jealousy in the one-year-old. He whined and ran up to get in on the affection.

"I don't want to watch Jakey's show again. I want to watch my show!" Jules declared. There were actual tears in her eyes. Already.

I jogged to the kitchen to get my coffee. I couldn't help but look at the clock to see how many hours until they would be at Doug's.

Jakey screamed. I turned to see Jules pulling him over by his neck.

"Jules!"

"He was standing in my way!" she shouted, as if that were a perfectly good reason to clothesline someone.

Just a few more hours, I coaxed myself. And then I could go to work and assure pregnant mothers that procreating is the apex of their womanhood.

I took a second to reflect on the irony of my life as I comforted my passionate offspring by promising screen time on random mobile devices. And drank my black coffee.

WHEN I POKED my head into the hospice room after dropping off the kids with Doug, Valentina declared in her raspy, Russian accent, "You came!"

I slunk in under the fluorescent light. "I came."

"You read my note."

"I did."

She was already unwrapping a white handkerchief in her lap—propped up in her hospital bed, appearing older than just yesterday. "Here it is. I am ready to tell you all the secrets I can remember."

I looked over to see the large, tarnished silver locket in her lap. I sat in her room's beige armchair, my back to the door, judging the size and heft of my chubby thighs splatted flat against the chair. "Valentina...you know this sounds insane, right? You hear yourself? Being alive in the 1890s. Being a ten-year-old boy...Are you sure you're not suffering from multiple personalities or something?"

She rested her crooked pointer finger on the locket. Her fingernail was a strange shade of gray. She tapped on the locket's cover. "This is the doorway to a greater understanding." She spoke as if my words hadn't even reached her ears.

"Okay," I sighed, crossing my arms. "Tell me all the secrets you can remember, then. I'll listen."

"When you open locket, you will see a mirror. It is not a mirror that you have ever known before. It holds the power to transport your soul through time." She paused to think. "At least I think it is your soul. Your inner self. Your spirit. It is shuttled through time and enters into someone else's body."

I couldn't stop my eyebrow from arching in skepticism. But I said nothing.

"When Zizi left me this locket, I knew nothing." She was shaking her head in self-pity. "I expected to see photo inside. Then suddenly, I was in Yacob. Or rather, I *was* Yacob. When I transported, I did not know how to speak Yiddish with the family. I did not even know my American history well enough to know I was in New York. Can you imagine my terror? It took me so many years to figure out rules of the mirror. I spent hours staring into every mirror I saw. But nothing ever happened. That is, until Yacob's body turned eighteen." She flapped her hands. "Never mind, never mind, that is all in the diary. The most important thing to remember is that the mirror is trying to show you something. Something of great importance. But I do not think the person you become is really a part of this great important moment. I think they—*you*—are merely a watcher."

I adjusted my weight in my chair, realizing my face had been scrunched in a form of impudence for most of her story.

"Just figure it out quicker than I," she added with a sullen undertone. "Use your memories. Your intuition. Figure out what you are supposed to see, and *then* are you able to use a mirror to come back. Remember, while you are gone, your body is still here…dying without you."

With that, she thrust the locket at me.

I took it. It dangled from my hand, silver and ornate. The chain was long and smelled like a jar of pennies. The oval case was covered with etchings of swirling vines and tiny flowers. It was heavy and cold. I touched the inscription on the back. It was in another language. "What does this say?"

Valentina's lips were pursed. She opened them with a smack. "It is Yiddish. *To see what you need to see, look past yourself.*"

"So... I just open it and look into the mirror?" I asked, running my fingers over the inscription.

"Yes."

"And I will see another time and place?"

"Exact-tally." Her Russian accent hung heavy in the air. "I think you will enter the body of someone dying at that very moment in time." She nodded, remembering. "Yacob was on his third week of typhoid fever. As he died, I became." She coughed. When she cleared her throat, she seemed agitated. "You are ready. Look! Look before I can no longer breathe! If you cannot see past yourself, I do not have much time to find someone else."

I swallowed and gave her a solemn look. "So you think only a select few people can see another time in here?"

She nodded. "I do not know why we are able to, but we are. I have tried to get others to see past themselves, and they could not."

With my fingernail, I unclicked the tiny, silver latch. The sound seemed to echo in the otherwise silent, clinical room. Before opening it, I looked at Valentina once more. "What will happen to me if this works?"

"You will fall into the past." Her eyes were dancing. "Immediately."

My mind projected several images of my smiling babies. "Maybe I shouldn't. What would happen to Jakey and Jules?"

Her face sneered at me. "But I thought you did not believe me?"

She was right. This whole thing was illogical. I would show her once and for all this was some sort of elaborate dream she created while she was in a coma. Like a defiant child being dared, I opened the antique locket and looked into the ordinary-looking mirror. I saw my reflection.

Yes, there I was, in all of my mom-glory. No makeup, smudged glasses, messy hair, new wrinkles…No wonder Jules had taken to calling me Uncle Mom.

I heard Valentina coughing again. And if I had been paying more attention to her, I would have realized how odd it was that the sound of her cough seemed to come from far away. Because she was still sitting next to me.

Staring at the mirror's reflection, something caught my eye over my shoulder. A movement. I saw the outline of the door…*sway* behind me. The doorway wavered. I should have just turned around to look at the doorway in real life. To assure myself that it was just the same metal doorway of the hospice room of Sunny Ridge in Saint Paul, Minnesota. But instead, I focused my eyes on the reflection of the area above my shoulder. I watched the mirror's version of the doorway.

Yes, the lines of the doorway definitely moved! As if from a cheesy dream sequence of a movie. I squinted—trying to make out the image coming into focus.

Oh! Was I literally looking past myself? I thought that was a metaphor!

And then it snapped into view. Hard definite lines appeared. Behind my face's reflection, I saw a narrow hallway appear. Several women were crowded together.

And before I could tear my eyes away from the scene, I felt as though I were punched in the stomach.

I lost my breath.

I was drowning…or being suffocated. Like being crushed by a weight so great I couldn't possibly survive its heft. The feeling was horrifying!

Everything was dark. The kind of palpable dark a person could feel around them. I had the fleeting memory of experiencing that kind of dark while on an underground cave tour as a child.

Terrified, I attempted to cry out for help. I think I screamed to God. My scream sounded choppy, like the sound of Jakey crying on the monitor when the battery was going dead.

And then, though my eyes were still closed, I sensed the darkness being replaced by light.

I felt soft hands on my arms and then on my face. I gasped in a deep breath. My lungs filled with air, thank goodness. I was still alive! But instead of the smell of the hospice room, there was an overwhelming scent of perfume. Muffled voices were talking all at once.

"I think she's coming back!" one of the voices called to the others.

CHAPTER 2

IT'S ALL ABOUT THE BENZEDRINES

I FELT A consistent waft of air over my face and realized I was being fanned. I peeked open my eyes. Blurry. I opened my mouth. Pasty.

"Dear heavens, she's still with us," an older woman proclaimed, making the sign of the cross over her head and shoulders over an old-fashioned dress. "Dottie, go grab some wet washcloths. Marjorie, run to her room and fetch a clean dress. We should get her out of this mess."

Inside my head, a steady throb kept the beat of my pulse. I had the spins. I lifted a hand to my temple. In doing so, I looked down at my body, crumpled on a carpeted hallway floor.

I screamed!

The older woman jumped, startled. "Now, now. No need for that, Barbara. We'll get you fixed up here. You're going to be just fine."

I was staring at my hand. But it wasn't my hand. Dear God, it truly wasn't. Valentina had been telling me the truth! This was not my body.

I looked up to see several faces staring down at me.

Focus. Figure this out. Where the hell was I?

The older woman started to pull me up. Apparently, my host body was young. Even near-death I was able to stand without clicking knees or slow muscles. Near-death...or dead?

I shivered. Was I in a dead woman's body?

"Barbara, do you know where you are? You look confused," the older woman said to me.

Opening my mouth, I croaked out the words, "I think I need to lie down."

Oh, that voice! Gravely and…seductive? How can that be my voice?

"Gracie, move out of the way. Let's get her to her room."

"Londa, I have the washcloths," a young girl said to the older woman.

She snatched them out of her hand. "Thank you. Now get back to your own business, ladies. All of you." The young women scattered.

Her arm was under my armpits, guiding my shaking, shapely legs down the hallway. The wet washcloth was now on my forehead. I tried not to tongue the grit on the backs of my teeth or choke on the burning in my throat.

So many beautiful women were looking at me. Classically beautiful. They were whispering and pointing. They held their hands over their mouths, as they said things about me. They leaned out of doorways to watch as I stumbled past them.

Was this some sort of dorm? Apartment building?

I swallowed. It hurt.

"I…I need water," I heard my body say.

"In a minute, dear. Let's get you back to your bed."

After following the dark red and gold carpet runner down a long, narrow hallway, we entered one of the identical doors. It was a sparse, modest room. I inventoried a single bed, miniscule, doily-covered dresser with a mirror, an armchair…and a girl digging in a beefy armoire where a closet should have been.

"She doesn't seem to have anything practical in here, Londa," she said to my helper.

I eyeballed the mirror, as we walked to the bed. I looked in and searched for anything out of the ordinary. Or some indication that I could transport back. But everything was out of the ordinary! Unfamiliar. Scary.

I was blonde, I saw from the reflection. Bouncy light hair with a side part. I looked like a black and white movie star. But in real life color. In my fleeting glance, I realized I might have won the weird-world jackpot. Apparently, I went back in time and came out looking like a blonde Audrey Hepburn!

"I'll take it from here, you can go," Londa said to the girl.

I felt hot tears sting my new eyes. This couldn't be happening to me. I was too boring. Too average. Too practical, realistic and unfantastic! Panting in a sort of hyperventilation, I realized I was losing it.

"Now, now," Londa doted. "Don't go messing up that expensive mascara." She dropped my body onto the small bed. The metal springs screeched in protest. "I'll go fetch your water, Barbara. Sit tight."

I heard her heavy footsteps echo in the long hallway. More whispers and snickers followed her.

Closing my eyes, I tried to think. But my new head was pounding. I could hear the blood pumping past my temples.

Don't cry.

I looked myself over. I was young, that I knew right away. Judging from the other women around me, I was in my late teens or early twenties. My blonde hair was light and groomed. Done in a hairstyle I recognized as the kind the girls were wearing at the swing dancing class Doug and I had taken before our wedding.

Oh God—Doug! He had Jules and Jakey!

Oh God—Right now the nurses were probably finding my comatose body in Valentina's room. What would they do with me? Was I in a coma? What would Doug do without me? And my babies!

Tears fell.

My babies would see me lying in a hospital bed, unconscious.

"What have I done?" I sobbed to myself.

"There, there," Londa said, reentering the bedroom. "We all make a few poor choices in life. But nothing in life is permanent...except maybe having a baby."

That fueled my self-pity. I sniffed back the snot. It hurt the inside of my nose and drummed up a terrible stinging.

She handed me a petite glass filled with semi-clear water. I took a gulp. It was only then I realized I was covered in barf. The horrible taste in my mouth was from vomit.

Londa was unbuttoning the long row of buttons down my back, as I sipped my water. Or was it Barbara's water? Since this appeared to be as real as real life ever was, I needed to learn things. Who was I now? Where was I now? And *when* was I now?

"I didn't want to say it in front of the other girls," Londa began, still working diligently on the buttons, "But I thought you were a goner."

My breathing sped up, and I gulped another swig of the rusty water. "I'm sorry if I scared you," I heard my body say. Minnesota nice, even in the thick of it.

"There," she proclaimed, freeing me from the last button. "Let's get you out of this dress."

And what a dress it was! From a land of yoga pants and T-shirts, I was now taking off a garment reminiscent of one in an exhibit at the History Center. It was a satin gown of sorts that wrapped and draped my new elegant body.

Londa tugged at my hand, motioning me to stand. I felt bewildered and awkward at the same time.

I did as she beckoned and balanced on shaky legs so she could help pull off the soiled dress. Being a mother and a birthing assistant, I was no stranger to being in someone else's vomit. But being drenched in puke from a dead woman's body was on a whole new level.

Londa didn't pry, nor did she gossip. She merely acted like any mother would while cleaning up a disobedient child. I used the chance to search the room for clues or hints as to where I was. But other than everything feeling small and a bit suffocating, I saw nothing in the stark room that might help.

"I'm guessing this is what you bought with the income tax money you took back from me?" Her tone was disapproving. She stood back to take in the sight of me.

Tax money?

I looked down to see what she was referring to. Under the satin gown was some sort of negligee. My hands went to it. I slid them down my new gorgeous frame. I was pale and bony, but it was sure better than the cellulite-infested, (almost) middle-aged body I came from.

If only Doug could see me now!

"Well, it seems that is what you'll have to make due with for now," Londa told me in an exasperated tone. "I don't know how you girls live without anything sensible in your wardrobe. Where are the nightgowns? The work dresses? You girls don't even know how good things are for you these days." As she lectured, she yanked down the scratchy blanket and stiff sheet. She shoved my legs under the covers.

I wasn't used to being touched by people I didn't know. I jerked away from her hands.

"Now, now!" she squawked. "You rest now." She was already drawing heavy curtains closed, blocking a view I hadn't thought to seek yet. "After you wake, come down to my office. I'm afraid we need to talk. I know the timing is bad, but…" She threw her hands in the air. "This is the reality we were dealt."

And on that cryptic note, she left the room, closing the door behind her.

I was alone.

I jumped up to rush to the window but was stopped midway by the blinding pain in my head. I tried to squeeze my eye and temple, as I held my eyes closed for a moment. When the majority of the pain had passed, I jerked the floor-to-ceiling, floral drapes out of my way to reveal the city below.

From my second or third story view, I saw a road full of classic cars! Cars in light yellow, peach, red… A gigantic, black Cadillac sped past the building. It seemed as long as a bus. A sidewalk busy with people—suits and hats on the men, dresses and heels on the women. American flags hanging from every streetlight.

Palm trees!

And then, just tucked behind a brick building, peeked a billboard. It was pink and gold and the glittery letters spelled out: HOLLYWOOD'S BEST.

I blinked. Hollywood?

The sky was a light, feathery blue. The clouds were visible, unlike the Weather Channel's constant smog report suggested for the L.A. area. I was definitely in a time long since gone.

Backing into the arm chair, I sat with a plop.

So I was a skinny bombshell and I lived in Hollywood? Seriously! Valentina had been shuttled off to the 1800s. She'd been a child. And a boy! If nothing else, I guess I should be thankful for my outstanding bit of luck in such an unbelievable situation.

The art deco mirror stood out from the pale green, busy wallpaper pattern of the small room. I hopped up with a jerk and stared into it. My eyesight was blurry, like I'd had one too many glasses of pinot. I lifted the hand my brain seemed to be in charge of now and placed it against the cold glass. I pushed once before looking away from the reflection. The drawer of the dresser caught my eye. Once I could focus, I dug past the thin, wispy undergarments and found what I was hoping to find. An ID card.

I was now Barbara Jane Miller. Twenty-one years old. Living on fucking Sunset Boulevard!

I felt like I should look around for a candid camera or at least wait for Ashton Kutcher to pop out and yell I'd been Punk'd.

I couldn't stop my mind from hurling questions at me. Why was I here? What was this momentous thing I was supposed to see? How long would I be stuck here? And why was a twenty-one-year-old, gorgeous woman lying in the hallway of a hotel…dying?

As if to answer my question, my eyelid began to twitch. I think I had noticed it earlier, but it was not high on the priority list.

I needed to get outside. I needed to smell fresh air and hear that those antique cars were there in real life.

Rushing to the armoire, I found a different dress to wear. My, the clothes were tedious to get on, yet so very beautiful. Ruby red, gathered at the neck. Tight sleeves, tight waist. But how to reach the row of tiny buttons that seemed to be up the back on everything I now owned?

As I twisted my arm behind my back to reach, I felt the dreaded feeling in the pit of my stomach. I was about to vomit again…

In a hurried frenzy, I looked around the room and realized there was no bathroom! I dumped the contents of the small woven trash basket onto the floor before flinging the door open and rushing into the hall.

I looked left, then right. Above a door about halfway down the hall I saw an arrow hanging overhead. Was it for the bathroom? Did everyone share the bathroom?

I was already running down the hall when the inevitable heave hit me. Too late to save the wicker garbage can. I watched in horror as the vomit threatened to drip between its woven cracks onto the Oriental carpet. At least none was on the red, gaping dress.

Glancing around, I heard a few doors open in response to the loud noise I had made. I didn't see any prying eyes, so I followed the arrow. And as the answer to my unspoken prayers, it did indeed lead to a bathroom.

Ladies Lavatory, the sign said.

Inside, there was one toilet, one sink, one mirror, one small table with towels and washcloths. And one occupant.

"Babs!" she proclaimed.

"Hi," I said in my new voice. I still wasn't used to the gravel it held.

She clamped her hands on my upper arms. I tried to jerk away, but she held tight. "I was so worried!"

Okay, so this woman knew me. She seemed to care about me. Maybe she could help me figure out a few things. But instead of anything helpful, I stuttered, "I...just puked in the hall."

She gave me an inquisitive look. After looking down at the mess in my trembling hands, clarity shown on her face. "Oh! Serendipity! Oh honey, that's okay. I'll help you clean it up before Londa sees it."

"Serendipity?" my voice asked.

She chuckled. "Remember, that's what my sister Kitty calls vomit? Sounds so much more pleasant, doesn't it? Telling people you just serendipitied."

I felt myself nodding though I didn't quite know why.

"Here," she offered, handing me another wet washcloth.

"Thanks," I muttered, wiping the perky corners of my new mouth.

"I just knew you should have come with me to Girl's Judo Gymnastics this morning," she started. "You always tease me about going, but before taking the classes I couldn't whip a cat!" She giggled before getting serious. "I only bring it up because if you'd come with me, you wouldn't have met up with Digger."

"Digger?"

She laughed again. It seemed like her nature to laugh often—easy and natural. "Don't you think for one second that I would take his side. I know how he is. But I got the impression you were going to call it quits." As she talked, she went about cleaning the basket for me.

I felt my new eyebrows arch.

She grabbed my hand and patted its back. "Hello, Babs. It's me, Sis." She laughed again. "Are you in there?"

My hand went to my temple again. The pounding pain was making things all the more difficult. "Where do you keep the Ibuprofen around here?"

"The what?" she shouted. "You are all out of sorts, Babsie."

I tried to force my mind to work. When was ibuprofen invented? What has been around forever? "Aspirin," I answered aloud. "Where is the aspirin?"

The girl called Sis shrugged. "I'm not sure I know. Maybe Dottie has some? Or Bess? We can go ask. Is your head hurting again?"

"Yes," I said with my pasty mouth. My tongue seemed like a lazy, swollen afterthought in the world of my mouth. And it wasn't playing nice.

"Well, let's go ask. But we should probably clean up that serendipity first," she said with way too much perkiness.

I nodded and grabbed the white towel from the wall rung.

"Oh, gee!" Sis gasped. "Londa would kill you for using that!" She pulled the towel from my hands.

What I wouldn't have given for some Lysol wipes. Or a smartphone. I still didn't know what time I was living in, though I was thankful to be among fellow English-speaking adults.

I watched as Sis finished rinsing out my waste basket. As she leaned over the sink, I checked her out. I stared, almost as if trying to place her. Soft, touchable, brown hair wrapped up in some sort of hairstyle I had never seen in real life. Bright red lips, stained the perfect shade. False eyelashes? I wondered if those had been invented yet.

Once she had finished, she pointed at the yellow tile floor. "Perhaps we should just do a little switcheroo and the ol' boss lady will never notice," she said with a wink.

After grabbing the bathroom's waste basket and leaving mine there, Sis led me out into the hallway. We followed the narrow hall back to the room I was using.

"Babs! You're completely undone in the back," she declared once we were back in the small, stuffy bedroom.

"Londa helped me get undressed and then when I needed to…serendipity," I stated, looking at her, "I just threw it on and ran."

She was laughing again. "You sure are acting off."

"Off?" Gah, I'd come back to life as a parrot. But I wasn't even thinking about acting like the person I inhabited. Would everyone know I wasn't Barbara?

"Yes." She was looking at the mess of garbage I had dumped onto the floor. "Darling, this simply won't do." Her long dress swung around her ankles as she put her hands on her hips. "You really are in a state, aren't you?"

She bent to pick up the discarded tissues, papers and…pill bottles.

"What's that?" I asked without thinking. It was a kind of bottle I had never seen before. It was dark brown glass.

"Barbara Miller, what has gotten into you?"

I snatched the glass bottle from the floor and read the label:

Benzedrine Sulfate Tablets (racemic amphetamine sulfate)
5-mg, Take 1-2 tablets as needed
Langdon Laboratories

I looked up at Sis. Her brow was furrowed. She crouched beside me and took my hand in hers. I wanted to pull away, but I didn't. "Something is wrong. Not a day goes by that I don't see you with your bennies. And now you're asking me what they are? Exactly what happened this morning?"

I took a deep breath. It was a strange feeling. Like the first time I had stopped to take a moment to just *feel* this new body I was living in. And the feel of Sis's petite hand sung through my senses.

Pushing away the thoughts of Jakey's soft hand in mine, I focused on the woman before me. "Something did happen this morning. And I need help making sense of it."

Sis dropped my hand and chuckled. "Well, aren't you one for dramatics. The auditions aren't until Sunday, sweetheart."

"Sis, I don't know what you're talking about! I don't know where I am. I don't even know who I am," I rambled, eager to have an ally.

Her eyes widened. She covered her mouth with her hand with a slight tremble. And when she removed it, out came the loudest shrieking I had ever heard, "Babs! You have amnesia!"

I swatted her upper arm. "Shush!" I said in my mom-tone.

She was pouting. "You'll be okay, Babsie," she mumbled, fumbling to open a gold cigarette case. "We will just have to call Doc…" She lit the end of a skinny cigarette before offering one to me. I declined. "Are you sure? Why, I'm simply an intolerable shrew if I don't get my ten a day."

I shook my head again, shocked at her admission. I hadn't so much as caught a whiff of cigarette smoke in years. It made my nauseous stomach churn.

I heard footsteps in the hall. It seemed I couldn't stop bringing attention to my situation. "Sis," I started, looking her in the eye. I urged her to stand with me. "I bet you can help me to remember."

Her shaky hand put the cigarette back to her lips. "Remember what? You remember me, don't you?"

"Sure, I do…I'm just a little rough around the edges. For instance, what day is it today?"

Relief shown on her youthful face. "Oh, is that all. It's Friday."

"Friday the…"

"The 5th of September…" she dragged out her words as though she were hoping that was the right answer.

"In the year…?"

"Babs! You don't remember what year it is?" Her eyes bulged. "It's 1947. What year did you think it was?"

Well, I'd figured the Fifties based on the little knowledge of classic cars and clothing I had. I wasn't too far off. "See, that's just what I thought! Thank goodness. I think things are coming back to me now."

She sat on the edge of my squeaky, single bed. Still puffing away, the small room was filling up with a smelly haze. It made me wonder what she'd think about second hand smoke research. I swatted the smoke away from my face and watched her for a moment, but I didn't know her well enough to imagine what was going through her mind.

"What else don't you remember? I've never heard of someone getting amnesia from pep pills—they're completely safe. Did you maybe hit your head when you fell?"

I was nodding. "I guess I must have." My hand was already on my temple. "I still need some aspirin."

"Oh, yes." She gave me a pitying smile. Her eyes widened. "You haven't truly forgotten about the audition on Sunday, have you?"

I mustered the part of me that had won the lead in the senior high school play. "I...I'm afraid I have." Forlorn look sent. Pity attained.

"Oh, Babs!" She looked like she might cry again. Such an emotional one. "Sunday is the day you set up to audition for the Ajax voiceover. It could be your big break!"

I said nothing.

"You know, down at the station?"

"The TV station?" I guessed.

My response was met by immediate giggles. "No. At HBC."

I was staring at her. Hoping she would elaborate. She did.

"HBC...the radio station where we are employed. You must at least remember that, Babs." Her pity turned to true concern.

I didn't want to take this too far and end up in a hospital. Would a hospital figure out this body wasn't mine? Or worse, would I end up in one of those horror movie psychiatric hospitals? "The radio station! Yes, it's coming back to me, Sis!"

She hopped up from the bed and clapped, her right hand still clutching her cigarette. "Goodie!"

"Maybe you should take me there now? I heard once that amnesia can best be cured by going to familiar places and jogging one's memory."

She twittered again. "You're talking like you've been tipping the flask."

I almost blurted, "I am?" but I kept my inner parrot to myself. This was working. I needed to keep Chipper Barbie on track. "Sis, won't you please take me there?"

She took the final drag of her cigarette and squashed it into a glass ashtray near the bed. Did my host body smoke too? Or were ashtrays just always around? I had the vague recollection of ashtrays laying around everywhere before cigarettes were banned.

"I will," she answered. "If you think you're feeling up to it, let's stop by."

I turned my back to her so she could finish my miniature, black buttons. The masochistic part of my mind was singing a round of *Miss Mary Mack all dressed in black with silver buttons all down her back*. It didn't make me feel any better or help the fact I felt inordinately overdressed. The dress—well, gown, really—was nicer than any holiday or business trip garment I had ever worn. Besides my wedding dress, it was the most graceful thing I'd ever had on my boring body. But, I reminded myself, this new body wasn't boring.

"Now you're decent," she announced. She looked around the room. I looked too. "Where in heavens is your clutch?"

I shook my head. "My ID is in the top drawer."

She laughed again. "Barbara Miller, you've positively become a comedian." She bent to look under the bed and checked the few feet of wardrobe space. "It's not here…" Her face registered sudden concern. "Oh, Babs! You didn't leave it with Digger, did you?"

"I… don't remember."

She was shaking her head. "Well, we can walk right now. But you should find your bus pass and coin purse before Sunday."

I nodded like a lost child. At this point, I would do anything she said just to have an ounce more information. Oh, how I longed to Google…

"I'll just stop in my room and fetch my things." Sis handed me a pair of black kitten heels. Or were they called sling backs? Did I mention how I missed all the world's information at my fingertips every waking moment? "Now, I don't mean to be a pig," she started, "but you really should stop in the powder room before we go."

I looked into the cloudy mirror attached to the three-drawer dresser. I winced at the stranger staring back. God, was I experiencing mirror PTSD?

Sis opened a large floral hatbox on the dresser. Under the round cover adorned with a blue bow, was a tiny collection of makeup products. With expertise, she plucked out two pencils and a gold tube of lipstick. "Come along."

She led me into the hallway. Just past the overhead arrow, the hallway turned to reveal a staircase. "I'll meet you down there in just a moment."

A short flight of stairs and I was on a balcony of sorts. I stopped to gaze down at the open, double-storied floor below. It was…regal. Potted ferns stood as tall as Doug. Gleaming tile in a geometric diamond pattern led to the trail of Oriental carpet creeping up the staircase and under my feet. A gargantuan chandelier hung in the center of the space. It showed off its lightbulbs with pride, displaying them as if a bare bulb was as attractive as a bare shoulder. It was dim. Small lanterns hung on the walls surrounding the gigantic front desk. From the stairway to where I stood, it seemed there was a mile of decadent, carved wood banister. My eyes followed it up to where I was standing. The hand-painted sign next to me declared, *Ladies Mezzanine*.

The perfect place to overlook the front desk, my hand slid across the varnished wood railing as I leaned in to hear Londa talking below. It seemed like a mother-daughter duo was getting some sort of tour.

"This is not a charm school, Mrs. Bunting, but rather a full-service ladies-only dormitory," Londa explained to her guests below.

"I see," the refined woman mused. Her high heels clicked with every step, echoing up to where I stood—frozen. Mesmerized on the mezzanine.

Londa handed the mother a pamphlet. "I'm sure you'll find our offerings top notch. Housed in our quarters, we have a fully-stocked library, three recital rooms, a sundeck, and a formal dining room where each meal is served by our all-female staff. Out-doors, we have a swimming pool and a tennis court. Each week, I act as the house social director and make sure to keep our young women bustling with activities." She paused and leaned in. "Idle hands, you know."

"Yes. And what is your policy on *visitors*?" Mother hen asked, her nose held high so she had to look down on Londa.

My mom-radar piqued. She was asking about boys. And her daughter blushed under the half-veil hanging from her petite, pillbox hat.

"Mrs. Bunting, I assure you that the doorman is the only male with permission to be on our grounds without checking in at our front desk first."

My eyes flew to judge the woman behind the mahogany front desk. Thin glasses were perched at the tip of her nose. So she was the gatekeeper. Her thick, wool-looking lady-suit reminded me of something from old Jackie Kennedy photos. She held a pen and was writing something—just to give off the appearance of being busy since the attention was all on her, I guessed. She never looked up.

Londa continued speaking, as she motioned up the grand staircase. "No male guests are allowed above the lobby without strict supervision. We, of course, always have chaperones avail-able."

I looked at the daughter—she was just a teenager. But oh so gorgeous already. It made me wonder what kind of beauty my Jules would grow into...

"Gee, she acts like we're a bunch of floozies," Sis observed. She had come up next to me without a sound. She nudged me in the side. "Takes one to know one!" She giggled loud enough for the sound to carry.

The tour below halted. All three women looked up at us.

"Gee..." Sis whispered again.

"Ladies," Londa greeted in her professional tone. She ges-tured for us to come down the stairs. Without hesitation, Sis followed orders, lifting the hem of her A-line, yellow dress and swaying down the staircase. Shifting her white gloves from one hand to the other, she let her hand slide with elegance down the shiny banister. Once at the bottom, she gave a slight tip of her head to the guests. "Good day," she said, her formality causing her to sound Stepford Wife-esque to me.

I followed her lead…the best I could considering I'd never had a formal bone in my body. One day I was spattered with blood and bodily fluids telling birthing women to breathe through the worst pain of their lives, the next I was a damn debutant.

My moves were jerky, obvious they had been planned. There was no flow. No dignity. But I forced myself to waltz past them anyway. "Good day," I repeated. Ah, but I did have this new, amazing voice.

Londa shot me a look. "Miss Miller," she said. "A word." Then she returned to her prospective clients. "As the Matron in Charge, I assure you this is an upstanding and very respectable dormitory for any young lady of her stature to reside." She led them to the portion of the lobby near the windows. Several round, wooden tables were set in a row in front of a bay window. A few girls were seated, playing cards. "Afternoon tea and nightly bridge games take place here in our solarium. If you will just excuse me a moment," Londa said to the two women, leaving them to peer over the shoulders of the card-players.

I saw the mother mouth the word "solarium" to her daughter. A bay window it was. A solarium, it wasn't.

Sis halted and watched as Londa approached. Londa lifted my hand and patted the back of it as she spoke, "What are you doing out of bed so soon?"

"I…" My eye twitched again.

"We were just going to stop by the station," Sis interjected. "She isn't feeling well. We thought perhaps stopping in would refresh her…" Sis's sentence trailed off, her eyes asking me if she could say more. I shook my head no in response.

"Aren't we allowed to leave?" I asked, a little too incredulous.

Sis's laughter bounced around the lobby. The tour attendees and card players all looked at us.

Londa appeared flustered. "Of course! But your condition…"

Sis patted my shoulder. Or rather the square shoulder pad of my gown. "I was just taking her to the powder room to freshen up before going. We won't be long. We'll be sure to return before dinner hour."

Our matron in charge looked back to her guests. They were getting impatient. "Yes. Well, Barbara, do not forget to come to my office after dinner. We still have important matters to discuss."

Sis yanked my wrist. "I'll be sure she does."

We clicked across the tile—or was it actually marble?—and Sis pushed open a swinging door to reveal an actual powder room.

Cream and rose-colored wallpaper was pasted from the carpet up to the ceiling. The pattern was of oversized fans. The kind of handheld fans debutants *had* used. I could picture them fluttering their eyelashes from behind the lacy fans of yore. But instead, I was staring at their cartoon cousins—exaggerated and made into an overbearing wallpaper design. Wallpaper that did not match the row of striped chairs.

The chairs lined the counter that stretched from one end of the room to the other. Here too, American flags sat in a glass vase as a substitute for fake flowers. The scent of talcum powder and cigarettes hung stale in the air, as Sis led me to an open chair. Three other women were using the room. All were seated behind the countertop, staring at their reflections in the wall to wall mirror, chatting away as they applied lip liner and powder.

"Hiya, Bess," Sis said to one of them, ever so jovial.

A perfectly groomed head twisted around to see us. Her smile disappeared when her eyes connected with my face. "Mercy! What happened to you, Babs?"

I threw her a sheepish smile and sat. The chair caught me by surprise when I sank in. Plush. It reminded me of the deck chairs

Doug and I used to have next to the grill...except they were black and white striped. And (judging based on my minimal experience with ugly designer things) expensive.

"You mean you didn't hear about her little incident this morning?" One of the other women chimed in.

Sis giggled. "Incident? Come off it, Ruth." She wasn't even looking at the other woman. She was focused on my image in the mirror.

And so was I.

To see what you need to see, you must look past yourself. I stared into the glass. Pushed my face closer for good measure. I watched the scenery behind me in the reflection. Nothing.

I was jerked back to my present situation by Sis tugging one of the jagged pencil's edges along my lips. Lips that—if on one of my patients—I would have diagnosed as being cracked by dehydration and malnutrition. Made me long for another gulp of the rusty water I'd been offered earlier.

I stifled a cry when she jammed the other pencil near my eye. I watched our reflections perfectly matching our real life actions. There was no funny business in this mirror. Well, unless you counted that I was now a sexy woman who didn't even need glasses to see in full clarity.

"All I'm saying is there better not be a stain next to my door," Ruth stated with a sniff. She stood, shoving the cushioned chair back with her legs. She sniffed again. "You positively stink, too."

Sis glared at her for me.

The rude buxom beauty turned and pushed open the swinging door with her gloved hand.

"Don't listen to her. We'll fix you up," Sis insisted, handing me the lipstick tube.

I actually gulped in response. Again, other than a handful of times in my life, I had never applied lipstick. And certainly not the chunky, chalky substance she was handing me. Maybe I needed to alter my lip diagnosis. Maybe it was this old-timey lip product that was causing these cracked lips.

The brunette Sis had called Bess approached us. Without so much as asking, she spritzed me with some sort of perfume. "It's from France," was all she said. And then she, too, turned and left the powder room.

Sis was busying herself fluffing my hair and combing my perfect part. "There! Good as new." Her smile could have made any guy I knew melt into a sloppy mess.

I smiled into the mirror as well. I didn't think it was obvious I had died earlier that day.

Sis was digging into her clutch. "Your pep pills, my lady," she offered. "You're looking a little peaked."

I put my hand out to catch the two small, white pills. "Aspirin?"

The last remaining girl in the room laughed along with Sis. "Since when is Babs such a stitch?" She puffed her cheeks with powder one last time and turned and left.

I looked down at the pills in my hand. "These are...my bennies?"

"Now you've got it! Oh, I just knew your memory would return. Come on, now. These will surely help you feel better. Take them and let's get going. Londa will have the doorman lock us out if we're not back in time for dinner."

I tossed the pills into the back of my throat and swallowed hard. They only stuck a moment and then went down with a lump. Again, she tugged me by the wrist. I was just not accustomed to this. To her. To the constant state of optimism, vivacity and...pep. Damn. It was actually pep. So she was on these Benzedrine pep pills, too?

She was poking each finger into a spot in her tight glove as we *click-clack-clicked* across the floor. She too held her nose angled upward. I had never realized real, living people could walk that way. How could so much have been lost—and gained—for women in so few years?

CHAPTER 3
DON'T ADJUST THAT RADIO DIAL

IN MR. O'KEEFE's eighth grade history class, I got a failing grade on my midterm. I later wowed him with my oral report. (Not a euphemism. It was an actual speech.) He came up to me after class to tell me I was an excellent public speaker. I convinced him in the midst of his praise to give me a passing grade on my midterm. That was the first time I considered a future in communications. And that pretty much summed up the extent of my history knowledge.

1947. Why had I been sent to 1947? What was happening in history at this point? World War II was over. What happened after that? The baby boom? When was the Cold War?

Sis got up to the large double doors leading outside and paused. A man in a full uniform opened the door and gave an ever so slight bow. "Evening, Miss Rose."

"Good evening, Henry." She trotted past him, her small hand purse swinging in rhythm with her curvy frame in those high heels.

I followed, trying so hard to emulate the same vibe. But then I stopped. Because I was out. Standing in Hollywood. In the past.

I whirled around to look at the building I had just exited.

The Heritage House Hotel for Women, a gold plaque stated on the brick building.

I took a deep breath and urged my feet to move again. A streetcar roared down the center of the road then blew past! There was a painted island right where the center lane should be. Men and women rushed across oncoming traffic to get to the island to board the streetcar. A woman in a fur and fancy hat pushed a baby in a pram. The tiny infant was just swaddled and laying in there. No straps or seatbelts. And there she went, trotting right to the center of a busy street.

I couldn't imagine having no baby belts or buckles. When we brought Jules back from the birth center, she was just four hours old. And the first thing we'd had to do was buckle her tiny body into a car seat. The buckle had been as large as her belly. And from there, it was being buckled into a rocker. Buckled into a swing. Buckled into a stroller...I suppose it was all for the best. Though I've never heard rattling statistics on the number of infants killed in rogue stroller accidents. But I always buckled. Always. So, I could not imagine the freedom that mother didn't even know she was experiencing. No wonder she was smiling.

I tried to keep pace behind Sis, but she too was walking with speed. The sounds of the city swallowed up the *clacking* of her heels and burped out revving engines and exhaust in its place. I looked into a store window to see what looked like a hand-painted sign. It was next to a hanging, fuzzy sweater on display that made me think of the one Valentina had described. *100% wool in big boxy style, 10 luscious colors $3.69.*

A sweater for three dollars? This was all too much. My senses were on overload. I didn't want this to be real. I didn't want to be a time traveler.

When we reached the corner, I looked up to see skyscraping palm trees and a street sign reassuring me that I was indeed on Sunset Boulevard. Sunset and Vine. My gaze was pulled to shouts coming from across the street. There was an honest-to-God newspaper boy! Oh, how a newspaper could help me. When one couldn't search online, good old print journalism was still there.

But I just kept hustling to catch up with Sis.

As I turned back for one last gander at the paper boy, I saw a man staring at me. He was in a light gray suit, sitting on a bench with one of the newspapers. His face was weathered, and he was small in stance. Nothing seemed out of the ordinary about him except his stare. It was directed right at me. Right, directly at me—just one out of several people walking down the street.

As I walked, his eyes followed me. I knew from my before-I-had-kids-and-ruined-my-body days that he wasn't *interested* in me. Unless maybe it was in a rape and murder sort of way. His look unnerved me. Like he was watching me for a reason.

Was it possible he could know I was from the future? Or know Barbara? Oh! What if Babs was being watched? What if she was a criminal? What did hitmen look like in the forties? Gangsters? Well, I didn't see a tommy gun…

He didn't unlatch or redirect his gaze, even though I was blatant in looking right back at him. So I turned first.

Sis looked both ways and jogged across the street. When she had crossed, she stopped and looked back for me.

"Whatever are you doing, Babs? Are you ill again?" she called.

I was, but that wasn't my current top-ranking issue so I just smiled at her. Throwing a final look over my shoulder, I saw the suited man watch me as I trotted across the street as well, narrowly avoiding the large, bubble-like chrome fenders of stopped traffic.

Sis linked arms with me and picked up pace again. Together, arm in arm, we sped along a street lined with retro-colored automobiles, fancy people, and a strange charm I had never beheld.

"I heard Ruth say she was going to the Brown Derby tonight, the lucky scamp," Sis said as our feet lowered and raised in unison.

I looked over to her point and saw a peculiar brown restaurant shaped like an actual derby hat.

"Like her beau could really afford it there." She sighed. "But if it's true…Well, it would sure trump the grilled cheese and cherry Coke date I had last week."

I had been to Hollywood once. When I was interning in college, I'd been asked to sit at an exhibiting booth for the company I worked for. Flying from Minneapolis to Los Angeles alone for the first time. Staying in a hotel alone for the first time. I'd still been in my twenties then. I had a grit about me. Before life, marriage and kids wore me down. I'd taken a shuttle to the conference center and manned the hell out of that booth, fielding questions from people of all walks of life. And after my work was done, I'd hopped on a tour bus and taken it down the bumper-to-bumper highway to get to the Hollywood Walk of Fame. I'd placed my fingers in star after star, feeling the energy and buzz surrounding the Chinese Theatre.

But this didn't even feel like the same town.

I lost count of the blocks Sis and I walked in our heels, but soon enough we were approaching the front doors of an enormous, square building. HBC. Hollywood Broadcasting Company.

Sis patted her hair before pushing into the revolving door. I snuck in the next entrance and whirled around with her.

Wow.

A bustle of people, sounds, sights and scenes surrounded me. Actual secretaries chasing men in business suits, men carrying large musical instruments and cases, kids on a noisy tour of the premises.

We hustled past men perched in small booths, much like ticket boys at old movie theaters. On our way past a flight of open stairs, we heard, "Hiya, Sis!" It was a young man jogging down the staircase. He approached us, seeming cocky and jovial.

"Hey there, Sonny." She did a full turn around so she could speak to him as he hurried past.

Sonny and Sis? That was just comical…

"See you back there?" he asked, walking with a group of guys into a restricted area.

"Maybe later," she cooed with a smile.

I nudged her. "Who's he?"

She flapped her hand and headed into the chaos, "Just a wolf we know." She smiled. With her usual sway, she wound through the marble lobby, past pillars that could pass as silos, through a narrow hallway and into double doors—waving to people all along the way. Huge red letters, backlit and beaming, declared *REHEARSAL* above the doorway. We stopped in front of a large viewing window.

I stepped closer to the window that was as wide as the wall and peered in. I was standing over an orchestra...an enormous orchestra filled with every instrument I could name and some I couldn't. At the helm was an aging man, furiously directing with his baton, sweating beads that I could see from the balcony. He was of course wearing a full suit. Though the sound was muffled, I could make out enough to know it was spectacular. There was an entire row of harps. Really. Harps!

In a flurry, everyone below turned the page of their sheet music, flipping the white pages against black music stands at the exact same instance. How majestic and robotic they looked from above.

I watched in awe as a wave of bouncing bows danced in time on instrument strings, all aiming toward the velvet curtain suspended behind them on the stage. Flanked by two white pillars, *magnificent* was the only word to describe what I was watching. Never in my life had I had the opportunity to be so close to something so perfectly harmonious, so perfectly *human*. There was nothing electronic. No technology whatsoever. Just talented people coming together to create something far superior than they could as individuals.

The conductor lifted and dropped his baton in three large motions. And then he pulled it to the side. Signaling, then sliding, into the big finish.

As he lowered his arm, the musicians lowered their instruments.

A loud buzzer sang through the room and the REHEARSAL letters blinked off. There was the sound of automatic doors unlocking.

"So is it all coming back to you now?" Sis asked, startling me out of my amazement.

Why would she have brought me here? We worked here...What job might we have? Considering I had a whopping two years of clarinet under my belt, I prayed it wasn't as musicians. "Uh...it's seeming very familiar. But how about a hint?"

She pouted. Pulling out another cigarette, she lit it before speaking. "I don't think your memory is coming back, Babs." She shook her head and took a long drag. "I think we need to tell someone about this."

I was eyeballing her cigarette when the doors opened. "Tell someone about what?" asked a firm female voice, approaching from behind.

Sis and I turned to see a young woman dressed in a strange sort of skirted uniform. A navy blue skirt went down to her shins. Below the skirt, were heels with straps around the ankles. On the top was a military-looking jacket with a gold tassel on the left shoulder that swooped down around her arm. Ha—kind of like Michael Jackson's red, tasseled bandleader's jacket. On her chest was a small nameplate with the name: ELAINE GLASS.

Sis leaned over and did a kiss-kiss on her cheeks. "Lainey, thank goodness! If I ever needed a confidant, it would be today!"

"How melodramatic!" Elaine teased. "You aren't on today's schedule, so I wondered why I saw you duck in here." She gave me a look. "I see all."

I glanced into the expansive window to see the orchestra members filing out of the room below.

Sis grabbed my shoulders and turned me back to her face. "Babs, I'm telling her."

"Telling me what?" Elaine asked. She eyed me up once more.

My mouth opened to protest, but Sis was already talking, "Babs had an episode this afternoon. She fainted and hit her head on the wall. And now she has AMNESIA!"

Elaine's blue eyes seemed to grow to the size of the giant plastic eyes on one of Jules's stupid stuffed cats. "What?"

Sis took my hand in her gloved palm. She patted the back of my hand like so many women had done since I arrived. She looked into my eyes and continued, "She remembers me and the year and nothing else. We came here to try and jog her memory."

Elaine looked at me, concern welling in her eyes. "Babs, you should call a doctor."

My head shook back and forth. "I'll be fine. I'm feeling so much better already." And that was true! My headache was gone, the cloudiness had passed, and I was no longer tired.

"Have you told Londa?"

Sis burst out laughing. "Oh, that was a hoot! I was about to tell her when Babsie glared at me. If looks could kill!"

I shrugged. "Sorry. I just don't think it's a big concern. I'm sure I'll be all right once I get my bearings again."

A tone dinged throughout the space.

"Oh!" Elaine cried, grabbing a pocket watch on a chain out of her jacket's front pocket. "That's my cue. I need to get back for the next tour."

Sis shoved me a little. "Babs, why don't you go with her? You need all the help you can get."

Movement below through the window caught my eye. Sis noticed too. It was a cute, young trumpet player with black wavy hair. He could have played a part in *Newsies* with his plain clothes and strong Italian features. And he seemed to be lingering.

Huh. Sis was trying to get rid of me.

"Come along, then," Elaine ordered. I did as I was told while Sis slipped through an unmarked door.

Back the way we had come, we wove through hallways and doors until we arrived at the front entrance. The place was enormous! No wonder they needed tour guides.

A small crowd of people was gathering in front of the staircase. Men, women and children—about a dozen of them. Seemed odd for the middle of the day.

Elaine blew the diminutive whistle around her neck. "Good afternoon, ladies and gentleman!" she shouted. The crowd shushed itself and gathered tighter to form a mob in front of Elaine. Several people looked at me, still standing next to Elaine, so I stepped back into the crowd. A cardigan was cloaked over the shoulders of the woman to my right. With only the top button buttoned, a tall hat on her head and glasses hanging from a chain around her neck, she was a living cliché. Every nosy neighbor in every old black and white movie. I was learning things from this time period became cliché because they were both true and common occurrences.

"Good afternoon and welcome to HBC!" The crowd clapped. The mood was cheerful. "My name is Elaine and I will be your HBC guide today. Did you know that the Hollywood Broadcasting Company welcomes more than half a million visitors each year?"

Nosy Neighbor gasped.

"Behind your air waves and radios at home, there are so many people coming together to make your favorite programs pour into your living rooms each day. Let's first take a walk into the back of the recording studio."

Elaine motioned for the dirty dozen to follow her. We all trooped along until stopping in front of a piece of radio equipment as big as my new hotel room. "When radio first began, one single man could run the radio station's panel board." She pointed at the machine and then led us to a steel door. "But today, our sophisticated technology requires an entire team of men!" With a dab of drama, she opened the door to reveal knobs, valves, buttons, switches—all connected to the biggest radio I had ever seen. Wall-to-wall, floor-to-ceiling. There were three captain's chairs filled with working guys and one man was who was standing, busy poking buttons and flipping switches.

He might as well have been manning an airport rather than the airwaves.

We took turns peeking our heads into the room. One of the men in the captain's chairs looked up to give us a tired grin before returning to his post in the stuffy room. Seriously stuffy. Could have doubled as a boy's locker room. Perhaps windows would have been a sensible design addition.

Elaine closed the door, leaving the radio captains in their airless tomb, and led us down another hall. "Next we'll see how our broadcasts can be heard by radio stations all around America."

We entered a large, open space filled with plugs and switches. Cords dangled off of every board and women and men were busy plugging and unplugging.

Now that was a huge switchboard.

"Really take a look at the men and women working behind the scenes. People that are integral to HBC, even though you won't hear them on the radio."

We hurried past more musicians and secretaries and stopped to look into a glass window, much like the one I'd used to spy on the orchestra. But instead of musicians, it was row after row of women ticking on typewriters.

"These are our teletypers," Elaine clarified. "They manage more than three thousand messages per day!"

The crowd ooh'd at that stat. I smiled at Elaine. She was dynamic. I had to hand it to her. But three thousand messages and it took this entire room of teletypers? What would they think when mass email was invented?

"If you'll look past our teletypers, you'll notice a time scheduling board. Our managers are detailing each day's schedule weeks in advance. It's noted on the board down to the second!" She turned back to the crowd with palms raised. "We aren't allowed to take the tour inside anymore for fear someone may pull a cue card from the board. That happened once in 1946, and people are still talking about what a ruckus it caused!" She swung her hands down, smiling to the side at her own words.

The crowd laughed along with Elaine, and we turned back in the direction we'd come. Her voice sang through the hall as she paced backwards. She seemed compelled to look her tour in the eye. Just as we were compelled to keep our eyes glued on her. "Now, I bet many of you are visiting from out of town. Where from?"

"Missouri!"

"Nevada."

"San Diego."

"Well, you may come from all over America, but you can bet that HBC has your best interests at heart when selecting programming for the radio. You'll be happy to know that neither sponsors nor network executives decide what types of programming we air here at HBC. Can anyone guess whose opinion is leading our way?"

The group was too busy walking up the stairs to answer. Elaine was still walking backwards. Yes, even up the stairs. "Well, to determine the most popular types of programming, we do constant research by telephone and through in-person sessions. We are continuously conducting surveys of radio listeners and inviting people to listen to newly-proposed radio programing by tracking and rating your opinions on our HBC reaction sheets."

At the top of the stairs, she stopped and pointed right at my face. "We just happen to have one of our actual reaction surveyists with us right now! Please give a warm welcome to Barbara Miller, who's been rating opinions and tallying reaction sheets for the past four months with HBC!"

My tour comrades gave me a weak round of applause, but even I could tell the natives were getting restless.

Elaine clasped her hands together and crouched like she was about to tell us a secret. "Well, I bet you nice folks didn't come all this way just to hear about *how* HBC runs. I bet you came to see *who* keeps HBC on top of the ratings, am I right?"

A few members of the crowd cheered, "Yes!"

I wasn't quite following. This entire tour was making me think about the thousands of people who would be put out of work the day technology advanced. Teams of people would no longer be needed. All replaced by tiny machines, cell phones and computers. Yet people like Barbara Miller would always have work. If only I could tell them the only jobs that would survive would be the telemarketers and tacky tour guides.

"Now, I could show you our master pianist who has to be available at a moment's notice to fill the airways with music in the case of an emergency dead air situation…" A man shook his head no. "Or I could show you our music library containing millions of songs in sheet music, all awaiting approval before our orchestra plays them on the air!" The woman in the cardigan made the "hurry up" impatient roll of her hands. "I could even show you our 120-piece orchestra, which is bound to impress." No one nay'd that idea, but she continued to walk backwards until we were right under another glowing red sign. ON THE AIR, it warned as we all approached. Her voice went down to a whisper. "But I bet you all came to see our *stars* at work. So how about I open this door and reveal to you who's broadcasting right this very minute. Any guesses?"

Our tiny crowd was buzzing in anticipation.

"Bob Hope?" one person called.

"Betty Grable?" another wanted to know.

"I'll give you a hint," Elaine twittered. "She's *too marvelous* for words! You may have heard her last month on *Your Hit Parade*!"

The woman next to me stifled a scream. She literally screamed into her gloved hand.

Who the hell were we about to meet?

The bright red ON THE AIR flashed to black and a loud buzzer sounded.

"Ladies and gentleman, let us enter the recording studio and see…Mrs. Doris Day!"

The crowd erupted into cheers and people pushed toward the door. I was half trampled as everyone stampeded through the small doorway.

As we entered, we saw Doris Day ready to exit through a door on the other side of the glass near oversized microphones and headsets. When she heard the roar of our entrance, she turned and flashed us a magical smile. She blew the young boy in the crowd a kiss. And then she was gone.

The members of the tour were ablaze with chatter. *Did you see her eyes? She winked at me! Did you see the scarf she was wearing? I always knew she was shorter than me. Do you think she styles her own hair?*

"Ladies and gentleman!" Elaine called before issuing a sharp tweet of her whistle. Now I saw the need for the whistle. "Let me now take you to a live rehearsal in Theater A. You will all have the chance to be seated as audience members. Now how would you like that?"

Our group would have followed Elaine anywhere she led. She was pretty much a goddess at that point—having led us to the oasis of Doris.

Meanwhile, I couldn't stop obsessing about cell phones. I'd been part of an actual Hollywood celebrity sighting, and no one had taken a picture. Not one click of a camera. Just a moment we had all lived without wasting the five seconds watching it from behind a cell phone case. Mystifying. And beautiful. But so ingrained in me I had reached for a back pocket out of instinct. Hell, one time I met Craig Culver—the CEO of the Culver's chain of Midwestern restaurants—and he gave me a coffee mug with a tiny, spin-able Butterburger on the handle. I snapped so many pictures of the exchange I might have helped the term *selfie* catch on. And that was my appropriate level of fanfare for a restaurant manager. I had never spent late nights snuggled into my couch watching any of *his* old movies.

Soon we were being herded into a row of theater seats. I hung back and went in last, seated at the aisle seat. After a verse of *Video Killed the Radio Star* finished playing in my mind, the buzzers went off, lights flashed, and a man stepped to center stage. The orchestra was seated in the pit. I scanned the trumpet section to see if Sis's cute guy was missing. But I wasn't sure.

From somewhere in the ominous back of the theater, a voice boomed, "Broadcasting tonight from Hollywood, California—the most glamorous city in the world. We hope you'll enjoy tonight's performance with your host Zeke Barrymore!"

The APPLAUSE sign started blinking, and we all began clapping. I craned to look behind me and saw the box where the voice had emerged. From behind a different viewing window, I watched a man signal a crescendo followed by a halt of the applause. Everyone did exactly as instructed. The director then pointed at the conductor and, right on cue, the orchestra sprang back to life, filling the theater with a symphony. A literal, goddamn symphony. For the opening of a nightly radio spot.

"Good evening and welcome," the host began. Wrapped in his graceful hands was a microphone pole as thick as a stripper pole. The microphone at the top was bigger than his head. In gold letters at the top of the microphone were the letters HBC. In case he forgot where he was broadcasting from?

I was engrossed and trying to figure out how none of the hundreds of people on stage—the choir members, speakers, musicians—tripped over the thick, black cords laying all over the stage when I felt a tapping on my shoulder. I looked up to see a man I hadn't yet met. He motioned for me to follow him. I looked around to search out Elaine or Sis, but neither were present.

I got up and, without a word, he again motioned for me to follow. I did. He pushed open the double doors to exit the theater. I followed. In the hallway he didn't stop, but rather looked around suspiciously and marched down the hall without making eye contact. Finally, we reached another set of double doors and entered with a clang as the doors closed behind us.

I looked around. I had no idea what I was standing in. Drawers as big as large-breed dog kennels surrounded me. They stretched up so high there were rolling ladders scattered around. The sign above the mysterious stranger's head clued me in: MUSIC LIBRARY. Hadn't Elaine said this room housed millions of orchestrations on file? I felt claustrophobic among the rows and rows of drawers. I noticed there was a framed warning sign with lettering in red bold: EVERY MUSICAL SELECTION MUST FIRST RECEIVE VERIFIED PERFORMANCE RIGHTS AND BE GIVEN CLEARANCE BEFORE DELIVERY TO THE COMPOSING STAFF!

I cringed. The thought of cataloguing millions of songs by hand was outrageous. Unthinkable. Kudos to iTunes...

"I have the latest," the man said, still not looking me in the eye. I noticed now that he was wearing a janitor's worksuit. He was teenager-young with messy blond hair. Thin and gangly, he seemed stuck in a permanent state of hunched. He jerked one of the bulky cabinets away from the wall with a thundering *bang*. Leaning into the shadow, he pulled out a lady's handbag. A clutch.

Hey, was that my missing purse?

I had no idea what to say or what to do. So I reached out and accepted it. It was crammed so full it looked odd and bulging. Curious, I opened it. And inside was a pile slim, aluminum tubes.

"Digger said same deal. Contact him when you have the dough." He gave the cabinet another rough jerk, and it was back in its original location.

Exit mysterious stranger.

Well...it was a pretty little clutch. I saw a coin purse next to the mystifying pile of containers. Sis would be pleased. Then I pulled out one of the tubes and read the tiny print on the side:

Benzedrine Inhaler

250-mg

Holy shit!

I snapped the clutch's small latch closed and took a deep breath. Tucking the petite, powder blue purse under my armpit, I hurried out of the library. Pretty much freaking out at that point, I just started walking.

So this was full-on drugs. Barbara Miller was…a drug addict? A drug *dealer*? Who were the customers? The women at the hotel? Is that why none of them seemed surprised at my "incident?" The incident that was so obviously an overdose?

And my bony little frame! I wasn't an Audrey Hepburn. I was a Courtney Love! Dammit!

I wandered back to Theater A and slipped into the room without disrupting much. I sat back in my seat, letting the symphony become the background music of my panic attack.

SIS, ELAINE AND I walked back into Heritage House together. Sis had looked right at my reunited accessory and I, but didn't say a thing about it. After Henry held the door, we made our way to the sweeping staircase together.

"Miss Miller," old Jackie Kennedy called from behind her front desk post. "Matron Mahoney has been awaiting your return. She'll see you in her office." She gestured to a door tucked under the stairs.

"Zing!" Sis called, mounting the staircase already. "She caught you after all!" She threw me one of her winning smiles as she and Elaine escaped to their rooms.

My heels echoed through the lobby. Approaching the door, I noticed a small, gold plate announcing OFFICE. Ms. Matron of Honor didn't get a lot of glory around here.

I knocked three times.

"You may enter."

I opened the door and hung back in the doorway. "Front desk lady said you were waiting for me."

She furrowed her brow. "Watch your words, young lady." She motioned for me to be seated. The room was asphyxiating. The ceiling sloped with the staircase. My guess, this was meant for storage, not for a house matron's office. I sat in the faux-velvet armchair. With the room's anxiety level mounting, I pushed at the bridge of my nose. But no glasses were there to push up. Huh. Did habits transport with a person's brain?

From behind her desk, she pulled out a file. I saw *Miller, Barbara* typed across the tab. I shifted in my chair.

"We must, I'm afraid, address your issue with back rent."

I crossed my legs and crammed the illegally-stuffed clutch tighter under my pit. I nodded that she should continue.

"Now, I know this is not good timing to address this issue, but you must have known it was coming. Rent was due September 1st. At $12 a week, I can't keep floating you in your single room. This is the third month in a row you've been late. And I suppose you will be short again?" She waited, but I said nothing. "And so, we need a solution."

She pulled a pamphlet out of a holder at the corner of her desk entitled, *Heritage House Hollywood*. Opening and pointing to a grainy image, she continued, "I think it's time to move you to shared quarters. They are priced at a manageable $8 a week and still include two meals per day."

The picture was of two girls sitting on a bed together while another filed her nails on a cot, looking ravishing in their button-up pajamas, of course. This was Hollywood, after all.

"Now, depending on the roommates, it wouldn't be all that bad. Our double beds are plenty big enough for two to sleep comfortably. And the studio couch isn't all bad. Some of the girls rotate day to day."

Sleep next to a perfect stranger? Was this real? "I'd rather not," I stated.

Matron Mahoney's lips pursed and eyebrows tightened at the center of her forehead. "Dear, I'm afraid I'm not asking. I'm giving you a final chance to show me you can be an independent woman. I know you strut around here telling everyone you're nineteen, but we both know you're approaching twenty-two. It's time you made realistic decisions. It's time to prove to yourself that you moved here from Milwaukee for a reason."

Ooh, Babs was from Wisconsin. I was still Midwestern!

"Now. Do you have this month's rent?" She looked down at a thin sheet of paper in my file. "You were $3 short in July and two short in August. That puts you at $17 due for September." She looked up, pity in her eyes. "Now, I know what you make at the station. If you aren't able to find a way to make some extra this month, I'm afraid I'll have to…turn you out." She looked down. I read a sense of failure in her expression. "And I don't want to turn you out. I'm no dummy. I know the sorts of things women have to resort to when they're down on their luck." She looked up with a burst of excitement. "Why don't you find a manager or director down at the station? You still have time to marry and have children!"

I furrowed my brow. "Thank you, Londa. Please tell me what room I should move to."

Disappointed at my lack of enthusiasm, she pawed through a few more files. "First floor. Room seven. You'll be in with Bess and Peggy." She looked up and scowled. "Now that they have a spot available."

I sighed and adjusted the sweaty clutch again, tracing the thin, painted pipe along the wall with my eyes and noting where it entered her dented radiator.

She cleared her throat. "So after breakfast tomorrow, I expect you moved downstairs. I'll let the girls know to expect you. They can clear out a space in the dresser for you. And as for your dresses…Well, I would ask a friend to hold on to those, if I were you. No wardrobes in the shared rooms, you know." She stood. The sound of her desk chair dragging across the floor startled me. "That will be all, Miss Miller."

I sighed again and heaved myself out of the chair.

When I left the room, I was met by Sis's smiling face. "And what did the old spinster want now?"

"It seems I will be moving down to first floor. With Bess and Peggy?"

Her mouth gaped open. "Ain't that a bite?"

I headed for the stairs.

She followed like my lost puppy. "You're behind on your rent? But we just went shopping last week! If I had known you were behind, I could have…well, I might have been able to ask my father to–"

"It's fine, Sis. I just need a place to hang my closet things. Apparently, the shared rooms don't even have a wardrobe."

"Oh, I know it! Such malarkey! Well you can sure use mine, Babs. In fact, we can move your dresses straight into my room right now. We have a few minutes before the dinner bell chimes." We rounded the corner and started down the long, carpeted hallway just as we had this morning—which now seemed like a year ago. Sis poked me with her elbow. "It's not like I'm overly excited to get down to my broiled chicken and creamed peas anyway."

AT LAST, I was able to shut the door for my first moment alone in Heritage House. I fumbled in the dark for a lock, but there was only a keyhole.

People seriously didn't have privacy in 1947, which frightened the hell out of me since I was carrying around a pile of drug inhalers.

With the light from the window, I took the few steps over to the curvy, art deco bedside table. I switched on the lamp, its light illuminating a portion of the quaint space. The room was small, but it did hold a certain charm.

Taking a moment to soak in the expanse of my view, I let out a sniff as a substitute for a laugh. Two lights on the hill had just switched off. The sight brought a memorized line from a Dr.

Seuss book to mind. *Every light between here and Far Foodle is out.*
I had read *The Sleep Book* a hundred times. So many times that
Jules started reciting a ridiculous rewrite. "Every butt crack from
here to Far Foodle is out!" she would announce each time Doug
bent down.

Turning away from the view and the homesick feeling, I
opened the clutch and dumped the contents onto the bed. A
quick scan revealed lucky number thirteen. What was I supposed to do with thirteen inhalers?

Inspecting one of the aluminum tubes, I was tempted to try
it. At 250-mg, it was way more potent than the 5-mg pep pills
Sis and I were always taking. I had never used an inhaler for
anything in my life. And I hadn't even realized they were around
in the forties.

Though I was alone, I shook my head.

How had a goodie-two-shoes ended up like this? And not
just the mind-blowing time travel piece, though that in itself
was a landmine. But how had a woman who'd made it 34 years
without *ever* having taken drugs ended up looking down on a
pile of paraphernalia?

Okay, one time I'd been pushed into eating a pot brownie, but
it hadn't done anything.

Other than that, the closest I'd come to drugs was while
vacationing in Miami with a friend. She had smuggled pot home
in her baggage in a travel-size shampoo bottle. Unbeknownst to
me, she'd also purchased a new bong in Miami. When we arrived
back at the airport, her bag hadn't made the trip home. Then she
informed me why she was in such a panic over her lost luggage.
With every minute seeming like an hour, we had paced the floor,
wondering if she would be hauled off to jail. Arrested. Fined.
Then four hours later, the doorbell chimed. And standing at the
door was a porter about the same age as we were at that time.
Just handing over the bag with no questions asked. Just a simple
apology from the airline, obviously memorized and repeated
with no meaning behind the words. Crisis averted.

I sighed and swept the pile of inhalers back into the clutch. Then I slipped off my shoes, expecting my feet to hurt. But they didn't. Ah, but I kept forgetting they were not my feet. And though I'd now actually walked a mile in someone else's shoes, I didn't feel all that enlightened. I felt like a strange voyeur. Like I was playing some virtual reality video game...while drunk.

I went to the dresser and stooped to look into the mirror. The darkness and the lamp's dim light played with my mind. As I stared, I kept thinking I saw movement behind me. Wishful thinking? Bad lighting?

I stared for a full minute or two. But all I saw was someone else's face staring back. Barbara Miller's. In fact, it was all Barbara Miller's. Her bony shoulder, her slender waist, her sprightly, young boobs. I could not think of a word strong enough to convey what it felt like being *in* someone else's body. I was afraid to look, even though it was all connected. Earlier, I had peed like I was holding the stall door closed for a friend—head turned, not peeking.

I fell to the bed, wondering what time it was, wondering if it was the same time in 2011. Thanks to Barbara's twenty-something stamina, I didn't feel tired. Was it bedtime for Jules and Jakey? I ached to hug them, to at least know I would once again be able to hug them.

Were they asking for their mommy? Had Doug taken them to see me at the hospital?

I snickered at the irony. Since I'd had both of them at a birth center, I had never spent the night at a hospital before. I got the heebie-jeebies being around so many sad, sick and dying people. Probably why the closest I'd come to healthcare was a job coaching women on how to push an organ out of their body and *not* be admitted to the hospital. (What? The placenta is an organ.)

Yet tonight my body was spending its first night in a hospital. Without me.

Valentina had been right to stutter her definition. Was it my brain? Soul? How was I still *me* without my body?

And how would I figure out how to get back to my body? I hadn't even come close to figuring out why I'd been sent here. Valentina had explained I was some sort of watcher. What was I watching? A person? A historical event?

Gah. I love how she had promised not to send me in without knowing "rules of mirror," and then she had done just that. She'd written me the note about New York…but I was in California. In 1947. With no money to my name. How the hell would I get to New York to find her diary?

I sat up and opened the single drawer in the bedside table. As I had hoped, there was a pen. No paper, but there was a postcard. I scanned the image. It was the typical Californian photo. A palm-lined street near the beach.

I looked back to the window out of instinct, wondering how far away I was from the ocean. Then checked the postcard. The back was blank. Barbara had never written it out.

Pushing aside the curiosity of her thinking, I went to work making myself a primitive list. All of the people I had met, situations I had been connected to. I couldn't get so sucked into the life here that I forgot to decipher the meaning of all of this.

When the postcard was full, I slipped it back into the drawer, sending myself a mental note to steal paper from HBC when I got the chance.

A sudden *tap, tap* on my door startled me. The door opened before I could ask who it was.

"Just me," Sis's voice whispered. "I figured with your memory lapse, you'd probably forget to take your sleeping pill." She was already next to me, hand outstretched.

I opened my palm and accepted the small pill. I guess she was my drug vending machine. And I guess it was okay I wasn't tired. There was a pill for that.

"Sleep well, Babsie. I hope tomorrow you wake up good as new. We'll get you all moved into Bess's room before we leave for work. Us bachelor girls need to stick together!" She giggled and backed to the door. "At least until we marry. Nighty night."

The door latched again and I sighed. My afternoon's cup of cloudy water was still on the bedside table. Again, doing as I was told, I gulped down my sleeping pill.

After all, it wasn't my body.

CHAPTER 4

NOIR AT THE NIGHTCLUB

I LOOKED AT the clock hanging in the HBC survey room, thanking God our shift was almost over. Most of my second day in 1947 had been spent in this room. The room was filled with women all appearing happy as pie to be working on a Saturday. (Can one really be as happy as pie? Is pie happy?) They sat two to a desk, facing each other. Between each was a giant switchboard. Black phones rang intermittently and sweet drawls of customer service sang through the room.

When we'd first arrived, Sis had been horrified I couldn't remember my job. "You simply ask the person on the line to rate the program they listened to and mark *good, fair* or *poor* on your reaction sheets," Sis had reminded me.

"That's it?"

"That's it," She'd answered. "Best $10 a week I ever earned."

And that's when my rent fiasco had come into focus.

I looked across the room. Sitting at her desk, Sis's shoulder-length, shiny hair was straight out of a shampoo commercial. It was parted at the side and somehow pinned to the top of her head. Near her ears, it cascaded out of the bobby pins and flowed right down to her double-row pearl necklace. Her light blue blouse was covered in flying doves, and it was double-breasted like a man's suit. Her glossy, pointed fingernail pushed the button on the switchboard and she was speaking in her calm and steady tone in an instant, "This is the HBC rating service. We are conducting a survey of radio listeners. Were you listening to your radio last night at six o'clock?" She paused and listened. "To what program were you listening, please?" She laughed at something the other person said. Just as she had done all day. Yet it never stopped feeling genuine.

I felt a great fondness for the ease of her being. She made living seem like a joy rather than a chore. She enjoyed people, her job. She made looking glamorous seem effortless. She made me envy her womanhood.

I filled out another reaction sheet with bogus information. No one around me seemed to notice, and it was far easier than figuring out the damn switchboard again. I was checking the "good" box for the thousandth time, when a chime tolled. Just as it had signaled Elaine to start her tour yesterday, it also signaled the end of our work day. The room of women rushed to finish phone calls, stood to chatter with coworkers and started gathering their personal things.

Sis was still laughing away on her call, oblivious to the five o'clock tone, so I gathered up my things as well. I pulled out my powder blue clutch, minus the pile of inhalers. I had stashed those in the pockets of a long coat before hanging it in Sis's wardrobe. Now that I shared a room (and dresser, and bed, and personal space of all kinds), I didn't have a lot of hiding places. I did, however, restock my clutch's stash of tiny, white pills. After the morning headache and eye twitch started to push back in, I'd popped one. Gone was my habitual morning coffee. Gained was my morning benny.

The plan I had devised during my long (long) day of telemarketing was to check out the library in Heritage House. I still hadn't managed to get to so much as a peek at a newspaper. There was so much I still wanted to know. I could feel Doug's imaginary mocking at my admission, but I didn't even know who was president of the United States in 1947.

"Now you have a pleasant day, too!" Sis was finishing up. "Oh, thank you. Yes, be sure to catch Zeke Barrymore again next

Friday. Bye!" She pulled off her massive headphones and looked at me. "My! Is it five o'clock already?"

I almost rolled my eyes. "It is. And if you're ready to head out, I'm looking forward to some time in the library."

She laughed so loud that everyone in the room turned. "If you aren't a regular Danny Kaye." She grabbed her hand purse and led the way out into the hall. "I suppose for your next bit you'll trip down the stairs!"

Guiding me just as she had since I arrived, she led me through the maze of hallways and doorways back to the front lobby.

"Oh!" she yelped, pointing. "I want to go wish Elaine good luck. Be back in a jiff."

I stood like the voyeur I was, pretty much paralyzed without her, second guessing just who was the master and who was the lost puppy. I watched. I judged.

The clothing. The accessories (briefcases, pencils and nametags—oh, my!) and the tedious hair.

Today I'd tried to leave Barbara's hair wild and free. Sis, of course, wouldn't hear of it. She'd spent a good twenty minutes in the powder room torturing me with bobby pins. It had taken us just over an hour to get ready for work, which was laughable by mom standards. At home I was lucky (lucky!) to get twenty minutes alone in the bathroom. But even before I had to get ready in seven minutes (the more usual occurrence), I still hadn't perfected the art of womanhood. I had never owned a curling iron, never learned to French braid, never understood why women would pay a hundred dollars for makeup. In fact, one Christmas, a family friend had given Jules an American Girl Doll. It had come with an insert just about caring for the doll's hair. Instructions on brushing, products, techniques (gah!). As I skimmed over the wording, I glanced at Jakey who—I kid you not—at that very moment had a glob of yogurt in the front of his hair *There's Something About Mary* style and was in the process of smearing snot up to his hairline as well. Knowing I couldn't even keep my own kid's hair clean, I tossed the insert in the trash, accepting I just wasn't that kind of woman and being fine with that.

But that part of me was not acceptable in the 1940s, it seemed.

I saw Sis and Elaine hug before noticing Strange Janitor Dude sulking behind them, hunched per usual. I turned away and pretended to scratch my neck.

"You won't believe this!" Sis was saying before she was even back to my side. "Your luck is changing, old girl. Elaine told me that Marjorie is sick again."

Oh, how she must have tired from my blank stares. "Okay. How does this indicate a change in my luck?"

She giggled again and linked arms. "This means you can be her stand-in again tonight at the club! Money, Babsie. Your rent! Isn't that just grand?"

"Too marvelous for words," I mumbled. Twittering again at my obvious sarcasm, I wondered if her face ever got sore from all the cheeriness. "Remind me again how I stand-in?"

We had just exited though HBC's rotating, glass doors when she whirled around. "Just when I tell myself you're getting better, you prove that you really don't remember a thing, Barbara Miller!"

I shrugged.

"That is simply *it*. You have to see Doc. I don't understand what's happening to you. You can't remember anything! I certainly don't mind helping you out, but you don't even act like you want to get better. You need help, Babs. Promise me you'll talk to Doc."

"I promise," I lied.

"Good," she asserted, fiddling with her pearls and resigning herself to get back to the cheeriness at hand. "Now, let's hurry home. We'll have to get Marjorie's frock. Oh, it *is* the best bit of luck that we'll both be waitressing tonight. Saturday nights are the best shifts! Why, you're liable to make a good five or six dollars in tips!"

A WOMAN NAMED Carol stood in front of us, around back of the nightclub a few hours later. We had toddled along Sunset Boulevard in our "working heels" until approaching an oval building full of pomp and lights. Following my master, I'd curved around the alleyway as she had. Still trying with desperation to emulate her womanly essence. (And failing.)

"Close your head!" Sis cried in disbelief. "Can you believe this, Babs? Cary Grant. Here. Tonight!" she gushed. "*This* is why I came to Hollywood." She flung her hands out in front of her body. Her smile was so wide it pushed her ears backward. "Have you been to see Hitchcock's *Notorious* yet? Thrilling!"

Carol took another drag of her cigarette, not even in the same realm of enthusiastic as dear Sis. "I heard Alfred Hitchcock doesn't have a navel," she inserted with a flat tone.

"What?" Sis shrieked.

"How is it possible to not have a belly button? Did he hatch?" I asked.

Carol had a masculine way about her movements. She demanded respect with her stance and tone. "Just what I heard." She stomped out her cigarette. "Well, I better get back in there. I also saw Miss Queen of Hollywood snooping around Cary Grant's table. Could be good press for me and the gals."

I looked to Sis to make sense of her words. As if we had an actual friendship, she smiled tenderly. "Hedda Hopper. Hollywood Gossip Column queen. Keep up, Babsie."

Carol gave me a look. "I haven't been drinking half as much as I should be." Then she flung open the back door with such force that it slammed against the wall. She was in high-waisted pants and a tight button-up shirt. Not what I imagined I'd see at the Palindrome, considering what I had been roped into wearing.

Sheer tulle draped down to ankles strapped into light pink heels. On the top, we wore something akin to a skanky Halloween costume. One shoulder strap not only held up the "dress" but was also adorned with the biggest carnation corsage I'd ever seen. It was so tight around the waist I could barely breathe (which was saying something since the new body was probably a size four in 2011 sizing), then flaring out at the hips to create a tutu effect. It made me wonder what Jules was wearing—she always had a fondness for mismatching clothes and twirling tutus. She'd love to see this strange getup. Probably call me a princess.

"Babs!" Sis was calling from the doorway. "Let's get you in here before the stage manager notices Marjorie isn't here." I followed her into the back entrance.

We had stopped in to see Marjorie to get this outfit. My diagnosis? One hell of a hangover. Marjorie's shift at the Palindrome the night before had leaked into the morning hours. While there, we had all taken our afternoon pep pills together to hear the story. Marjorie had been lurking outside when Henry manned his post at the front entrance of Heritage House, so the gossip was told. Spent the night shivering on the stoop and banging on the front door. Londa refused to let her in until sunup. This was all explained while passing around a View-Master filled with dirty pictures. Shocked they had the same toy I had played with in the eighties filled with a sailor undressing, I had clicked through each frame…twice.

Following Sis's tiny frame through a dimly lit back hallway, we emerged into a cluster of commotion. There were several women dressed in identical frocks. (Yes, I used the word frock. Their language was contagious.) Waitresses, I presumed. The women were groaning and complaining. And standing in a long line.

Sis butted right in. "What's going on here?"

The young woman she was asking looked a little terrified to answer. "Al is demanding we all have smallpox vaccinations. Right now. Right here."

The disbelief was obvious as I registered her words. "Smallpox?"

The young woman looked at me, noticing Sis's companion was not who she expected. "Oh, he is not going to be happy to see Marjorie isn't here again! Is she sick again? Oh my! No smallpox symptoms, I hope."

"Psh, her symptoms all point to the bottle flu," Sis retorted, getting in line in front of several others waiting.

I looked ahead and saw a thick old woman in an actual white nurse's uniform hiking up a girl's tulle and jabbing her thigh with a long needle. "This is as hard to swallow as my Granny's peanut butter and butter sandwiches…" I mumbled.

The other waitress chuckled and nudged me. "It gets better." She pointed to a handsome man in a suit, leaning in and taking photos of the entire process. "Word is, he's here with Hedda Hopper."

"No!" Sis exclaimed, patting her hair and standing a bit straighter. "Well, God bless America." She was loving this.

"Yes," the waitress replied. "Publicity for the efforts the club is taking to keep us all safe."

"Next!" Mean Nurse called. We all stepped forward.

"You better look your best," the waitress warned Sis. "No wincing or crying. One never knows what Hopper will caption a photo!"

Sis adjusted her corsage. "Well, the good news is the nurse doesn't know us. When it's your turn, just tell her you're Marjorie Meyers. Al will never know she wasn't here."

"Next!"

We watched as the friendly waitress lifted her tulle up to her waist and propped her high heel on the wood chair in front of her. She unclipped her nylon stocking and rolled it to her knee. I couldn't look away. Not just because of my disbelief, but also because her legs were unreal. Like didn't physically look real. From the land of photoshopped celebrities, I was almost disheartened to see it indeed *was* physically possible to have legs that looked that good.

"Great gams, eh?" Sis said to my opened-mouth gape.

"Unreal…"

"This is just her lamplight gig. She's a professional roller skater."

I whipped around to face her. "That can't be real!"

Her laugh was full of glee. "Sure it is. She's hired to do a choreographed skate around tennis courts, parking lots, lobbies—she's big in the party scene. Unique, graceful entertainment, wouldn't you say?"

I turned back to look at those legs again. The nurse jabbed her and she did indeed wince. Snap, went her photo. "Oh dear…" she whispered, heading off toward the front of the nightclub, snapping her stocking back in place.

Next up was Sis. Patting her hair once more, she marched right up to the nurse, but directed herself at the photographer. "The name is Sis Rose." Jab, went the needle. Click, went the camera. Ever-poised was dear Sis.

With a wink, she was gone.

"Next!"

Trying not to panic, I did as the others had. Gingerly raising my skirt, Mean Nurse was glaring at me. "Name?" was all she said.

"Uh, Marjorie Meyers." I fumbled with the nylon clip and paused to check out my own leg situation.

I was in the midst of being pleased at the lack of cellulite when she jabbed and I yelped. Actually yelped!

Thankfully, the camera man was too busy watching a woman in a gargantuan hat beckoning him to the front to get a photo of my less-than-demure reaction.

Mean Nurse marked something on a clipboard and yelled, "Next!"

Rubbing my leg, I too went in the direction of the others. No one back home would believe this. I just got a mandatory nightclub vaccination wearing a tutu.

In a rush, I remembered the face I'd made while listening to Valentina explain what had happened to her. I'd thought she was crazy! I had gone so far as to suggest multiple personalities. Yuck. I hope I hadn't been right. I hope this wasn't all some fantastical mind maze I had created on my own.

After dropping my things off in a little room, I pushed the double-wide doors open to enter into the main room. I saw Sis about a mile away, behind a long bar. Walking out into the ballroom to make my way back to the bar, I wanted to do a full-circle with my arms stretched wide *Sound of Music* style. The Palindrome was beautiful and enormous!

I had come out of a door that stretched up to the ceiling. The stage next to it seemed large enough to hold an army. (And something told me it had, since World War II was still fresh in everyone's mind.) Again with the swooping, velvet curtain—but unlike the one at HBC, this one was mustard yellow...a yellow color that definitely had a name. Citrus? No, citrine! Hey, my mind still worked!

Satisfied I could indeed survive without looking every single thing up on the Internet, I marched over part of the oval dance floor and into the seemingly millions of chairs and tables.

The chatter of conversation and clinking glasses made me feel like I was attending a large wedding—a wedding with like a thousand other people. The guests were all dressed well and drinking. And most eyes were at the front of the room. There was a buzzing in the air. A shiny feeling that I recalled from my clubbing days. Maybe it was the extrovert in me, but I could feel the energy in the room. People were here to be happy. People were here to have a good time.

And I was going to liquor them up so they could! Perhaps I had missed my life's calling.

I glanced back to see Carol, the woman we'd talked to out in the alley, leading the band! I couldn't help but smile. Part of me wanted to throw a fist up in the air and declare, "You go, girl!" But I contained myself.

Aside from the thick cigarette and cigar smoke devouring all of the air in the room, being a part of this scene was like a dream come true.

And I longed for my cell phone camera to freeze the moment in time.

Finally back to the bar, Sis was already loading up a black tray and balancing it on one palm. "You're gonna hafta keep up here, Babsie ol' girl. I sure hope you remember the ins and outs of cocktail waitressing because I certainly won't be able to help tonight." And she was off, weaving through chairs and customers, also seeming happy to be part of the coming-together set before us.

I turned back to the bar and was met by a pair of giant, brown eyes. Leaning in to be heard, he said, "Well, well, well...look who came back to Vinny."

I smiled. It was automatic. The guy made my heart race. I felt flush. The look in his eye, the smirk on his lips.

Oh, yeah. We'd done stuff before.

"It's me...Babs," I blurted, sucked back into the rush of being wanted. There was a look in his eye I hadn't seen in oh so long.

He chuckled and wiped the bar top. "Maybe after your first round you needs to get some more glasses from the back?" His eyebrow arched in proposition.

"Perhaps," I flirted, grabbing a round tray from the pile.

Someone patted my back. I turned to see Sis again. "He's here! Really, truly here!"

My eyes looked to her aim and I too gasped. "He really *is* here!"

There before me was yet another beyond-handsome man—Mr. Cary Grant. Glossy, black hair, just as it had always appeared in the late night TCM movies my mom and I used to binge watch. Sideways smirk. Swelling with charm.

Sis was squeezing my arm so hard I had to slap her away. "I want to hear him talk," I stated robotically.

Must. Hear. Accent.

In a daze, I sent my starstruck host body in the direction of Grant. When I was about halfway to his back booth, I felt the familiar hand on my shoulder. "Barbara! You can't!" Sis declared.

I looked back at her. She was pointing to a small sign near the booth that scrawled PRIVATE PARTY in a decorative font. Then she nodded to the rock of a man seated in the corner booth next to it.

"But surely bodyguards won't stop lil' ol' me," I cooed to her.

She yanked again. "Oh yes they most certainly will!' she hollered over the music into my ear. "Besides, it looks like your dance card may already be full."

We both looked back to the bar and saw Yummy Vinny, watching our every move as he whipped up some kind of red mixed drink and plopped in an olive.

With longing, I looked back for another glance of Cary Grant. My, he was gorgeous. He was under colored accent lighting within his private dome-top cocktail lounge area, oozing a captivating brand of charming—even when a giant pineapple centerpiece surrounded by a line of tiny shrimps threatened to humanize him.

"Maybe you can have the tables over that way, though I doubt Miriam will give them up, considering. But you can always host that way and overhear him, if that's all you want."

"Oh, it's not all I want…"

Sis slapped me. "You're positively beastly!" She was smiling despite her verdict.

Soaking in his features, I sighed. "I suppose he really is too classically handsome to be straight."

Sis appeared puzzled. I realized it would be years before anyone in Hollywood knew the truth about Archibald Leach—which was Cary Grant's real name, and which I could somehow recall even though I still hadn't even figured out who the hell the president was.

"Chop, chop," Sis called, marching to a specific table. How she kept it straight from the others was beyond me. I followed, my tray empty, only to realize hers was full of drinks.

She chattered something at the patrons and tossed them her winning smile before sliding the drinks around to each of them.

When she stepped back, she stepped on my toe. "Babs!" she yelled, appearing cross for the first instant since I had met her. "Get to your tables." And then, the familiar nervous laugh. "Your tables are right over there, old gal." She pointed, grinning once again.

Stumbling away, I walked up to one of the tables I guessed to be mine. With not a minute of waitressing on my resume, I did what I assumed I should do. "Can I take your order?"

A round man in a checkered suit squeezed my right butt cheek. I squealed and darted away from his grasp, causing the table to roar with laughter. "We got ourselves a jumpy one tonight, boys!"

Forcing a smile, I repeated, "Can I take your order?"

"We're good, cupcake. But come on back to papa when your shift ends." He winked.

I held back a gag.

The song ended, and for a moment, there was silence. My gaze shot to the stage in time to see Carol at the mic. She introduced a singer I had never heard of and the singer revealed herself from behind the citrine curtain.

The audience applauded and the next song began. The vibrato of the woman's sultry voice resonated through the room. It was a perfect scene around me. A chandelier hung on the left side of the dance floor, signaling the "nice section" where Cary Grant and probably the Queen of Hollywood were seated. All of the tables held a vase with a single, red carnation. Huh. Red carnations, I noticed, that matched the giant corsage adorning my chest. I was part of the vibe.

I headed back to the bar, but someone caught my wrist. "Miss, two fingers of Scotch on the double," he said.

I nodded to him and hustled back to the bar where Yummy Vinny was shaking a cocktail in a chrome shaker—an act that never ceased to charm me.

Was that on the double? Or make that a double? Waitressing was not proving to be my life's calling after all.

Mid-shake, Vinny leaned over to me once again. And waited.

After a moment, I realized he was waiting for my table's order. "Uh, Scotch…make it a double."

He wrinkled his forehead, but kept moving—fulfilling several orders already.

He pushed a full shot glass over to me using his forearm. Looking into his eyes, I realized it was meant for me to drink while I waited. So I drank it.

Met with the burning liquid, I wanted to let out a loud, "Woo!" The sense of possibility ringing through my host body reminded me of a stupid Facebook meme I'd read a while back. It showed three cartoon women. One was barely wearing any clothes and screaming they should all do shots, go to a strip club, get matching tattoos, and fly to Vegas. The accurate caption stated: *When stay-at-home-moms get a night out.*

So true. Even before I was trapped in old Hollywood in a hot, young body.

I nodded in thanks, my face beaming in a flirtatious smile meant just for him. As he filled a waitress's tray, he slid another over to me with a wink.

I threw my head back in a laugh, wondering if he was trying to get me drunk for unsavory purposes. But considering all I'd been through in the past 48 hours, it was a relief to be offered a moment to escape. I shot it back into my throat, feeling it sting all the way down.

"You looked like yous needed a drink," he said in his gruff, Neanderthal tone.

Laughing again, I said, "I did. Thank you."

He chuckled at my words, his shoulders heaving in happiness. "Never thought I'd hear you say thanks for nothin."

I nodded, not knowing how to respond but getting to know Barbara Miller just a little bit more.

Then he bobbed his handsome head to acknowledge someone behind me. I turned to see another waitress bellowing her order over my head and batting her eyelashes over her bosom. One of the other bartenders was free, yet this waitress was pushing past me to get to Yummy Vinny. She pressed in so close I felt a shove against my new injection site.

I glared at her and looked down. Somehow my lowly, single glass had been placed on my tray without me even noticing. I picked it up, squeezed past Miss Flirty and headed back out into the crowd.

Now which one was his table…?

As I wandered, trying to remember what Scotch guy looked like, I spotted the checkered suit creep and oriented myself from his (overweight) position. Scotch guy was two tables over from him.

"Here you are, sir," I offered, setting down the crystal glass of brown liquid with a slow hand. My movement was not fluid. Was I already feeling buzzed from two shots?

The man looked at his drink and looked at me. He didn't look satisfied but tossed a nickel onto my black tray nonetheless.

A nickel. Five fricken cents. Man, to make $5 in a night's tips I would have to serve so many drinks! Like…(five, ten, fifteen, twenty…) Dammit, when did I get so stupid? I seriously couldn't do simple math without my smartphone calculator anymore?

"What's the matter, doll? You look troubled," a man called from a nearby table.

I turned toward him. Maybe it was the two shots of Scotch hot inside me, but I bellied right up to him. "If I make five cents per drink, how many drinks do I need to serve to earn $5 tonight?" I bellowed into his ear.

Without missing a beat, he said, "Why that's easy, dollface. A hundred."

I crumpled my mouth in a form of disgust at both his answer and his ability to do math.

"But not everyone tips a nickel, see?" He flipped a dime onto my tray. "Run and fetch me a martini, doll, and there's more where that came from. And make it dry."

I nodded, the music engulfing any chance of speaking without yelling, and ran to fetch.

I trotted around the tableclothed tables, making a straight shot back to the booze. Just as I was starting to get a feel for the layout of the room, the waitress from the smallpox line rushed up to me. "Barbara!" she called.

I stopped and waited until she was next to my ear. "Sis told me to tell you to meet her at table eight." She pointed to the front of the room. I hadn't noticed earlier, but the tables closest to the stage all held numbers next to RESERVED signs. "Right now."

"Why?" I didn't see Sis up there, though my view wasn't clear.

She shrugged and headed back to the bar—the bar where the Scotch and sultry smiles were. The bar I needed to get back to so I could earn 10 cents for a martini.

I bit my lip and headed toward table eight, bopping a bit to the catchy tune on the way. When I got closer, I saw Sis crouched next to the table, next to a red-faced man in a suit. If I was being observant, I would have stopped trying to differentiate men from their clothing since they were all wearing suits.

"Babs!" Sis hailed.

When I was in earshot, the drunkard grabbed my hand with both of his. "My dear…amnesia? Why didn't you call me earlier?"

Glaring at Sis, I was met with concern in her eyes. "Doc can help us figure this out, Babsie. Just chat with him a moment and I'll cover your tables." She looked across the vast room. "Or I'll start your tables! Babs, have you served anyone yet?" She shook her head, though she was chuckling at me. Then she disappeared into the crowd, leaving me and old red-face alone.

Doc tugged my waist, forcing me to sit on his lap. I struggled to stand, but he held tight. Panic spread warm across my cheeks. "Now, now," he croaked into my ear. "No need for that. You really are out of sorts, aren't you? Now tell Doc the truth—did you indulge in a few too many inhalers before this incident in the hallway?" He laughed at his own joke.

I hated that he knew everything. Why had Sis left me with this creep? I shifted my weight on his sweaty lap, as uncomfortable as I'd ever been. The hairs were standing on my arms. "Yes. A few too many," I barked, hoping to end this weird intervention.

"Funny. I've never heard of amnesia in a Benzedrine overdose. I just may need to look that one up." He nodded and breathed into my neck.

I shuddered.

"You seem uneasy. Why?"

Receiving such a nonchalant question from a dirty old man made me even more nervous. "I don't like to be touched," I blurted, again trying to stand.

This time he let me. "Well, why didn't you say so? That's a new one on me. Usually you're eager to climb up here and tell Doc just what you want for Christmas," he stated with a sneer and a slap of his legs. "And it's usually another hit of the ol' white stuff."

I couldn't tell what that was referring to, but I didn't care. I wanted out of this space. Out of his red face. "Well, things are different now."

He nodded, his face changing from pervy to professional. "Actual behavior changes. Curious. And Sis said you hit your head on the way down?"

I reached up and felt the lump on my head. "Yes."

He took a drink of his dark alcohol, then reached over to grab me again.

When I yanked out of his reach, he tsk-tsk-tsk'd me. "Checking your pulse, my dear."

My brain screamed I shouldn't let him examine me too closely. What if I didn't have a pulse? I nearly laughed at my own mind. Oh, judging from the extreme range of emotions I'd felt just since entering the doors to the Palindrome, I had a pulse.

"Have you felt nauseous? Headaches?"

I nodded.

"Do you recall any memories of your life before you fell? Do any people or places seem familiar to you?"

I shook my head, wondering if he really was an M.D.

He took another sip and then looked at me in earnest. "Not much you can do for amnesia except stick to routine. I recommend you keep doing what you're doing. Something will come back. Meanwhile, go ahead and drink and continue your pills. Maybe getting you into a half-conscious state will help your mind get back to normal—couldn't hurt."

My eyes widened. Was that my prescription? Drink and do drugs?

He picked up his fat cigar and took a puff. "I'll catch Sissy Rose and tell her you'll be fine. I'll let her know she's doing all she can for you by leading you through the motions." With that, he turned back to face the stage.

I took a deep breath. When I turned to head back to the bar, I saw Sis was up near the stage, too. She was hopping up and down and hugging a familiar woman near the double doors leading out to the corridor. The woman turned, and I saw it was Elaine from HBC—the tour guide. With a sideways glance to the awaiting 10-cent-tipper, I headed over to them just as they ducked out into the corridor.

When I pushed the doors open, I met them. They both turned to look at me—excitement was in the air. "What's up?" I asked, curious and wondering if they were now my friends since I felt so invested in the answer.

"My good luck charm worked!" Sis exclaimed. "Elaine was chosen to be interviewed at HBC headquarters in New York City."

"New York!" I chimed in, if only for my personal gain.

Elaine was beaming. "New York, here I come."

"Wow, great news, Elaine," I congratulated. "You will move there?"

She shrugged. "I don't know. It all depends. But HBC is paying my way there by train. I leave tomorrow morning! I'm being interviewed by the president of the station."

"This is Fourth of July, kid!" Sis cheered, hugging Elaine again. "You'll be married in no time."

My brow furrowed without my consent. "What does this have to do with marriage?"

They both twittered, still clasping hands. "Think of the future husbands out there. This could be Elaine's chance to become a real Gatsby Girl," Sis chirped.

"But it's a job interview. What's the job?"

"Lead Tour Guide. I would assist in writing the scripts for tour guides at all of the stations. I'd do the training as well," Elaine explained. "My mother is thrilled since we have family out that way. Though I've never met any of them."

"Well, I just can't believe you leave tomorrow morning! Thanks for coming in to tell us," Sis said, straightening her dress in preparation to head back to her tables.

"Will you be doing any sightseeing while you're there?" I queried.

"Oh, perhaps. I'll have one free afternoon."

"Don't look now, but here comes Hopper's cute photographer!" Sis told us in a hushed whisper.

The three of us watched as he approached from the men's bathroom farther down the hallway. He was still lugging around his gigantic camera. "Hiya, ladies!" he greeted, tipping his hat.

"Well, hiya yourself!" Sis tossed back with a coy smile.

He was already lifting his camera when he approached. "Mind if I take a photograph of the three of you? Such lovely ladies. Why, you'll double the Palindrome's business the day I print!"

Elaine grinned. "You're too much." She continued the cigarette in her hand.

He smiled and herded us together with a simple hand gesture.

I was silent. Grimly comparing photo ethics of the forties with 2011. No selfies. And he asked permission! No sly clicks and posts for the world to see. This photo would never be uploaded to any social media site. Perhaps printed in the newspaper's gossip column though. Was that the same as social media in 1947?

"Babs!" Sis was scolding, a smile permanently frozen on her face in preparation for the photograph.

I scooted in closer. We stood in a line, smiles on our young faces, hair-dos all in place, dresses perfectly puffed.

"On the count of three, ladies." He bent and looked through the lens. (Remember photo lenses?) "One, two, three!"

Click.

The moment it was over, I wondered if it had been a good idea to have photographic evidence of the time I was trapped in Barbara Miller's body.

And then, when my hand brushed against Elaine's stomach, I did a double-take. Slight bulge. Hard as a rock. Oh, Lainey…

"Have an enchanting evening, ladies," he said with another tip of his hat. He pushed open the doors causing the music to triple in volume and was gone.

Sis wasted no time turning back to Elaine. "I simply can't wait to hear all the details, Lainey. But I really have to trot. Ta-ta!" Sis said with a smile (that suggested she was going to chase down the handsome photographer). She hugged her again and headed back into the main ballroom, back to her tables and tips.

"I don't suppose you would do me a favor while you're in New York…?" I started, also wasting no time. Trying not to assess her bulge in fetal age.

"Oh! Well…what did you have in mind?"

"A visit to Orchard Street? I hear there are brilliant shops there."

Her face twisted. Uncomfortable with a touch of growing curiosity was my guess.

"You see, I have cousins there," I lied, spinning a tale on the fly. "And one of them has left me a book. She hid it in the boy's bathroom of her father's shop."

"The men's lavatory? Why?"

"Oh, to avoid prying eyes of her sisters, I'm sure. This is a diary of sorts."

Skepticism and a dash of impatience. "Why would she want you to have her diary?"

"Well...it was her dying wish. Her final request. I wasn't sure how I would ever be able to get to New York, but then this happened. It's just so...serendipitous!" I tried to cheer, mimicking the ways that made everyone so eager to help Sis.

"I'm sorry for your loss," she mumbled, sucking in another drag of the cigarette she shouldn't have been smoking.

I nodded. "Please, Elaine. This would mean so much to me," I pleaded as solemn as I could muster. "It would be such a quick stop. In and out and you're on your way. Maybe you'll even meet a handsome stranger!"

She was coming around.

I grabbed her hands. In the same way people kept doing to me. "Elaine. I will repay you somehow, someday. I truly need this book...for my cousin."

She sighed.

Bingo!

"Okay." She fished in her handbag and pulled out a pen and small tablet of paper. "Write down the address. I'll call you at Heritage House if I run up against any issues finding it."

I scribbled all I could remember—all I knew: *Hal's Men's Suits on Orchard Street, New York, New York.*

"And it's actually in the men's restroom? How do you suggest I go about collecting it?"

"I guess just ask to use the bathroom and slip into the wrong one. My cousin said she hid it inside the vent, behind the grate."

Elaine's eyes widened. "And how do you expect me to get it out then?"

I looked at her gloved hands. "Bring a screwdriver."

Elaine was huffing in disbelief, when the door was pushed open. The music escaped into the corridor. It was Vinny. And he had that look in his eye.

Without a word, he passed us. I could feel the attraction as he moved quick enough to blow the tulle of my skirt with his gate. In a split second of eye contact, I knew he was requesting I follow.

I mindlessly handed Elaine the pen and pad. "Good luck," I muttered, already following the lug of a man down the hallway.

She huffed again behind me, but I was focused.

Was I about to do this? Host body or not, was I really the kind of woman to meet a stranger in the back room?

Once, just after college, my best friend and I had gone to Cancun for spring break. We'd used our tax return money to book an all-inclusive resort. It was my first time out of the country (unless you counted driving to Canada). We were wild and free—touring everything from ancient temples to newly-completed jungle waterparks. One night, we went to a local club. It was so jammed full of people we couldn't walk without touching about a dozen others. We went to the upper floor of the club and it was not as violating-fire-code full, but it was even hotter than the first floor. Thick, Caribbean air made everyone sweat through their clothing. Most guys weren't even wearing shirts. Combine that with alcohol, drugs and dancing and it was downright suffocating. Anyway, my best friend had found a group of Australians who were on holiday. They were all beefed up and on the prowl. Arms as thick as tires, though they were all shorter than me. My friend guessed steroids, but still liked what she saw. I guessed dimwits and was disappointed to be correct. The one who seemed to be assigned to me couldn't hold a conversation to save his life. The whole night, he tried to kiss me. My friend had even pulled me aside, "It's just one kiss with a handsome stranger. What's the big deal?" But the big deal was the fact I couldn't be attracted to someone with no personality. Not even for just one kiss.

And yet I was following an exquisite, dimwitted man back to a secret rendezvous spot.

Vinny looked back, catching my gaze as he pushed through a door.

The tap of my heels in the empty hallway caused me to look around more than once, wondering if I would be missed, wondering if Mr. Martini had ordered from someone else…wondering what my mother would think of my behavior.

Heart racing, I too went through the door.

His broad back was to me. He was reaching up to hoist down a large cardboard box. It chimed as bottles clinked together inside. He must have felt me like I felt him because he spoke without looking back. "You're *fugazi* today," he stated, twisting to slam the box to the ground. He turned to get another.

I let out a breath. I didn't need to understand Italian to assume he was saying what everyone else had been. I wasn't being *Barbara* enough. "It's been a crazy few days."

He hefted another box down and set it on the first with another clank. The boxes came up to his thighs.

Finally looking at me, he reached out his hand.

I was nervous, excited, unsure…but I let him take my hand. He pulled me to the boxes. I sat on them, as he'd suggested with his pull.

His brown eyes held urgency and—wow—was it nice to be the object of his desire. His sigh was part growl, as he scooted my body closer to him with his huge paws.

Sucking in an enormous breath, I felt the need to know something—anything—about this man before he kissed me. "So, you're Italian?" I blurted, soaking in his dark hair and eyes.

His face twisted. "Is that suddenly a problem for yous?" His voice was defensive. "You gonna call me a commie next?"

Stammering, I took a different direction. "Uh, can you believe Cary Grant is really out there? Did you see that comical pineapple appetizer on his table?"

Now his brow furrowed. He took a step back. "You didn't hafta meet me back here." He was shaking his head.

I reached out toward him, but didn't make contact—disappointed to find I stunk at intimacy no matter what the lifetime.

His scowl was frozen in place, thick eyebrows scrunched together. "I better get back then," he blurted, shoving me off the boxes.

I yelped at his gruff nature and watched him hoist the box of bottles up to his chest and barrel through the doorway.

Damn.

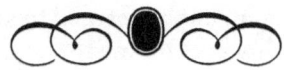

BACK OUT IN the masses, I searched for Mr. Martini. I had missed my chance at that dime, judging by the drink in his hand.

Full of defeat, I spent the next several hours doing the job I'd been asked to do. I emptied ashtrays, fetched drinks (from bartenders other than Vinny), and wiped down tables. I collected change on my little round tray and tried not to wonder if Elaine would be successful in her mission or not.

Numerous times throughout the night I met some of the other waitresses in the corridor for a swig from a communal bottle of some sort of schnapps. Being buzzed seemed to help the time pass.

The vibe of the Palindrome had changed. Gone was the fresh, new night. Now time was dragging. Patrons around me were more obnoxious. Pushier, louder and thirstier. My eyes were red and stinging from the constant cloak of smoke. And Vinny still wasn't looking at me.

Judging by the lull of the music, the loss of pep in the wait-resses' steps and the clock above the bar, it was almost clos-ing time.

I was leaving the bathroom, marveling I wasn't exhausted, but still feeling defeated as I counted pennies, nickels and dimes in my palm, when it happened.

A massive, sweaty hand was around my neck. The force of it pushed me back to the wall with a slam! Large fingers pressed up under my jaw and a palm was flattening my airway like a cheap straw in a thick malt.

"What the *fuck* are you doing here?" The *f* had been spat rather than spoken. The foamy saliva spattered across my face was proof of that. The smell of stale coffee breath, whiskey and cigarette smoke engulfed me. I heard the sound of people approaching behind him, but he seemed to know who they were. He didn't take his steely eyes off me for an instant.

Maybe it was the copious amounts of true crime TV I'd binged back home, but my instincts told me to memorize his features. I soaked in the dark, greasy hair under a gray fedora. The large frame hidden under a floppy trench coat. The gold watch that was gouging my collarbone. And the steel blue eyes, devoid of any connection or character. Filled to the brim with pure rage.

"I asked you a question!" he roared, slamming my head against the wall once more.

I opened my trembling mouth, but I couldn't muster more than a hollow moan. How could he expect me to make so much as a peep with his iron hand around my throat?

"Are you here to see *him*?"

I registered his tone as jealousy, but I was involuntarily gasp-ing and things around me were getting cloudy. I gasped again before hearing the familiar *click-clack-clicking* of expensive shoes. I prayed to God it was Sis.

"Digger!" I heard her scream, the clicking of her high heels picking up pace.

So this was the infamous Digger.

I was flickering out of consciousness.

As I started to slump, I heard a jolly, familiar voice in the distance. Like catching the radio station from a passing car. "Have I not commanded you be strong and courageous...."

"Jules!" I gasped, collapsing on the cold floor below me.

CHAPTER 5

TWEAKING WITH A SIDE OF BLACKMAIL

I WENT TO see a hypnotherapist once. A coworker from the Birth Center—an acupuncturist with serious anxiety—had coaxed me into going to a group session so she wouldn't have to go alone. I had never been hypnotized before, though in my thirty-plus years I had witnessed group hypnotizing twice. Deeming myself *too mentally aware* to be hypnotized, I went to the group session with no real expectations. Acupuncturist Annie, on the other hand, had gone in search of answers. Could she tap into the forgotten memories lost in the depths of her temporal lobe that could give her clues about her constant state of anxiety and stress? Could she discover causes for her phobias and concerns? Could she find peace?

At first, the hypnotherapist detailed the two camps of belief surrounding her craft. In her own non-medical, non-scientific words, she explained one camp believed through the use of regression therapy, individuals could remember past lives. The other believed hypnotizing was a way to tap into the almost 90 percent of the human brain that went unused. Affirming to myself my participation wasn't total bullshit because I was in camp number two, I allowed her to continue.

But when she explained what her process was, I scoffed out loud. A woman in her fifties, clearly still identifying as a hippie, glared at my response.

The process would be to relax, find that state of mind you settle in to just before you fall asleep, let go of all conscious thoughts, then fall into a trancelike state.

The hypnotherapist did this by using some sort of singing bowl that reverberated a tone through the dark room, while chanting in a calm, sing-songy voice.

Lining the floor on yoga mats like a high school gym sleep-over, she regressed us, supposedly, to the womb. Fascinating? Yes. Believable? Not to me.

"Feel yourself floating within your mother's body," she had chanted.

My conscious mind screamed and taunted the foolishness.

"What do you see?" she asked the group.

My inner voice screamed, *Nothing! It's impossible to have memories as an unborn fetus, lady!*

"Now, focus on your mother. Feel what she feels. What is your mother feeling as she places her hand on her pregnant belly?" she questioned the group.

But that was when I felt overcome. Overwhelmed. I felt such a strong emotional reaction, that a single tear dribbled out of the corner of my closed eye. I felt relieved and ecstatic, grateful and overjoyed.

My mother's emotions or my own, I was unsure. But I was *feeling.*

Panicked to be showing raw emotion in front of strangers (who were also hypnotized with their eyes closed), I tried to raise my hand to brush away the tear.

But I couldn't lift my hand!

It was then—amid my conscious mind freaking out, and my subconscious mind drowning in mental images and emotions—I realized I had been hypnotized. That I was aware, but not able. I was alive and partially awake, but dreaming. I was momentarily paralyzed. Lost in my own subconsciousness.

And I was trapped in the exact same mental space being choked out by Digger.

I had a vague awareness of chaos—a sixth sense that unpleasant and angry things were happening around me, but I wasn't there. Not really, anyway.

I was with my babies. I was in a sunny grove, singing with Jules and carrying Jakey on my shoulders. I was watching my sweet little girl hop off a large rock, and then a picnic table bench. I was laughing as Jakey stuck his finger in my ear and slapped the top of my head playfully. I was enveloped in love and relief. Relief I was with them again. Together with my other pieces. Whole once more.

My eyes fluttered open as hands raised me up to a sitting position. I was still in the hallway of the Palindrome. I looked to see who was touching me. It was red-faced Doc and Sis, doing their best to get me off the floor.

I was still Barbara. And my babies weren't with me.

Terror was in the air. I sensed it more than saw it at first. Sis was silent. Her face was flushed, and her makeup smeared. I followed the fix of her stare.

To my left, there was a corpse.

The dead, bleeding body of Vinny...inches away from me.

The sight of his beautiful, lifeless face smothered me. The river of red flowing from his chest asphyxiated me. Seeing my dainty shoes diverting the river finally caused a gasp for air.

I scrambled, eager to get away, squelching a scream of horror. My deep inner voice was roaring I needed to run from danger. Frantic, I searched for Digger. But we were alone. Me, Sis, Doc and the corpse of the man I'd been too timid to kiss.

His blood was on my dress.

I scurried behind the others—breathless. "What happened?" I blurted.

"Shh!" Doc scolded.

We all looked around.

The music was still thumping in the hall, distorted as it seeped into the corridor, as if coming from far away. Voices, too, were muffled from beyond. But it was dark in this back hallway. It was near the alleyway where we'd first entered the Palindrome

"If you're able to walk now, let's go," Doc ordered.

Sis was in a frantic state. Her face reminded me of the open-eyed panic an animal displayed when the fur stood up on its back. She followed Doc's directions without hesitation. She and Doc were pushing the metal bar to open the back door by the time I looked at them again.

"Now!" Doc demanded.

I ripped my gaze from Vinny—knowing it would be the last time I ever saw him, hating the sight of my handful of change scattered around the floor like a bloody wishing well—and ran to be with them.

Outside, the darkness made me realize two things: one, I was still drunk, and two, Barbara had fantastic eyesight! It had been years since I'd seen so well in the dark.

We hurried along the sidewalk, our heads down. Doc and Sis were silent.

But my brain was in overdrive, so I was not. "What happened? Did Digger kill Vinny? Because of me?"

Neither replied. We were still marching at a rapid pace. I thought I heard Sis start crying, but I couldn't be sure.

"Do you think he would be alive if I hadn't…Digger *did* kill him, right?"

We went under a streetlamp. Its illumination confirmed my hunch. Tears.

I held back my questions for a couple blocks, but then I could no longer contain them. "Won't it look bad that we left?" I asked, spinning a full circle to search the darkness between us and the Palindrome. "We didn't clock out or whatever to end our shift. We will seem suspicious. Won't people be looking for us? Maybe we should go back?"

"No," was all Doc replied to my barrage. He was wheezing from our breakneck pace.

"Well, did either of you see where Digger went? What if he's following us?" My words caused the hairs on my neck to stand on end. I peered around, searching for anything scary lurking.

And found it.

"There!" I yelped, pointing. I almost reached for my cell phone camera, desperate to have evidence of what I was seeing.

My companions looked across the street, but then went back to their focus. We were not quite a block from Heritage House.

But I couldn't tear my gaze from the man across the street—the same man as the day before. The same man, in the same gray suit, on the same bench near the newspaper stand. He was staring at me. Again. "Don't you see him? Please tell me you see him!" I begged them.

"Keep your voice down," Doc instructed once again.

"But he looks like he knows something!" I cried, emotions emblazoned by trauma and schnapps.

"He's been camped out there for weeks. Always there," Doc growled.

I watched as the man laid a finger on the side of his nose. It was directed at me...And I recognized it as an old gesture my grandfather used to mean "you got it right on the nose."

Creep or not, I buried myself into Doc's armpit upon seeing that. Terrified, I figured if nothing else, Doc was someone Sis trusted.

Doc put his other arm around Sis as we walked into the glow of Heritage House. He bent his head to our level. In a hushed tone, he spelled out the plan. "Our only hope here is to play on Mahoney's sensitivities. Babs, there's blood on your dress and shoes. Sis, it's clear you've been crying. Let me do the convincing here. The story is that Babs had another fainting spell and hit her face this time. That will explain Sis's state, and the blood—if she even sees it." He reached up and turned the door chime. Its ringing echoed in the front parlor of Heritage House. "Not a word," Doc insisted.

After a full minute, Doc twisted the entry chime a second time.

A siren blared behind us. I spun around just as it passed. It was a white ambulance, heading in the direction we'd come from. I searched the scene just past the road and streetcar station, and squinted to see if the man was still on the bench, but I couldn't tell in the darkness. "Do you think they found him already?"

"Shh!" Doc shushed with a squeeze.

The heavy clunk of the door unlocking redirected my focus. Instead of a disheveled, pajamaed matron, we were met with a rather fancy looking one. Londa was stuffed into a dress straight out of a movie. Her makeup and hair were overdone. It was painful how obvious she was in trying to look younger, more glamorous and less matronly. "What is going on here!" she bellowed, pulling us into the lobby.

"I'm afraid I wanted to deliver these young ladies to you in person, Mrs. Mahoney," Doc said. "And might I add that you look lovely this evening."

Londa didn't smile. She was too busy glaring at Sis and me like a scolding mother. "Do you know what time it is? I don't allow late entry. I would have ignored you outright had I not seen the doctor with you." She paused and lifted Sis's chin with her hand. "Have you been crying?"

Doc gave us a little shove in the direction of the staircase. "I'm afraid Barbara had another fall, Mrs. Mahoney. Gave Sissy quite the scare."

Londa squinted at me but said nothing.

"I wanted to escort them home to be sure they arrived safely. I've asked Sis to keep a close eye on Barbara, as she recovers."

Approaching the staircase, I saw the door to Londa's office had been left open a crack. I swear I heard someone clear their throat from inside as we stepped up the first stair. I wondered if Sis heard it too, but saw she was still in her state of shock. "Sis…" I whispered, climbing the staircase next to her. "When did you grab my purse?"

She looked down at her wrist, saw my bag swinging alongside hers, and continued climbing without a word.

"Please say something," I coaxed, rounding the corner as we headed toward her room.

Silence and darkness were entangled in an age-old rendezvous when Sis wandered into her room and snapped on her bedside lamp, sending light in to chaperone the room's secret activities. She fell to the bed.

I hovered in the doorway, feeling awkward and uneasy—a strange feeling while with Sis.

Taking a step toward her, I shut the door behind us. "Sis…did you see it happen?"

She stuffed her face into the pillow and sobbed.

I stifled the urge to throw up. My drunk was wearing off, but that meant the gravity of what had just happened was seeping in with more force.

"It's my fault!" she cried abruptly.

I rushed to her side. Gently touching her back, I spoke in my mothering tone. "Shh, it's certainly not your fault, Sis. No one could ever think this mess was your fault! Digger! What kind of a man kills over a girl like me?" My tone was shrill by the time I'd finished my thought.

She popped her head up. "When I saw him choking you, I ran to get Vinny. I thought he could help! But when he went back there, Digger *stabbed* him! Just stabbed him like it meant nothing to kill him in cold blood!"

I was staring at her trembling hands. I couldn't say what I was thinking…because I was thinking maybe this *was* a little bit her fault for bringing the cause of the jealousy directly into the sights of the killer.

I shook my head, shook the thought away. I was panicking, too. "So then he just left? Left me? Left the body?"

Gulping, she nodded in response. "After he left, I ran to get Doc. I needed someone to help us, but I didn't know who to trust."

I sucked in a breath and let it out, pushing the thick hair on top of my head back. "What do you think will happen? Will the police be able to link this to us?"

Her eyes widened. "Oh! Do you think they could? But how?"

"Well I don't know about you, but I'm sure I left hairs and fibers and fingerprints and who knows what else *all* over that crime scene!"

She gave me a look like I was speaking in French.

Forensic evidence in the forties could work in my favor, I realized from her expression. "My tips were all over," I continued, thinking aloud.

She finally looked at me. "They were! Oh, this is terrible all around. How will you be able to pay your rent?"

I scoffed. "The least of our worries right now."

She agreed.

"Do you think Londa will be up to check on us?" I asked.

She shook her head, dabbing her nose with a handkerchief. "I'm sure she went right to bed."

I shrugged, standing to go to the window. "She was dressed pretty nice to be on her way to bed." I peeked out through the glass. Seeing nothing out of the ordinary—or what I guessed to be ordinary for Hollywood at night—I went back to her. "Maybe she's on a date."

Sis let out a small laugh. It made the whole room seem a little more…normal. "At this hour? Come off it."

"I'm worried about that man on the bench, Sis. Why did Doc say he is always sitting there? Have you noticed him before?"

She bit her bottom lip before answering. "I have. And Babs, this is strange to say to your face, but I think you know him and just don't remember."

"Really? Why do you think that?"

She shrugged. "Just things you said to me a few weeks ago. It's just been seeming like…well…like you're working for Digger now."

Hot guilt crept into me. "So I didn't use to sell drugs? But now I do?"

She giggled and stood abruptly. "I don't know, I don't know. So…" She began in her upbeat tone. "…you'll have to stay in here tonight. You simply can't creep into your shared room at this hour on your first night. The girls would simply abhor you." She nodded toward her crisp-cornered bed. "We can sleep head to toe—just like my sister and I used to do back home!"

That made me smile, despite the new revelation about ol' Babsie. "So you really are a sister?"

She let out another small chuckle. "Of course. You don't get a nickname like Sis being an only child. I have six brothers and sisters. You used to know that…" She trailed off, seeming sad again.

I reached up to feel the back of my head. "Go easy on me. You heard Doc. I really am suffering from amnesia." And there was a part of me starting to worry I really was…

No. There was no way I invented Jules and Jakey. This was happening. It was real.

She sighed and stood to remove her shoes. "Well, I'm going to get ready for bed. Coming to the lavatory with me?" She started gathering things from her dresser.

I shook my head, looking over my blood-stained tulle. "I don't think I'll be able to sleep, Sis. And I'm truly not sure what to do with Marjorie's dress. Just having it here is evidence. How do I get rid of it?"

Sis's face was scrunched so tightly, it was red. "I don't do well in these situations. I'd rather never talk of it again. Pretend it never happened. Live in oblivion."

"The Isle of Denial," I quoted my previous marriage counselor. "I know it well."

During the divorce, the counselor made mention of my preference to "skim over real life" and live in denial. She called me an escapist and accused me of being the communication barrier in the marriage. She talked of it so often she thought she had coined the phrase "living on the isle of denial" until I showed her the search results proving that it was an actual place in New Orleans, named after Hurricane Katrina had swept through. But that would be decades from now. So perhaps I had just coined the phrase.

Sis was holding out her hand when I focused again. I took a nightgown and two white pills from her. "Your sleeping pills will help. Let's just go on as if everything is normal. Because it should be. We just had an ordinary night. It's not your fault for being at the club tonight. It's not my fault for leading Vinny to Digger."

I put my hand on her shoulder. "It's truly not. You were helping me. This is completely Digger's fault. And I, for one, sincerely hope he is caught by the police *immediately*."

Sis nodded and touched the doorknob. "I'll be back in a few minutes. Just knock if you need to join me." And she slipped out into the dark hallway.

I looked down. The spattering of Vinny's blood was dark now. It blended into the black material and barely showed. Still, I was eager to remove it from my body.

I changed into the nightgown and gathered the wad of clothing I'd been wearing. I hadn't a clue what to do with it. Stuff it in the kitchen garbage? Steal Sis's pillowcase to shove it into? Throw it out the window?

No, those all seemed suspicious. More suspicious than I needed to be, considering no one knew I was a witness.

Speaking of being a witness, should I send the police an anonymous tip? That had to be pretty easy in 1947. Every phone was anonymous, wasn't it?

But I didn't even know Digger's last name. Or if Digger was his real name.

I eyed the two sleeping pills on the dresser. Then the twin bed. And in an act that even surprised myself, I sashayed right over to the wardrobe, stuck my hand into the long coat and pulled out one of the thirteen unlucky inhalers.

Fidgeting with the small tube of aluminum, I wondered who it belonged to. Digger? The man at the bench? Strange Janitor Dude? Me?

Heaving the biggest sigh I could muster with a throat that burned from its Digger damage, I left Sis's room and headed back downstairs. I noticed there were shower facilities through a doorway in the powder room.

Shoeless and in just a silky (yet conservative) nightgown, it was easy to slip down the wooden staircase with only a few creaks. I hugged the tulle tighter and dashed to the powder room on tiptoes. As if I was a teenager sneaking in after curfew, I literally dashed. Ah, to be young again.

Inside was pitch dark, which created feelings of déjà vu from my recent entrance into Barbara's body that sent shivers through me…

I felt around for a light switch. When I felt a round shape, I pushed it—summoning a vague memory of push light switches in an old bed and breakfast Doug and I had once stayed in. With a click, the sconce on the wall partially illuminated the long room.

The padded, striped chairs looked even more ridiculous with no primping women to occupy them. And the oversized fans on the wallpaper took on an unnerving identity, drenched in dancing shadows, looming over me.

I stepped closer to the wall-to-wall mirror. Barbara barely even appeared tired. And hardly a hair was out of place. A smear of eyeliner was the only tell that I had just been witness to a murder.

A gruesome, senseless murder. A murder that I didn't fully grasp yet.

One wish overwhelmed me: I wanted to go home.

In the silence of the night, the aloneness of my situation, the dread that still ricocheted around in my belly…I needed to get out of here. I needed to leave. I could *not* be Valentina and be sentenced to decades in a world in which I did not belong.

Still staring into the mirror, I saw nothing but Barbara and her pile of blood-stained clothing. "I wish I could go home!" I demanded of the mirror.

But nothing happened. So I wrestled open the inhaler with fumbling fingers. I unscrewed the cap from the end, put it in my mouth and tried to do what my asthmatic friend had done so many times in front of me—inhale.

Coughing, I tried again.

How would I find time to decipher the reason I'd been sent here when I didn't even have a moment to think without someone giving me drugs or murdering someone?

One more inhale to be sure it worked.

Kicking the stupid striped chair, I followed the length of the counter and mirror to the door on the other end of the rectangular room. Again, searching for a switch, I managed to shed light into the dank and unpleasant shower room.

A third inhale from the thin, metal container full of drugs, and I set it on the counter.

Getting straight to work, I turned the water on and held the dress under the shower spigot. I imagined a stream of red flowing from the material, but there was not one. In the bad lighting and wet darkness of the garment, I could no longer even see the spatter. I soaked the entire thing for good measure.

Laying it on the ground next to the drain, I next wiped down the high heel shoes. Only then did I see a tiny trickle of red-stained water dive down the floor drain. I worried suddenly if I had left bloody footprints. Judging from the red in the grooves of the soles, I may have.

With a gulp and a shake of my head, I finished my disgusting task. I hung the gown on the neighboring showerhead and tossed the shoes out of the shower area with a double-thud.

Since I'd come this far, I turned the water to hot and shed my damp nightgown and undergarments. I stepped under the short faucet. At that height, it was easy to keep my hair from getting wet.

When the water hit me, I realized how alien it felt to run my hands over Barbara's smooth body. There was no protruding mole on my side, no stretch marks on my underbelly, and Barbara was an outie instead of an innie. (A *waaay* innie ever since Jakey.)

As I washed a foreign body that wasn't really mine, my mind spun me a little ditty: *With this water, I thee shed. Rinse away the blood. Wash away the sight. Let the crushing weight go. It was a man you didn't know.*

I was delirious.

And towel-less.

One more exhausted sigh and I begrudgingly used my damp tulle dress to dab some of the water away. Thankful I hadn't submerged my head, I tugged the nightgown on over a drippy body... and froze as still as a statue.

A noise. The door. Someone was in here.

"Hello?" I asserted into the shadows.

The echoes of the *drip, drip,* dripping from the shower were the only sounds.

I hustled to hike up the gigantic granny panties. Holding my breath, I emerged out of the shower area as if I were holding a dueling sword. "Ah-ha!" I bellowed, hopping into the light.

Drip, drip, drip.

Glancing around, no one was in the powder room. The black and white chairs were untouched, all in a row. I went to the swinging door and pushed it open a crack. Peeking outside, my mind flashed me scenario after scenario. Was it Digger coming back for me? The gray-suited man from the bench? The police to imprison me for life?

Suddenly, I heard the noise again. Almost like a scraping. What I thought to be the swinging door opening, was actually coming from the area under the stairs. Londa's office.

Remembering the guttural sound I had heard when we were shame-walking back up the stairs, I realized someone might be lurking in the office. Lurking with the intent to harm Londa? Or me? Or kidnap one of the gorgeous young girls here?

Oh, crap! *My* new body was gorgeous. Were they waiting to kidnap me?

I let the swinging door close in front of my face and flung my hands to my chest. My heart was racing. Zooming!

God, had this body overdosed on Benzedrine for a second time?

With the feeling of about three Vodka Red Bulls in me, I decided Barbara needed to face the wrath that lay before me...us...her...Whoever! The time was now!

As my brain calculated whether or not I would feel pain when Barbara's body was hurt, I grabbed one of the damp shoes as a potential weapon.

Once again pushing the swinging door open, I tiptoed—with rushed, hyper steps—over to Londa's office door.

The closer I got, the more distinctive the sound was. My mind was buzzing, and the urge to hop up and down was *surging* through me, but I forced focus and pressed on.

At the door, I took a deep breath. I could hear my own heartbeat in my head...or Barbara's head—whatever!

One...two...

I thrust the door open and bellowed into the semi-darkness, "Three, motherfucker!"

Two female screams filled the small space. And neither came from me. I don't know how loud they were. I was too busy soaking in the scene before me.

Two women. Barely clothed and leaning over the desk. Scrambling to cover themselves, distance themselves. Oh, they had hopped apart quickly, but I had seen it all.

"What!" Londa screeched. "Miss Miller, what are you doing in here?"

As if she had the right to be asking questions after this. I looked at the other woman. She looked young. She had flushed cheeks, and was still scurrying around trying to button and clasp and cover things.

Realizing my mouth was still hanging open, I closed the door again, wondering if Londa had seen my hands shaking.

Sis's words echoed in my mind. Ain't that a bite?

Feeling my own cheeks hot with embarrassment, I stumbled in the darkness, through the length of the lobby to an area I hadn't yet been.

Turning a squeaky, metal doorknob, I opened another door.

Through large windows, light from the streetlamps outside made it possible to see I had staggered into a haven. The library!

Hearing sounds of harsh whispers and squeaking stairs behind me, I pushed the light switch on the wall and again was barely met with enough light to see a path before me.

Overhead lighting. Just another perk of life in the twenty-first century.

Looking around with darting eyeballs, I felt a bit of relief. This was just what I needed: information. I longed for it. Craved it!

I had just started reacquainting myself with the Dewey Decimal System, when I heard heavy breathing from the doorway. I assumed it to be Londa, huffing at what I had just observed, so I carried on. Running my hands over the book spines, delighting in the feel of the hardcovers and smell of the paper, I pulled out an encyclopedia as she stepped closer.

"Listen, here," she started, her voice sounding about as puffed out as a primate about to beat her chest. "What you just did was inexcusable."

I hadn't bothered to look her way. I was like a toddler in a room of tiny, breakable tchotchkes—I *had* to touch everything!

"Are you listening to me, Barbara?"

I nearly stuck my tongue out at her. "Oh, Londa, Londa, Londa...don't play it this way." I finally looked at her face. She was still red and heaving her breaths. Fury or embarrassment, I wasn't sure. "You see, how you play your hand right now will determine my counter." I slapped a book on the wood table. "Know when to hold 'em. Know when to fold 'em. Know when to walk away."

Her scowl deepened. "What are you talking about?"

I was lost in thought... Kenny Loggins? No, Kenny Rogers? Amazing how many pop culture references were buried inside me.

Before I reconnected with the unfolding scene before me, I felt her fingers clasp over my earlobe. "Listen here, Missie," she hissed through clenched teeth. I yelped and tried to pull her off me, but she relentlessly continued, "I've dealt with floozies and vagabonds aplenty. You will not be the one misfit who takes me down!" She started dragging me to the library's door. She finally let go in a dramatic shove in the direction of the exit. "Pack your things immediately. You are being evicted."

"Ha!" I shrieked incredulously. "On what grounds? Seeing you face-deep in one of the girls in your care? Are you forgetting I work at a broadcasting company? Are you forgetting that at a moment's notice the entire city of Hollywood could know about the real things that happen at Heritage House?"

Her nostrils flared. Her face was frozen. Petrified.

"Look, I didn't want to get nasty with you. I couldn't care less who you want to be with! I'm far more concerned that it might not have been mutual, than the fact that you're a lesbian."

"Shhhhh!" she flared, stepping closer and clamping a hand on my shoulder.

I shrugged her off.

"Of course it was mutual, I'm no monster," she spit at me.

I sniffed and looked back at the library, still feeling a level of heightened senses I had never felt before. "I didn't say you were. Just making sure. Hey, I'm all for free love."

She shook her head and crumpled her forehead.

Silence crept in. Heavy, uncomfortable and hot.

"So," I started. "Let's just say I can move back into my old room and get another extension on the rent. And let's just say this is our little secret, huh?" I watched her face. "I will find a way to pay you the back rent. I just don't have it now." In the shadows of the night she appeared younger. The look on her face was the same face Jakey gave me when I took away something he knew he shouldn't have been playing with in the first place.

After an eternity, she swallowed. "Not a word or you're on the street."

Mid-nod, she was already headed back to her office. The door shut, and I was once again alone.

I reminded myself to breathe. Holy shit, was I high. Never before had my heartbeat been its own entity.

Though it was literally the middle of the night, I was on overdrive. Hopped up and ready for action. Spinning around to shelves of information, I felt like I had just walked into the Internet. Just opened a door, and there was all the Google.

The time had come to harness my inner student. It was time to study.

CHAPTER 6

TO CATCH A COMMUNIST

"**B**ARBARA JANE MILLER, there you are!"

The grit in my eyes caused me to squint up at Sis. Groggy and thirsty, I twisted to look at her from my position at the wooden table.

"What on earth are you doing down here? You didn't come to bed!"

I opened and closed my mouth a few times, again cursing the fat tongue of Barbara's mouth and glanced toward the window. Bright.

Sis yanked me up by the arms. "Here I thought you were just getting a good night's sleep with your roommates, and you were down here growing bags under your eyes just in time for your audition today!" Her tone was at maximum shrill.

"Ajax audition on Sunday," I regurgitated. "Today is Sunday?"

She crinkled her face. "Babs, you know perfectly well that it is. Now get up!"

I stood. Stretched. Yawned. "What time is it?"

"It's 8 a.m., my dear. And you don't have much time to get prepared. I suppose you don't recall your line, either?"

"Amnesia," I stated with a nod.

Exit one very exasperated sigh from dear Sis. "All you have to say is 'Use Ajax, the foaming cleanser,'" she demonstrated in a high voice.

I was busy surveying the mass of books I had ingested on my college-esque bender. And as my eyes hit the books, all of the information (or at least what wasn't asphyxiated by Benzedrine) rushed back to me. Excitement became my natural pep pill. It was my turn to grab her by the shoulders. "Sis, I discovered so much last night. World War II ended two years ago this month! Our president is Harry S. Truman because Roosevelt croaked. It's all there in the newspapers! 'So ended an era, and so began another,'" I said in my presidential tone. "And Jackie Robinson—the first black man to be allowed on a professional league! Tremendous. And don't even get me started on Roswell."

"Roswell?" She continued to give me her motherly look, crossing her arms over her pert chest.

"UFOs, Sis. UFOs."

She shook her head and shoved me away. "Lovely that you have this new interest in learning, but Babs—please get ready. It took you months to get this audition. Please don't spoil it. You need rent money!"

"Ha!" I cried in victory. "I talked Londa into giving me another extension."

Her face turned skeptical. "Another extension? How?"

"I can be very persuasive when I want to be."

"Good! Then use that persuasive personality to convince them you're their new Ajax girl!" She pushed me toward the door. "And I don't even want to know when you found time to appeal to Londa. But right now, go. I mean it, young lady. I'm taking you to the station whether you're dressed or not!" She bubbled at her own words. "Well, that's what I would like to do. But we both know I would never let you exit this building looking like you do right now. Egads, woman."

I walked with her toward the stairs. I saw a few women dressed in their actual Sunday best. They eyed me and my nightgown with a flair of disgust. I looked away. "Sunday," I began. "So Elaine left for New York today? Maybe she'll call me today." I felt the urge to check the time on my cell phone again. Perhaps I should invest in a watch.

Sis threw her head back and laughed. "It's like Bob Hope is holding up cue cards these days, Babsie. Yes, Elaine leaves this morning *for Sacramento*. She is due to arrive for her interview next Monday. Seven days of traveling by train each way. She's not due home until the twenty-second."

"No!" I hollered. My voice echoed. Everyone looked.

"Get it together, old gal. Are you expecting her to call you? Since when do you even care about Lainey? You two have never gotten along before. She's lectured me more than once on keeping company with you."

We completed the stairs. "Why do you then?" I asked sincerely. "Stay my friend?"

She twittered. "You're fun. And a lot more exciting than Elaine Glass could ever dream of being. And you don't care who knows it."

"Okay, well, does Elaine have a boyfriend?"

"Not that I know of…" We rounded the corner.

"Then maybe she's more fun than you give her credit for."

"Now that's a curious thing to say."

We were almost back to her room. "Did you take care of me this much before I hit my head?"

She laughed her perfect Sissy Rose laugh. "I always was a mother hen. And what's a mother hen without any chicks?"

"Free," I said.

Laughing again, she shoved into my hip with hers in a hip bump. "Lonely," she said.

AFTER MOTHER HEN assisted me with wardrobe, hair and make-up, I was like a new woman. After putting on the final touches in the powder room, no one would have known I had only slept a handful of hours the night before.

My quest for information had led me on such a trip. I read about being in a coma, time travel, religious experiences. I found books on medical practices, and magazines about current fashion. And I read enough style articles to know the ladies in this house *were* the face of fashion.

With a perfectly perched hat upon my head, and tiny white gloves that Sis deemed *absolutely pertinent*, I felt ready to walk the red carpet.

"Hey, who left a frock hanging in the shower room?" a half-dressed girl called.

I jumped up, electrified by her words. Dear God! How had I forgotten to remove it?

"There's just something so different about you, Babs," Sis was saying to me when I came back to the chair, dank dress in tow.

I nodded. "Like what?"

She clicked a necklace behind my neck and motioned for me to stand. "Just something." She took the dress from my hands and looked at my reflection in the mirror. "There! Ready. And in the nick of time."

Looking at our reflections in the mirror, I smiled at her.

"Hey, Dottie, would you bring this dress back up to my room? We're late for an audition," Sis called.

The girl I hadn't yet met was happy to help Sis. She took the incriminating dress and left the powder room.

I looked into Sis's kind eyes. We both knew what that dress could mean. "You do so much for me, Sis. I don't know how I'll ever be able to repay you."

She let out her boisterous laugh. "Just get this part and then we can talk about repaying me! Right now you don't have a nickel to buy me coffee and pie." She poked me with her elbow. "And you know how I *love* pie!"

We pushed through the swinging door, leaving the expressive striped chairs to themselves, and emerged into the grand lobby once again.

And that's when we saw him.

I felt Sis's fingers squeeze into my upper arm one by one. Jabbing me through the layers of jacket and gloves.

"Don't panic," I told her as we stared at the police officer in the entranceway. "Act natural. We have an appointment to keep. Just head for the door."

Sis let out a squeaky *mm-hmm* and kept pace with me.

I was much more self-confident without Scotch or meth clouding my mind. Oh, yes! Meth. I did my research. Benzedrine was a form of actual meth. And they handed them out to everyone! According to the paper I'd devoured last night, the U.S. military supplied 5-mg tablets of Benzedrine to servicemen during the war. They just handed them out like aspirin, issuing it as a cure for depression and fatigue, for weight loss and to fight the urge to sleep. Pep pills, indeed. Shit! I even saw an ad for them. Just a one-page ad in a magazine selling meth. No big deal.

We were walking straight for the front door—straight toward him.

But my mind was on my inhalers. Apparently, I had used that the wrong way, too. After a bunch of prisoners of war started geeking out, the government found out they were cracking open those things and actually *eating* the insides. Eating them! Those *mothers* were like 250-mg a piece. Illegal to possess? No. Illegal to sell though? Probably...

The officer was pointing to a clipboard in a confrontational way, right in Londa's face. At least the bright side was Londa and I wouldn't have the chance for our awkward first meeting after seeing her half naked.

"I think most of those girls are here right now, officer. I will gather them. Won't you wait in the solarium?" she nearly begged, sweeping her hand toward the bay windows she insisted were more notable than they really were.

His face was sharp and authoritarian. I couldn't look away.

"Miss Rose," Londa said. We were so close to the door. "I'm afraid you are on the list."

"I am? What list?" she yelped.

Sis and I glanced at the clipboard, now in Londa's hand. I recognized the paper it contained as Mean Nurse's smallpox check-in list. I stared at Sis's face to see if she had noticed, too.

"I will explain it all once I get the girls together. Please go with Officer Wright to the solarium while I find the rest of these ladies."

Sis visibly gulped. She had the same terror in her eyes as last night, reminding me of a quivering, furry baby bunny.

Londa was turning for the staircase. "Aren't I on the list?" I asked her.

Without looking back, she shook her head and continued on.

But I bet Marjorie was...

"Get to the station and get that audition!" Sis cried, clutching her purse with both hands in a death grip, stumbling over toward the table near the windows. "Then come find me."

The officer squinted at Sis. Why was she being so dramatic? Didn't she realize how guilty she seemed?

How guilty she was...

I stumbled out the door with Henry eyeing me up. Once the warm California air hit my face, I inhaled, the heat making me think of the time Jules asked me if the weather had a fever. And had the most intense craving to pull out a long, slim cigarette and light it up. I settled for popping a benny. I was getting good at swallowing them without a drink.

Looking away from the clownishly large police car parked in front of Heritage House and down at my demure heels, I hit the pavement, trying to remember the way to HBC without Sis to lead me.

I passed the streetcar stop in the middle of the road. Passed the store selling the luscious sweaters. There was a new ad in the window. It was a color poster board starring Lucille Ball. *The new lipstick from Hollywood,* the poster proclaimed. *Available in rose red, blue red and clear red.* I slowed my pace to see what *blue red* meant, but it looked like standard dark red to me.

Walking along, I was just about to the corner of Sunset and Vine, when I remembered to look for the bench man.

There was the paper boy, but the bench beside him was empty. Had the police officer scared him away?

Picking up speed, I became entranced in the clocklike clicking of each heel.

If Barbara was dead, that meant she would not have made it to this audition. So, if I went and actually got the part, would I be messing with time? With the future? With some other woman's life when she didn't get the part she was destined for?

Ugh…if I hadn't been at the Palindrome, would Digger have killed Vinny? Had I already altered the future?

Waiting more than two weeks to get the diary from Second-Trimester Elaine would be torturous. That is, if she even went to get it.

THE INSTANT MY hands pushed the glass in the rotating front door, I knew something was amiss. Something was off.

Instead of the rush and bustle I had experienced yesterday, there were long faces and fewer people. I reminded myself it was a Sunday. But the men perched in the "ticket towers" each had a stern look. Like they were acting as gate-keepers.

I approached the first. "Excuse me, can you point me in the direction of the Ajax auditions?"

He looked down at me. "Canceled. We're closed to the public today."

"Oh," I muttered, looking up at the clock. I was probably late anyway. "Can you tell me why?"

"You will receive more information, as it becomes available. Now please, we are to keep the public and press out today."

"Oh. Well, I work here."

He looked down at me. "Who is your manager?" He seemed irrationally angry at my answer.

"No matter. I'll just check in tomorrow." I backed away.

He scowled.

When I turned to leave, I saw a familiar face headed down the staircase. It was the once-jovial man Sis had called a wolf. His face seemed beat down. He fit his hat onto his head in a way that seemed familiar somehow.

We reached the glass doors at the same time.

"Rough day?" I offered.

"Honey, you don't know the half of it." We twirled around in the glass exit and were spit out onto the street. And with that, he thrust his fists into his pockets and marched off.

Layoffs? Bomb threat? What the heck was going on?

I watched him walk away, ready to leave myself, when the revolving door swished out another familiar man. It was Sis's cute trumpet player. "Hi," I greeted.

He looked me in the eye, trying to place me. "Sis's friend, right?" He stopped to light a cigarette. He offered me one and out of habit, I declined. Though the itchy, twitchy feeling inside me wondered if I should have.

"Can you believe this *sciocchezza*?" He clicked his lighter closed and stuffed it into his pants pocket. "This foolishness?"

"I'm afraid I'm not quite sure what's going on," I said, noticing similarities between his features and Vinny's.

He scoffed. "Aren't you the lucky one? I was just interrogated for an hour!" He spit toward the building.

"About what? By who?"

"Eh, some bozos calling themselves the House of Un-American Activities Committee." He took a drag. Then dramatically barked in my face, "Are you *now* or have you *ever been* a member of the Communist Party!"

I stumbled back.

"Those bozos." He glanced at his watch.

I took a breath. "And why are they here at HBC?"

"There's some new garbage being spread about secret communist agents concealing propaganda in radio and films. They've been at this all day! Going after writers, directors, actors—Italians!—practically all of Hollywood. Some *stupido* mission to smoke out active members of the American Communist Party."

"Oh. I didn't know. Is being a communist against the law?"

He scoffed again. "Well, they can fire or suspend you without pay. But they can do that even if you swear you're not a commie." He took another drag before squashing his cigarette in the sidewalk. "Hell, they can do that to me just for being *Italiano*. But this time, they're serious. A buddy of mine told me they subpoenaed Walt Disney and Ronald Reagan—goin' after the entire Screen Actors Guild." He looked me up and down. "Were you called in? Is that why you're here on a Sunday?"

I shook my head. "I was coming in for the Ajax audition."

He threw his head back in a mocking laugh. "You were interested in being the voice of an Ajax elf? One of those silly little cartoon elves?"

I jutted my lips out, not knowing how to respond. "Well, it was a voiceover audition. I guess I wasn't sure of the particulars."

He chuckled at me again. "The particulars being that those damned cartoon elves aren't even memorable enough for you to remember 'em. *Use Ajax, the foaming cleanser!*" he squeaked. "Ah," he interjected with a point of his large finger, "my streetcar. Well, you go and give Sissy a squeeze from Dino, will ya?" He winked and clicked his tongue in the side of his mouth. Macho, I suppose. But made me smile without realizing I was.

After I'd watched him board the streetcar, I rewound my way back (silently thanking the ridiculous Brown Derby for sending me in the right direction) and got back to the paperboy stand. With the man in the gray suit gone, I scampered through traffic, over the streetcar tracks and looked down at the dreaded bench. But there was no longer anything to dread about it.

So I sat.

What a vantage point. I could see all floors of Heritage House. I could see the police car in front, Henry lighting a cigarette, women entering and exiting. Because of the distance and the hill, it wasn't obvious either. I bet I could have sat there all day without bringing attention to myself.

Not eager to enter during a different interrogation, I just sat there. Pondering.

How strange was the evolution of a parent. Smothered by my young children, I had become increasingly grumpy. Less social. More trapped-feeling. My inner voice couldn't always be squelched. There had been times I had yelled terrible things at my children. *I can't wait to get out of here today! Go away!* And at work, my digital self was affecting my ability to talk to people in real life.

One afternoon I had been chatting with a coworker about Twitter. My boss had joined us to hear more. I was in the process of explaining how to "mention" someone using their username. The example I went with—without any forethought about the words spewing from my mouth—was to look my boss in the eye and say, "It would be like if someone tweeted *@Ellen you're a big fat slob.*" Thankfully, I had kept explaining how that would appear in the feed, not stopping to acknowledge the wide eyes from my coworker. Socially awkward. That's what I had been slipping into. But that's not who I used to be. I used to be fun and free. A party girl. Someone people loved to be around. Gregarious.

And here I was in a different time and place—a different body—and I was still the same boring person. Should I be making the most of this? Spending each day like the lottery ticket winning that it could be? Or should I be more desperate to unravel the riddle and get back to where I belonged?

To see what you need to see, look past yourself. Well, I was looking. I was seeing. But for all Valentina had tried to warn, she hadn't said much. She hadn't explained why she had stayed for twenty-nine years. Had it been because she was trapped? Or had it been a choice? There was a certain appeal to getting a do-over. But she hadn't even told me the most obvious—what had she seen? How had she returned? How had she looked past herself?

I looked down at my slim ankles, crossed like always. It had always been a fantasy to be thin and beautiful. But now that I was, I kept thinking of the advice my mother had given to me as a teen. *Sexy is a secret, not a proclamation.* And there was something inherently unsexy about being a drug-addicted, desperate young woman who, for as far as I could tell, tried to proclaim her attractiveness. I felt a small gleam of pride for old, chubby-thighed Liza. At least she was sturdy and supple.

A man in a tie and fedora sauntered past walking a large dog. My mind shouted, "Look, Jakey! A ruppy!" because, adorably, that's what he called dogs.

Sighing, I put my arm over the back of the bench.

Yes, a man was murdered. Yes, I was a drug addict. Yes, I had an angry man or two out there looking for me. But I also had youth, beauty and smarts. Should I stop worrying so much about getting home, relax and take a taxi to see the ocean? The past few days had triggered something inside me. Started an unintentional inner project of adapting. Things and people were less vague and more purposeful. I was establishing a life. Or maybe assimilating into an already established life.

But just because I'd stopped sticking my hands under bathroom faucets and waiting for automatic water didn't mean I belonged here. My heart ached for my children. Like somehow, metaphysically, I could sense how far away they were. *Feel* how much distance was between us. And it created a deep aching within me. A part of motherhood I hadn't even known until separated from my other pieces.

I saw Officer Wright exit the building, nodding at Henry as he did so. After he had climbed back into his squad car, I stood.

Perhaps the man in the grey suit was just sitting here to ponder life. Perhaps I'd come back and sit here again.

"OH, THAT VOICE!" Bess moaned. She was sitting closest to the radio. "He's a Lip."

The girls were teaching me how to play *Sip, Lip, Steal*—a game they'd invented over a long weekend with no plans. The rules were to listen to the radio, and state whether you would rather sip from the flask (usually reserved for female singers), lip the singer or steal their fame. It was on a first-yell-first-get basis.

"Steal," Marjorie stated, filing her nails without so much as a look in the direction of her remark. "I heard he's an absolute tyrant to his family."

"Does it matter if he is? Bing Crosby's voice melts me. Simply melts me!" Bess affirmed, causing the ties substituting for night rollers in her hair to bob.

We were piled into the shared room of Bess and Peggy, though Peggy wasn't with us. Sis and I had popped in when we'd heard giggling while on our way back from HBC. We'd been gabbing about the strange animated film we'd been forced to watch during our shift at the station. The gist was that cartoon characters were learning how to be "anti-isms" (they never dared to actually say communism or socialism) and being lectured on the pros of democracy and America. The kind of stuff a corporation certainly couldn't get away with in 2011.

When we'd passed by the room, the girls had been playing a round of *Sip, Lip, Steal* and asked us to join in.

Sis and I sipped from the flask, having no other options left.

"If you used your head more than your heart, you'd know Bing is a Steal. He has to be rich, by now," Marjorie opined, sipping from the flask regardless of her answer.

"I don't think that was her heart talking," I teased, causing Bess to blush, and the other girls to giggle.

It was Tuesday on the afternoon of my twelfth day as Babs. I had only cried once out of self-pity and longing for my family. I'd been sinking myself into the new daily grind—staying in my single room, working at HBC with Sis, reading in the library, avoiding shifts at the Palindrome and alone time with Londa. More than a week had passed since Vinny's death. Sis and I had barely uttered a word about it since.

After I'd returned to Heritage House after the interrogations, Marjorie and I had scuffled a bit. She was mad I'd gotten her interrogated by the police when she hadn't even been there. I was angry she made me go there and pretend to be her in the first place. But after the girls all verified the story, we accepted that Officer Wright had only been gathering statements from the girls working the late shift. He accused no one. He hadn't even mentioned the murder, just asked a bunch of questions about patrons and coworkers. So Marjorie and I had ended our mini-feud.

Once Officer Wright had finished talking to every girl on the list, he invited Sis out to dinner. Her frightened bunny bit must have appealed to him. Out of fear she would blurt something she shouldn't, she politely declined his offer. But she and I assumed she was off the hook after that. And then nothing else happened. There was nothing in the paper, nothing said at the club (so Sis informed me since I wouldn't set foot there again), and there had been no sign of Digger, either.

I found myself staring at a framed photo of a young uniformed man, wondering if he had been one of the unfortunates, when the girls started screaming—*Sip! Steal! Sip!*

The voice on the radio sounded distinctive, but I couldn't name him. "Who sings this one?" I asked.

Sis laughed uproariously. "Jimmy Durante! And you, my dear, are the one stuck necking the old goat!" She took a puff of her cigarette, making a new stain of red on its tip.

They held out the flask for me and then stole it away before I could take it. "Ah, ah, ah! No sip for you," Bess teased. "You're too busy trying to find his old lips under that gigantic schnoz."

We were still laughing, as I heard the thudding of footsteps running up the hall. "Hey, is Babs in here?" a girl called, poking her head in the doorway.

We all looked at her. "Yeah, I'm here. Why?"

"Phone call. Long distance."

"Oooh!" Marjorie called, too many sips in to count. "Who could that be, you little tease?"

I was too frantic to give her a look. I hopped up and followed the girl's directions to the nearest communal phone in the mezzanine. I trotted over and lifted the receiver—eager, to say the least.

"Hello?"

"Barbara?" There was crackling and swooshing behind the voice.

"Elaine?" I hoped.

"Babs, thank goodness! I'm calling from a phone booth at the train station. I'm about to board."

"Did you get the diary? Please tell me you found it!"

"Yes, but…" Crackling kept me from hearing the beginning of her response. "…so strange so I ran. I didn't know what to do. I'm so scared!"

"What was so strange? Why are you scared?"

"The mirrors were all backwards. Why would they hang mirrors with only the backs…" The swooshing sound got louder. "…you should meet me at the train station on Monday. I can only hope he hasn't followed me. Meet me there, Babs. You have to!"

"I'm sorry, Elaine," my panic was in full swing. "I didn't know it would be dangerous! I would never have asked you to go. Especially in your condition."

"My condition!" she shouted over the crackles. "How did you…"

The whooshing of air made it impossible to establish another clear connection. After a moment, there was a *click*. "Your call has been disconnected due to a bad connection," a woman told me. "Would you like me to try to reconnect?"

I yanked the black phone receiver away from my face and stared at it. Live operators. I'd forgotten that was a thing! Did I have to reply? Had she heard our conversation?

I hung up. Perhaps a rude millennial thing to do, but I did it.

I bit my bottom lip, a new habit I'd developed. It stung, but I continued my chomping anyway, staggering back to the room.

Listening to the girls chatter and play, I turned away from the doorway. Changing destinations, I ran down to my newest haven—the library.

Knowing just where to look, I ran my fingers along the thirty identical spines of *The Encyclopedia Americana* set, grabbing the book marked, 'M.'

> *Mirror definition, mirror meaning, mirror in religion…* "Mirrors are covered out of respect for the dead during sitting of shiva as a mourning ritual of Orthodox Jews. *See Judaism, Torah.*"

So perhaps Elaine's discovery wasn't as creepy, as it had first appeared. Perhaps the family store she visited on Orchard Street had merely been a Jewish family in mourning. Though she hadn't said they were covered. She'd said they were backwards. Was there a difference?

Slapping the volume closed, I fidgeted with the pocket of my tall pants. Feeling the slender stick inside, I headed for the lobby as if on autopilot. Though it wasn't necessary to smoke outside, I did so out of respect. Or habit. Or social conditioning. Whatever the reason, I began this new habit only five days ago and was already hooked.

"Evening, Miss Miller," Henry greeted, opening the door for me.

I nodded, lighting the Pall Mall like I had far too many times already. Taking in a long drag, I wandered over to the side of the building near the alleyway. My new hideout. My new escape. Where I could go to ponder Liza Anderson and stop being Barbara Miller for a moment...though where one stopped and the other began was increasingly blurry.

I puffed in another hit of the sensory-dulling tobacco product and leaned back against the bricks. I could feel this body start to relax a bit. This body that I could poison with cigarettes without regret. Since it was already dead and all.

Elaine had Valentina's book. Soon I would be able to read more. Understand more. Perhaps this would be the end of my little escapade through time. Maybe this was the beginning of the end. A story I could tell Jules and Jakey at bedtime. Just *that time I fell through the mirror*.

Calmer, I picked at the row of white buttons that climbed up my navy blue hip. I'd never worn pants—excuse me, slacks—that buttoned up both hips to above my belly button. Strange. Flattering on ol' Babsie's body, though.

Absent-mindedly humming the Bing Crosby song from earlier, I realized it had been nearly two weeks since I'd changed a poopy diaper. The first time since Jules was born I could say that. I was just finishing up my lipstick-stained cigarette when I heard a noise.

My reaction was too late.

"Hiya, cookie," the gruff voice cooed. "Where ya been?" It was Digger. Crazy, murderer Digger. And he'd just ducked into the alleyway with me. "Been watching you, cookie. And you have not been a good girl, lately." He stepped closer.

I attempted to march right past him, back toward the front entrance. But he moved in front of me. Fear had risen, causing the hairs on my arms to stand on end. Terrified I would once again be choked. Or worse.

"We need to have a little business discussion."

My senses were flooded with his stale breath, steel eyes, and jet-black, greasy hair. "Business?" I squeaked.

He pushed his hulk of a body closer to me, sending me skittering back to the brick wall like a daddy longlegs spider. His gold watch glinted in the single stream of sunlight that graced the alleyway.

I cursed myself for ever taking up smoking.

"Are you that dim of a broad? Have you been hitting the bottle? We had a deal. I waited. You didn't deliver."

"The inhalers?"

He shoved me back with both his huge hands against my shoulders. I flew back and hit the brick wall with a thud so great I lost my breath. "Knock off the cute stuff. It don't work on me no more. You tellin' me you don't have the money?"

"I...I still have the inhalers."

He growled, pushing his face inches from mine. "You didn't sell a fuckin' one?"

I shook my head, still trembling.

Between clenched teeth, he ordered, "Go get 'em. All twelve of 'em. Now!"

I breathed in, hating the feeling of doing his bidding as much as the feeling of getting the breath knocked out of me. I cringed passing him, but made the corner and rushed up to Henry.

He opened the door for me and I *click-clack-clicked* through the expansive lobby, up the stairs, around the corner and into my room. Sweating and breathing heavily, I did stop to wonder if it would be safer just to stay inside. Or to call the police. But the other part of me wanted to get rid of these things. To be done hiding them.

I pulled them out two by two, out of the deep trench coat's pockets. Desperate, I looked around for something to put them in. Going with the little I knew, I grabbed the powder blue clutch and stuffed them back in, marveling at the wonder that

I had used one and he had only asked for twelve. Had Barbara always intended to keep one for herself?

Packing the bag full, I clasped it shut and crammed it, once again, under my sweaty pit. Shutting the door behind me, I marched my walk of shame right back the way I'd come, hoping-not-hoping someone would see me and ask where I was off to.

Henry gave me a sideways glance, but his job was not to judge. Not to ask questions. Just as it was apparently not mine.

Around the corner, I was met with his tall frame and the stench of his cologne.

"What is that?"

I lifted the clutch with shaking hands. "It's the inhalers."

"What the hell," he grumbled, pulling out a brown paper bag from his baggy trench coat pocket. He dumped a half-eaten sandwich onto the dirty ground next to a tin garbage can.

After he'd transferred the inhalers into the bag, he thrust the clutch back to me—using it as an opportunity to shove me again. I stumbled back.

He slid his hand into his pocket and casually revealed a pocketknife.

My heart raced faster, but I just stared.

He stared, too. A long moment, nothing happened. "There's something different about you, cookie. I can see it. You don't act the same. You don't even have the same look in your eye."

My eyes got large and I shook my head again. Still against the brick wall, wishing I could dissolve through it back into the safety of Heritage House. I said nothing.

Flicking open the pocketknife, he used it to pick at his dirty fingernail. Making it obvious threatening me was not an issue for him. His chin was sharp and his eyebrows thick. If he wasn't such a fucking psycho, I would have said he was handsome. Without looking up, he continued speaking in his growling voice, "You've been slipping lately." He looked up. His eyes met mine.

My nostrils flared. I was petrified. Waiting to see what would happen next. Knowing it could be anything.

He was toying with the handle of the knife. Staring right into my eyes. "This is your warning, cookie. Time to get back on your good behavior again."

There was only a moment of time between his words and the dramatic, exaggerated stab of the knife. His whole body lunged toward me faster than I could wince. When the knife's blade hit the brick wall a breath away from the side of my face, I finally winced—thinking it was the end. Thinking it made contact even though I felt no pain.

In that hair of a second, his large body was leaned over mine, invading my personal space, breathing into my face. "Next time you won't be so lucky. You remember who says jump," he rumbled.

I was looking down, watching my host body's chest rise and fall at a quick, jagged pace, seeing the dropped clutch's powder blue color contrast with the dingy, dirtiness of the alleyway. He finally pulled back, once again, as casual as if he'd handed me a new book for book club. He tried to fold his pocketknife, but it was too bent to retract into the handle. He tossed it into the tin can next to us with a loud *Ting*! "Guess I'm gonna need a new knife."

He looked both ways down the alley. He sniffed and then sneered. "That's all the time I got for you." He paused, still staring at me. An uncomfortable moment of silence passed between us. "What, no kiss for your old man?"

I was frozen in place.

When I didn't come closer, he spat on the ground near my feet, secured the hat on his head and walked off. Away from Heritage House. Away from me.

Letting out the breath I was holding, I jogged right to the door and barely waited until Henry had opened it far enough for me to fit before ducking in. I ran right up the staircase and back to the safety of the girls. The safety of friendship.

The giggling got louder as I got closer.

"Well, it's about time, Babs!" Sis said. "That must have been some phone call."

Still trembling, I nodded and took my place on the single bed.

"I was just telling the girls about the Committee of Un-American activities, or whatever it's called."

"It sounds tantalizing, Barbara!" Marjorie gasped, taking another hit from the flask. "I can't imagine anyone in this country being anti-American."

I hugged myself instead of responding. My eyes lingering on the doorway, and my mind thanking Londa for not allowing men above the first floor.

"I heard," Sis started, "that all employees with any ties to *certain segments* are being put on a list. And if they don't renounce the communist party right then and there, they will be banned from working in Hollywood altogether!" Sis continued, her cheeks red from the nips of alcohol.

"Does that mean your handsome Italian friend?" Bess asked her with a wink. "Oh, if he wasn't so green, I'd take him for a spin."

"Bessy!" Sis scolded.

"Really? The Italian boy?" Marjorie chimed in. "Here I thought you were going for the hearty Jewish stock. Sonny made it through the war with a medal! He's older and more established."

"She means he has more money," Bess stated with a snicker.

"And he's a bit of a wolf," Sis interjected. "He's too serious for me. Killing all those Nazis did something to him."

The ladies all nodded. The room grew quiet. I looked at the framed picture of the soldier again, wondering who he had belonged to.

"So tell us then, Sis. Which one of those fellas is gonna end up being your old man?" Marjorie asked, breaking the silence and passing the flask.

My eyes snapped to her face. "*Old man* as in husband?"

They all laughed at me. "Yes, as in husband."

"Does everyone call their husband their 'old man?'" I swallowed, already sickened by the answer I guessed was coming.

They took turns giggling at me and calling me teasing names. The consensus was in, though. Everyone did use that phrase. And it always meant husband. Unless it was used for a father, which was rare, so said Sis.

No...No, no, no, no. Was Digger my husband?

The next song started, featuring a female voice.

"Sip!"

"Sip!"

"Steal!"

"And now you're kissing a commie, Babs," Bess said to me, the others laughing at my bad luck at the game. "Though we all know it's not your first."

They all agreed with their giggles except for Sis. I wondered if they knew they were speaking ill of the dead and sighed. Maybe being twenty-one again was not all it was cracked up to be.

CHAPTER 7

GREY MATTERS

"**N**OW ARRIVING FROM Sacramento," the overhead voice boomed.

My eyes scanned every single face as it exited the train. Where was she? Eighteen days in 1947 were enough for me. I was more than ready to read the message from Valentina, figure out what I needed to see and get home.

"You sure seem tense," Sis said. She was puffing her hair with one hand while holding a hand mirror in the other. "Just worried she wasted all this money and didn't get the job?"

"No," I stated matter-of-factly. I looked into her mirror for good measure. Nothing. Back to people watching.

"Still upset about Digger?"

I shrugged. "I'm not going to go to city hall or wherever and go searching for a marriage license. I would hope if I was married, I would know."

"No ring." She pointed. "You're probably not. Plus, like I said, I just can't imagine you marrying that beast and not even telling me." She stopped puffing and looked at me. "But it does seem rather odd. His using those words, how much time you were spending together... Are you sure you don't want me to go check for you?"

I shrugged, still scanning faces leaving the train and regretting letting Sis talk me into this morning's pep pill. I was pepped up with enough Benzedrine and adrenaline to lift a car. I scratched at my shoulder with the verve of a camper varnished with poison ivy. I was too agitated to deal with the day's wool jacket ensemble. I missed cotton. And stretchy pants.

I gave up scratching and slapped the nagging itch instead.

Sis startled. "Well if that's not why you're acting so tense, why are you?"

Distracted, I answered her without meaning to. "I asked Elaine to find something for me in New York. And I think she did."

"What did you need from New York? A souvenir?"

"You could say that." Then I blurted, "There!"

We started moving forward, into the herd of people and luggage and hugs. When my eyes met Elaine's, I felt kicked in the stomach. This was really it! Today could be the day I went back.

"Let's go," Elaine said, grasping my gloved hands and pulling me back the way we'd just come.

"What's wrong, Lainey?" Sis asked, worried and hurrying to keep up.

"He was on the train," Elaine hissed, hustling toward the streetcar lane.

"Who was on the train?" Sis's panic was escalating.

Elaine's hand was still clenched in mine. She was dragging me. "Do you know who he is?" I hollered over the crowd.

"No! But I know it's all your fault that he was on this train. And in my sleeper!" We were almost to the platform.

"In your sleeper! Who is this man?" Sis stopped and crossed her arms. "I insist you tell me what's going on, you two!"

The streetcar came into view. We shoved ourselves on, cutting in front of several people. One with children in tow.

"Sissy Rose, you get on this car *now*!" Elaine shouted. She was going to be a great mother.

Sis ran toward us and made it onto the car. There were no more spots near us though. She had to stand in the center row.

Seated, I wrenched her closer. "What the hell is going on, Elaine? I had no idea this would be dangerous."

With darting eyes, she finally looked at me. Our faces were so close I could have kissed her without moving more than two or three inches. "He took it. He had to have. No one else but you even knew about it." She eyed a man in a suit near us. The streetcar surged to life. We were moving. "I spent a lot of time looking at it after leaving New York. I couldn't make sense of it, though I thought I recognized one of the words. But it's not in English."

"It's not?"

"Are you girls talking about the job?" Sis interjected, trying to squirm closer to hear us. "Did you get the job, Elaine?"

Elaine nodded to her. She didn't even try to fake a smile.

"That's simply spectacular!" Sis yelped, clapping her gloved hands. A woman in front of her fixed her hat. *Fixed her hat* in a nonverbal way to say "stop shouting over my head."

"What is this book? Is it really just a diary?" Elaine was looking me in the eye. Her eyes were pretty. Sparkling with emotion.

"I can't really tell you. Not the truth. I'm sorry."

The sparkle turned to flaring. "I just risked my life, and you won't even tell me what for?"

I sent her a look of pity. "I don't think you want to know."

"Are you a spy or something?"

I snorted. "God, no." Well, maybe I was in a sense. I was certainly a fly on the wall to this whole patriotic-American-postwar mentality.

"And you still haven't told me how you knew about...the other thing."

I glanced to Sis before looking back to Elaine. "I used to work in a midwifery," I said. I wasn't sure how much Elaine knew about Barbara's background. "Can I see the book?"

"He took it! I told you. He must have come into my sleeper room at night. I had it for the first few nights and then it was just gone. It is so troubling to know a strange man was in there while I was asleep."

"Maybe he wasn't. Maybe he pickpocketed it while you were in the dining car or something. Don't jump to conclusions," I tried to sooth. People were starting to look. And Sis had not stopped staring. Probably trying to put the pieces together. "Do you know who this man is?"

"A man from the shop. I was not prepared for what you sent me into. I went to a shop I wasn't buying anything from, to use the ladies' room so I could end up in the men's room! What was I even thinking?"

"That you were helping out a friend," I tried.

She glared. "So I got in there and the man behind the counter didn't want me to use the facilities. Insisted I buy something first. He was acting strange. Stranger still when he caught me looking at the *three* different mirrors hanging on the wall, *all* facing the wrong way! I convinced him to let me use the bathroom, broke open the vent and found the old book." She took a breath. "Babs, the date on the first page says it's from 1898. That's too old to be your cousin's."

"What's too old? Did you meet a man there?" Sis yelled again.

"God love her," Elaine sighed, "she's driving me crazy. Why did you bring her if you didn't even tell her about this book?"

I shrugged and smiled at Sis. "She insisted."

"Well, you need to decide if we're telling her or not," Elaine hissed.

"I really don't think I should even tell you, Elaine."

"Oh, you're telling me."

Sis's face was long. Unusual for her. She looked ready to kick a rock across the road she looked so glum.

Sighing, I looked up. I had come this far without involving or scaring Sis. "Meet me in the library five minutes after we stop. She has a shift to get ready for." If Sis heard me, she didn't let on. "I feel like she's jealous."

"Of what?" Elaine asked.

"Of us. Before coming to the station, she pointed out we were never friends before."

Elaine looked away at my accusation. Then looked back, "Are we even friends now? You seem to have complicated my life."

I looked at her stomach, concealed in a flowy skirt and jacket. "You seem to have done that yourself."

That was apparently her limit. She stood and shoved over to Sis.

And remained there until our stop at Sunset and Vine.

THE LIBRARY DOOR opened. Elaine looked both ways before entering. Then she ever-so-slowly closed the door behind her. "You have a lot to explain," she spat at me, sitting at my side by the long, wooden table. "Let's start with you explaining how you knew about a book in a vent in New York."

I looked out the window. Rays of sunshine beamed in, shining on the table and creating our shadows on the opposite wall. "I was told about it by a friend."

"So what is it? What does it say?"

I whipped back to her. "I don't know. That's why I needed it. I didn't realize it would be written in a different language. Do you know what language it was?"

She shrugged. "No." She leaned back in a way I was familiar with. The baby was making breathing more difficult.

I leaned in closer. "How far along are you?"

She made a face and then lifted her chin. "Nearing the end, I hope. I figured it out five months ago. Please tell me how you knew? Is it too obvious to hide?"

I shook my head, wondering how far along she had been five months ago. "You're barely showing for several months in. It's only obvious to someone familiar with the process."

She placed her hand on her stomach and started rounding circles. A comforting movement I'd seen every mother-to-be do. "I don't know what to do next," she confided, still not looking at me.

"The father isn't in the picture?"

She shook her head. "I didn't dare tell him. I'm not keeping her."

My eyes felt misty. My heart longed for Jules, imagined her scent and snuggle. "Do you know it's a girl?"

"How would I know?" She gave me a face that caused me to remember some of my obstetric history. No ultrasounds yet. She shrugged. "It's just some sort of mother's intuition, I suppose."

I nodded. "Why can't you stick with the plan you put in place?"

She looked down. "I was planning to take time off at work and reappear afterwards with no one knowing a thing. But if I'm in New York, I don't know how to do that. I don't know any safe places to have her or leave her. And I don't know if it will be more obvious with those tight uniforms they wear there—I've heard there's even a uniform fitting! Plus, I'm sure they won't let me take time off."

"So you know when you will start? When you will move?"

"No. They said they would be in contact."

"Would they wait for you?"

She shook her head. "I truly don't know. But I don't even have a good reason to give them. I can't tell them the truth. I can't tell them I made a mistake with a wolf from the station."

I opened my mouth to ask the obvious, when the library door opened. "I will not act as your personal secretary again, Miss Miller." It was Old Jackie Kennedy in her wool suit. And she was agitated. "A gentleman dropped this off and asked that I give it to you directly. A rather gruff sort, with an accent. Now, I don't want to know the details of your degenerate lifestyle, but I will say that you run with rough company. I asked that Henry not let him return. I did not like his attitude one iota."

I looked to her hand. So did Elaine. Seeing what was being offered to us, she stood so hard she doubled the chair over backwards.

"Miss Glass!" Old Jackie scolded.

With a steady hand, I reached out and took Valentina's diary.

"Sorry," Elaine mumbled, righting the chair.

Old Jackie spun on her heel and left us alone with the small, leather book.

"He was here?" Elaine hooted in a hushed tone. "He followed us!"

"But to give it back to you?" I pondered, opening the faded, leather book to the first page. I ran my fingers along the words, smeared and indented into the page with an actual fountain pen full of blots of ink. At the top of page one, it began with *1898*.

"See," Elaine pointed. "This is certainly not in English."

I put the pieces together in my mind. The shop owners were Orthodox Jews, according to their website. "Perhaps it's Jewish?"

Elaine gave me a disapproving face. "You mean Hebrew?"

I blushed. "Yes, of course."

"Okay," Elaine started, pacing back to the window. "Well, my father's side of the family is Jewish. And I know a few guys down at the station who might speak Hebrew, but I don't really want to–"

"People you trust?"

She tugged at her bottom lip. "Well, you still haven't even told me what this is. Is it going to get more people in trouble?"

"Probably."

Her nostrils flared. I smiled at her. Oh, those radioactive pregnancy emotions. "I fail to see what's so humorous about this situation. A man followed me across the country, stole something and then handed it back. Why?"

"Maybe he can't read it either?" I mused, flipping through the pages. "Earlier, you mentioned you thought you recognized one of the words. Which one?"

She pointed to squiggles on the page. "Those symbols there appear to be the same as the ones from my father's family tree painting. He had it hanging in his study. When I asked about it, he showed me where it said Shoshanah because that's my grandmother's name, as well as my middle name."

When I moved the book closer, a small piece of paper drifted out of the back cover, floating to the floor as if in slow motion. My brain registered the words before I had even stooped to grab it. "I return in four days for translation. Be ready," I read aloud.

"What!" Elaine gasped, covering her mouth. "That's from him? The man from the shop?"

"It must be," I said, flipping through the book again. No other threats fell out, so that was a plus. "I guess I was right. He can't read this thing either. Now what do we do?"

"Ohhh, no," Elaine refuted, shaking her palms at me. "There's no *we* here. You leave me out of this, Barbara Miller. I never asked to be involved in any of this!"

"Neither did I," I mumbled back.

She was on her way out of the library. "I'm telling you as directly as I can," she said from the doorway, "Leave me out of this!"

I sighed and flipped through the book again. It looked like garbled symbols. It was useless to me.

Useless to the New Yorker as well.

With Sis busy at work and Elaine shutting me out, I had no one else to go to.

Elaine's words stuck with me. *Leave me out of this!* That's just what my mother had said when I'd first told her my plan to reconnect with Gramps. When I suggested the plan, I was about as far along as Elaine in my pregnancy. And I, too, had soothed my baby with circles on my belly. Mom had called Gramps a liar and untrustworthy. She was so mad at him that she was on year seventeen of not speaking a word to him. This from a woman who had a canvas painting over her entryway touting, "Family is Forever." So I'd discovered Sunny Ridge on my own. She hadn't seemed angry at me for reconnecting. But she had reacted as though the relationship between them could never be repaired. Later, when I'd gotten to know Gramps better, I'd asked him to explain the feud. Being just as vague as mom, he'd answered, "I made a mistake. I meant to protect your mother, but instead I deceived her." Then he'd launched into some spiel about the Revolutionary War or Imperial Britain or Native American culture—something completely random that he had way too much knowledge of—and never spoken of their rift again.

I wandered upstairs, intending to go to my room, but stopped along the way. Marjorie was in her room. Guessing from the voices, Bess was in there, too. The door was open in the usual, inviting way. So I accepted the invitation.

"Hiya, ladies," I sang, leaning in the doorway to their small room.

"Well, look what the cat dragged in," Marjorie teased. "What are you up to? You look like trouble."

"I do?" I said with feigned innocence.

Bess giggled. "Have you fully recovered from your tongue tango with Jimmy Durante?"

Marjorie's laugh seemed to echo.

"Not fully," I replied, eager to switch gears from the immature drinking game. "I actually came in to ask a strange question."

Marjorie hopped up onto her knees. "Oh, well you have me intrigued. Go on."

I fumbled with the diary. "Do you know any linguists?"

Bess's forehead crumpled. "Any what?"

"Do you know anyone who might be able to translate something for me?"

The girls stared at me like *I* was the one speaking Hebrew.

"Anyone at all. I'm willing to ask around."

Bess and Marjorie looked at one another, as if there was some sort of collective consciousness between them. They tossed out a few names—a John, a Randall and a Patricia—before Marjorie snapped her fingers. "Just ask Doc!"

I cringed. "Doc?"

"Yes, great idea," Bess agreed.

I shook my head, accepting my fate to talk once again to the creepy old man who had helped me avoid being interrogated about a murder. "Okay. Where can I find him?"

"Uh…his office." Bess chuckled. "Or just wait till tonight when we all know he'll be at the Palindrome scaring off the meek and innocent."

"Remind me where his office is?"

Marjorie shook her head at me, much the way Sis tended to do. She scribbled an address onto a small scrap of paper. "Your memory lately," she mumbled, handing it to me.

"Thanks. Maybe later I can fill you in on my night of sultry necking with Durante."

THE BUS PASS had come in handy in my trek across Hollywood. Eager to get this meeting over with, I knocked on the half-glass office door in front of me. It reminded me of the old-style door a private eye would use. Except Doc's name wasn't on the semi-transparent glass, which struck me as shady for a physician.

"Babs?" he asked, shocked at my presence at his door. "What are you doing here?"

"I have a favor," I blurted. Not exactly the words I'd rehearsed on the bus ride over. Adding a stalking New Yorker to the list of people wishing me harm had eliminated my ability to beat around the bush.

He walked to his rich, wood desk and gestured I should sit in the arm chair across from him. "What sort of favor?" His face was just as red as I'd remembered it. He was uglier in the light of day. "I'm hoping this has something to do with your amnesia and not the other night."

"No." I glanced around. A globe stood in a floor-stand. A mantel clock with roman numerals ticked in the background. Shelves of books and the diploma on the wall fit together like a puzzle. "You're a psychiatrist?"

He crossed his arms and leaned back, peering at me. "A psychotherapist, yes. You know this, Barbara. So you are still having problems with your memory?"

His belly bulged under his tight sweater-vest. He matched the name on his diploma. He looked like a Bernard Gillinghardt.

"Yeah. But that's not why I'm here, Bernie." He winced at his new nickname as I pulled the leather book from my purse and tossed it onto the table in front of him. It slid on the smooth surface. "I was told you might be able to translate this for me?"

His fat fingers clamped over the diary. He took a moment to fan through the pages. "What is it?"

"I'm asking that you translate it without too many questions."

He arched an eyebrow. Scraggly eyebrows I knew Jules would refer to as *eye-beard*, as she often did. He scanned my tight shirt without shame. "What will I receive as payment if I agree?"

I shifted in the chair. "What do you feel is a fair?" I held myself back from running away when he licked his lips. "I need it back in four days."

"Four days?" He opened to a random page and scanned the words. "Seems like plenty of work to get done in just four days."

"I don't have a lot of money," I blurted.

He laughed at me. "This, I know. But you do have something I want."

"Yeah, and what's that?" If the old creeper was asking for sexual favors, I was gonna make him say the words outright.

He pulled out a pad of paper—maybe his prescription pad—and scribbled. Tearing it off, he handed it across the table. "If you can get *that* to me in four days, I can return this to you in four days."

I read his note. "But how could I...?" Digger. Oh, God. He wanted me to go back to that murdering monster and get more drugs.

He grinned again. "So you *can* get it. I thought so. Do we have a deal?"

I stood. "You're sure you can translate that?"

He closed the book. "I'm sure." Then he stood as well.

Thankful for the desk between us, I extended my hand. "Deal."

"A bit old fashioned to shake on it, but if you insist." He slid his clammy hand into mine. We shook, and I pulled away, wiping my palm on my skirt. He glared. "That was uncalled for."

"I'll be back here in four days."

"Wait."

I did a quick spin. "What?"

"Should we talk about the timing of this *amnesia* of yours?"

My forehead scrunched. I didn't know what he was getting at, which seemed to be just what he wanted. "Well, you're the doctor. You tell me."

He stood and walked to his bookshelf. He removed a navy blue, hardcover book with gold-edged pages. "Then you truly don't remember our sessions?"

Intrigued, I stepped closer. "I didn't even know we had sessions together."

He flipped through thin pages with a flutter. "You were under my care for several private sessions while you tried to uncover some," he stopped flipping pages, "information that may be locked in your unconscious." He held out the book.

> *Episodic memories, or precise individual experiences and corresponding details of the experiences, occur within the grey matter of the medial temporal lobe. Therefore, by directly interacting with this area of the brain, access to unconscious memories may be possible.*

Setting the book on his desk, he motioned for me to sit on the chaise lounge. "I see how much you dislike me now," he started. "That wasn't true just a few days ago. There have been major behavioral changes."

I sat, bewildered at his words.

He sat, too, on the chair beside the chaise. "The day Sis told me you fell was the same day as our last session." His fat fingers fluttered with nervous energy. "Well, I just wouldn't feel right with myself if I didn't at least ask if you'd like me to try and put things right again."

I swallowed. "So you think you can just—what? Hypnotize me back?"

He shook his palms. "It's a series of meditation exercises we practice. No swinging pocket watches in this office." He stared at me, itching his neck. Appearing guilty. Causing me to wonder if he really had done something.

"Remind me what our last session was regarding?"

He tried to shrug off my request with nonchalance that wasn't successful. "Oh, just your emotional state."

"I'm leaving right now unless you tell me."

He sighed. "If you don't remember, perhaps that's even better than what we were striving for." My glare caused him to continue. "You were seeing me to try to help you with your reoccurring nightmares."

I scoffed. Of course Barbara had nightmares. "What kind of nightmares?"

"Those of loss, fear, disconnection," he rattled. "We were making progress, though it was of the more mysterious variety."

"Meaning?"

He rubbed the tips of his fat, red fingers together in an anxious motion. "It seems I may have sent you to an unconscious state where you believed to have seen some sort of energy world."

"What the heck is an energy world?"

He raised his eyebrows. "We didn't figure that out yet. But you awoke to tell me about your *twin soul*. And you were seeming much more at peace."

"I've never heard that term before. Is that a soulmate?"

His shoulders raised, matching my question. "I've read stories about people coming back from meditation recognizing people in their current life as people from past lives. That the reincarnation progression tends to..." He twirled his hands, searching for a word. "...*process* some souls at the same rate, sending them into bodies at the same time again and again. And stories exist of these souls finding each other."

My face was twisted in the same form of impudence as when Valentina had first told me about the mirror. But seeing as how that had turned out to be true, I conceded. "Fine," I agreed. "If you think it might help, you can hypnotize me again. No funny business, though."

If he'd been the kind of man to roll his eyes, that would have caused one. "Despite my apparent shortcomings, I do hold a doctorate in clinical psychology." He nodded toward his framed degree.

Taking a deep breath, I reclined back onto the chaise. Reluctant to be this vulnerable. Sickened by the naked feeling. Ashamed at the level of my anxiety.

The scene prompted a memory of sitting in front of two midwives when I'd been pregnant with Jules. As a lover of fast food, the crushing diagnosis of gestational diabetes and pricking my finger three times a day had sent me into a panic. But then the appointments full of food diaries and blood glucose levels that followed felt like being on trial, being judged from the inside out by a professional. *Why did you eat that? Try adding more kale.* One such occasion involved Doug ratting me out. "Why are your numbers so high in the afternoon?" one midwife wanted to know. Shrugging it off, I'd hoped to move on. But Doug had interjected, "Probably because of the chocolates." The two midwives and I turned to face him and his admission. They lectured me on the dangers of spiking glucose levels while building a human inside my unstable body. I felt shame for not taking better care of my growing baby. Outside the birth center, I interrogated him. How had he known about my afternoon chocolates? "Cuz you can't screw, babe," was his answer. Unclear what he meant, he went on to list a myriad of screwtop items he followed me around righting: peanut butter jars, shampoo covers, coffee thermoses, *bulk chocolate containers*. I remember how I stood in place, listening to Doug explain something he knew so well about me when I was completely unaware. So I was unable to screw covers on correctly. All the jars and containers in our house were in a constant state of off-kilter. This was a minor annoyance he lived with. And one I had just discovered about myself.

Uncomfortable, I sighed, feeling as though Doc *also* knew something about me I didn't.

He started chanting numbers in descending order and asking me to concentrate on my breathing.

"NAME AND REGISTRATION," the clerk announced, motioning for me to come forward in the line at the Los Angeles County Clerk's Office about an hour after my regression.

I fumbled the I.D. card out of my purse, eager to get the answer I needed. "Barbara Miller." Sliding my card over the counter to her, I couldn't help but find ironic that every aspect of life had changed between the forties and the new millennium—except for dealing with the government. "I need a copy of my marriage certificate."

Her face held a kind of permanent pucker, reminding me of the face I made when the clock hit 7:30 at night, and my kids were still running around half-dressed, singing and sobbing instead of getting in bed. One part exasperation and one part rage.

She disappeared into a room. From the little I could see, it was a file cabinet library back there. So maybe government dealings really had changed. The sign over the door said, "PRIVATE DATA STORAGE."

I scoffed. That was data storage? No wonder so many people my mom's age didn't understand how to back up a fricken hard drive.

Old Lady Rage Pucker returned and leaned over to me, "Middle name. Too many Barbara Millers back there."

"Jane. Barbara Jane Miller."

Apprehension started to rise in me. There was too much in my head, now that it was holding some of Barbara's actual memories with my own. Just this one fact check for evidence for myself, and then I'd have proof the memory was real.

Rage Pucker came back holding a paper. A white piece of paper holding sacred, secret information.

"That will be two dollars and twenty-five cents," she said, placing the license into a manila envelope.

I pulled out change from my coin purse and paid her—pleased, in some malicious way, I was paying for a government document with change.

I hurried up the marble stairs and stopped before the glass doors. Without bothering to sit on the wooden bench next to me, I tore open the envelope.

John M. Digrokowski and Barbara Jane Miller
Married July 10, 1947

So it was true. I was legally Mrs. Digger. Mrs. Digrokowski.

And, just as I had remembered, there was an address for a shared apartment. The piece of memory that had forced me to find out, once and for all, if I was married to a murderer.

I flung a hand to my forehead. "Woo!" My exhale echoed in the entryway.

My brain was like two women who had always been friends reconnecting after a long time apart. Like it was having a conversation with itself. Doc's mind-melt had caused me to remember details about Barbara. But how could I have memories of Barbara when I was Liza?

I looked at the clock, knowing I should head back to Heritage House. Londa had been *extra eagle eye* toward me ever since the incident. She was just waiting for me to mess up so she could kick me out. But at least if I pissed her off again, I now knew of another address I could cohabitate.

"JIMINY CRICKET!" Bess yelped, dropping her fork down to her plate. "You're a married woman?"

Sis was still avoiding my gaze, though I was looking right at her. "Since July, Sis."

After staring at the silly napkin holder between us for a century, she finally looked up. "You didn't tell me." She went back to her tapioca.

I shook my head, wondering what kind of fool Barbara was ostracizing her best friend and marrying a man like Digger. Digger who made Doug seem more like whiny, self-absorbed Ted wandering through the maze of *How I Met Your Mother* than the man I'd divorced for irreconcilable differences.

Maybe with another session with Doc, I would be able to remember what she'd been thinking…Why she had done it. Why it was a secret.

Bess's mouth was full of dry baked potato. "You've been acting so strange lately. I guess now we know why."

I shoved the strange meat lump across my plate. A smirk came over me thinking about what Jules would have to say about this meal. She'd call it something hilarious like *kitty nibbles* or *smushed up sweet potato booty*. My smirk faded. "What *is* this?"

"Minced meat rissoles," Marjorie explained, though that helped me none. Then she leaned in to whisper, "Are you in the family way?"

Elaine, who was seated a few seats down, prickled and sat up straight. Not subtle, that one.

"No," I stated, cutting into my minced meat. Though I hadn't thought to check…Eh, I would have noticed that by now.

"That's good," Marjorie said. "That's how Bess and Peggy lost their roommate, you know. It wasn't owing rent. It was for canoodling a little too well with the iceman. Londa wouldn't allow anyone to know a *Heritage* girl had gone and gotten herself pregnant." She shook her head.

Now it was me who couldn't be subtle, shooting Elaine a look.

"But," Bess began, going back to the topic at hand. "I want to know why you aren't living with your husband. It's your womanly duty to keep his home, Babs. And isn't there something in the Bible about sharing a bed with your husband, too?" She scanned the other women, hoping someone would chime in.

No one did.

"I'm just not that kind of woman."

Bess laughed as Sis, at last, looked at me. "Well, we all want to say that, don't we?" Sis barraged. "That's why we're all here, isn't it? We all want fortune and fame. Or to marry a millionaire. Get the Bogey and Bacall ending, right?"

Guilt struck me. Had it been so long since I was a single girl I had lost touch with the awful emptiness of living lonely?

All the ladies were nodding in agreement with Sis. She continued, "Otherwise, why would we live like this? With no one to care for or spend our nights with. With the dreadful aching of loneliness. With only the company of other women." She paused to glare at me. "Sometimes catty women are not what a girl needs."

Marjorie finished a sip from her child-sized glass cup before adding, "What I wouldn't give to see a pair of pants around here. This bachelor girl lifestyle is not something any of us wanted. It's the price we are paying to find better."

The table was silent as we all soaked in their words. After Marjorie finished chewing, she turned to me. "As for you, Babs, maybe you felt forced into marrying?"

Sis, Bess and I looked to her face, waiting for her to continue.

"How so?" I asked, intrigued. Though I'd had a memory about Digger and I living together in an apartment, I did not have one of the wedding.

"You're not with child, not using his last name or address, not sharing his bed, and you haven't resigned from your job."

Bess was so interested in Marjorie's words, I just knew she would be ecstatic when the Lifetime channel was invented. "But if he's not living with her, why would a man want to be married?" she asked the group.

I was too busy eyeing up Londa's young lesbian friend to brainstorm with them. The girl carried her plate past our table, stiffening at the sight of me. Ashamed. Scurrying away to eat alone.

Was she feeling banished because of what I'd seen? Had she been this isolated before I humiliated her and blackmailed her girlfriend?

"Does she ever sit at your table?" I asked the girls, nodding my head toward Londa's girl.

"Nah, she always sits alone, that one," Elaine said. The other girls agreed.

"She's an odd duck," Bess interjected. "Don't get wrapped up with her. Word is, she's a degenerate."

The rest of the girls nodded in agreement. Then went back to eating and discussing secret marriages.

Such a social difference. For as much as people of my time complain about sexism, racism and other-isms, we don't know what we're spouting off about. In my circle, we don't ostracize someone for being gay. We don't ask that women resign from their jobs upon marriage.

Before the 2008 election, I tallied an alarming number of friends and acquaintances who were not even planning to vote. We, the passionate people, all have a pet cause. Mine happened to be women's rights. I ranted to everyone who would listen about our grandmothers being the first to ever have a vote in America. How they were beaten, humiliated, jailed. Then picketed and rallied and faced terrifying consequences just to be heard. Just to be counted as a citizen with a vote. Just to stand alongside their husbands and say, "We *each* have a voice." These women wanted a voice for themselves, yes. But they also wanted a better tomorrow for their daughters. And they got it! Yet less than ninety years later—while we faced kind neighbors standing in line rather than violent bullies, and received a sticker, not a fine after casting our ballot—women I knew were not voting. I had accused a coworker of "metaphorically sucker punching Susan B. Anthony in the gut" by not voting. Nearly lost my job.

And the women sitting in front of me at the table were the daughters of those brave women. Stuck halfway between *the way it's always been* and *the way it will be.*

So instead of participating in the debate about why a man would marry a woman with nothing to offer, I abandoned my dry potato and meat cake.

"You're done?" Bess asked as I stood.

"I'm done," I said.

CHAPTER 8

WHAT'S THE OPPOSITE OF HOUSEWIFE

"**I** NEED HELP," Elaine sobbed. "I only just discovered this, and I don't have much time left."

It was day twenty-one in the ditty doo-wop world of Old Hollywood, and the day New Yorker was expecting the translation. Yet instead of hurrying along, I was in the music library at HBC among the aisles of drawers, hiding in the back corner. And Elaine was in hysterics. "You're sure about this?" I double-checked.

"Yes!" she declared in a hushed tone. "Judy said they don't allow you to make telephone calls or accept visitors. They make you use a false name. Judy said it was like being imprisoned! Not even allowed to talk to other mothers there with you. I just can't do this, Babs. You have to help me. You said you knew about these things."

"It's okay, Elaine. You just need to rethink this a little. Can your obstetrician help?"

"I don't have one!" she bellowed.

"What? Oh, Elaine. You haven't been seeing a doctor or midwife?"

"No, that's why I was getting ready to go to the maternity home. It's time now. This is what I thought was best."

"Well, I can certainly look you over. See how things are progressing. I've seen many women give birth." I set my hand on top of hers. "Many of them feeling just as scared and unsure as you are right now. You have the strength in you to do this. But I do not want you to try and do this alone. Do you hear me?"

She was dabbing her eyes with a handkerchief. "I don't have anyone I can trust."

"Sure you do. You have your sisters. Your friends. Your roommates at Heritage House. We will find someone to be with you."

"You mean you won't help me when the time comes?"

"I can certainly try. But for now, I can get you prepared. I can explain what will happen. How it will happen. What you'll need to do. I'll come to your room tonight. We'll brainstorm. I just know there are trustworthy women in your life you can call on for this."

"Well, I suppose Judy trusted me with her secret. And she's gone through it before."

"There you go!" I cheered. "Ask Judy to meet us in your room tonight. And if you're sure you want to keep this a secret, we'll get you prepared."

"I don't have any other choice." She sounded so small. "I'll have to invite her. Judy isn't a Heritage Girl. I met her through HBC. At the party that started this whole mess."

I didn't want to be rude, but I was trying hard to wrap up this little powwow. My shift had ended fifteen minutes ago, and I had to get to Digger. With a quick hug, I said, "Tonight. I'll meet you in your room tonight."

Racing out the doors, I headed for the street. Things weren't cleared up around the station yet, but it was business as usual until we heard otherwise. There were a few faces missing from the ranks of the employees and higher-ups, but there was little news about the witch-hunt for communists.

Outside, I was just in time to catch the streetcar that headed to Mr. Digrokowski's neighborhood. I boarded.

New Yorker would be appearing at my side any minute, and I still didn't have a way to pay for the translation. Not for lack of trying. Each day I'd boarded the bus to Digger's apartment, preparing for the worst, preparing for a potential beating when I asked for drugs to sell, knowing they would be given to Doc.

But Digger hadn't been there. Not on Tuesday. Not on Wednesday. I was running low on funds for this trip across town.

During my painful shift of phone call surveys, I'd primed myself for the possibility of breaking and entering. In fact, I'd popped an extra pep pill just for the added oomph. I had thought ahead and brought the big girl purse to work, rather than the tiny clutch. Huge mom-bags were not in vogue in 1947, so it did garner a few looks, prompting me to ponder the origins of the term "bag lady." But hidden inside, my megapurse concealed a small mallet, stolen from the basement of Heritage House. My plan was simple: knock out the hinge pins and open the door from the hinged side.

Having inspected the apartment door twice already, I had confidence it could be done. Thanks to the shitty craftsmanship of the divey apartment Digger lived in, the doors were all hung backwards with the hinges exposed from the hall. I'd seen my dad remove hinges once when we were locked out of the bathroom. He had made it look easy—a few taps, and the pins fell loose.

The problem was, once I was in—I had no idea if I would find anything. Though Doc had shaken a memory loose from Barbara's brainwaves, I didn't have a clear picture. I had glimpses. The address, the layout, the smell and an idea where to look.

And no other choice I could come up with.

"Good evening," an older woman greeted, sitting next to me on the streetcar bench.

"Hi," I squeaked, lost in my thoughts and not prepared to speak.

"Nice night out there," she engaged, unwrapping her hair from a scarf.

"Mmm-hmm."

She eyed up megapurse. "Going somewhere special?"

"Nope." I sensed my answers were rude somehow, but wasn't sure how to make small talk in my own time, let alone this one.

I threw her a line. "Needed a bigger purse to carry all the kids' stuff." I patted the side of the bag.

"Ah, you have little ones! How old?"

"Three and one," I answered, wishing they could try out the neat old streetcar we were riding.

The lady chuckled. "My, that's a wonderful age. Wonderful time in life. If only they'd stay small forever."

My smile was sheepish. Not a sentiment I often agreed with, but considering the circumstances, I did. I wish time had stopped the instant I looked into the mirror so I hadn't missed a day with them. But Valentina had made it quite clear time was ticking there as well as here. And that I was wasting away in a hospital room.

"Where are they now?"

I looked down. "With my husband." I felt so awkward I couldn't look at her face. It seemed like I was breaking unwritten rules speaking about my real self.

"Oh, you are one of those modern mothers then? My Paulie didn't help a stitch with the little ones." She leaned in. "Didn't make me love him any less though. Good provider, he was. Been gone two years now."

"I'm sorry." I obliged.

"Oh, that's life, isn't it? We had a good time, Paulie and I. Had a good run. The kids are all grown up now." She nodded at her own words. "Yes, you're in a very good place in life."

I pursed my lips. "May I ask, wasn't it difficult? Being the caregiver for the children? Never having any help? Didn't you resent your husband and his freedom?"

"Ack!" she exclaimed, flapping her hand. "He didn't have anything I wanted. Wearing a suit in this California heat, sitting at a desk all day? No. Not for me. I enjoyed being with my little ones. And I was good at keeping house." She nodded again. "I was a good wife even then."

I sighed. "I fear I am not a good wife."

"Oh, come now. We all have our moments of weakness, but that doesn't mean we're bad wives. As long as your husband is being served his dinner plate first, and you're good at keeping each other company, you'll be fine."

"Serve him his plate first?" This was a concept lost on me. Our children were our world. They ate before we ate, bathed before we showered, slept before we slept. Had Doug and I been dooming ourselves?

She was smiling again. Reminding me of the Mrs. Butterworth syrup container. "You must know what I mean. He needs to know he comes first. We are fortunate enough to get to choose our husbands. Lord knows we can't choose our kids," she chirped. "As for feeling down on yourself, don't you have sisters or girlfriends to lean on when the kids and dishes are too dirty to handle?" She was waiting for a happy answer.

Her words sounded so similar to those I had just preached to Elaine. "I don't…"

Her smile melted and turned into pity. "Sorry to hear that, dear. You know, I'm in a Thursday night bridge club. You should join me, since you have a husband willing to sit with the children."

Without knowing it, she had just hit on one of my soapbox issues. If they were *his* kids how could he be babysitting? Mothers didn't babysit their own children.

But she was saved by the approaching bus stop. Instead of a rant, I said, "Thank you so much, but I don't know how to play bridge." I stood, shimmying past her knees to get into the aisle the best I could with such a full skirt. "I will take your advice though, and reconnect with some old friends. It was nice meeting you."

"You too, dear. Have a pleasant evening."

Ha. My night was going to be anything but pleasant.

The car came to its stop, and I stepped out onto the sidewalk in front of the apartment building. Focused, I propelled myself up the front stoop and into the entryway. Up the stairwell, my shoes echoed the timing of the pounding of my heart. I swallowed the lump in my throat, lifted my hand and knocked.

Waiting was excruciating. I fiddled with the shiny, slim belt cinched around the waist of my swishy, A-line dress.

Would he answer? Would he be angry? Would he hit me or shove me or choke me?

One more timid rapping for good measure.

Waiting.

Listening.

Praying.

Letting out the breath I didn't realize I was holding, I opened megapurse, which actually may have been luggage. Wrapping my fingers around the wooden handle of the small mallet, I glanced around to be sure I was alone in the hallway. One thing I hadn't thought of was the sound level.

The door's hinges were large. Not rusty. The pins were just jammed in place. Good.

Tap, tap, tap went the mallet, light and reserved, mirroring the elves of North Pole as they built rocking horses for the good girls and boys.

I froze and listened. Someone was coming up the stairs.

TAP-TAP-TAP the mallet smacked the pin again with force and panic and gusto.

My heartbeat was in my ears, adrenaline I had rarely known in real life surging through Barbara's thin veins. At least, I assumed they were thin; everything else on her was.

With a final *TAP*, the pin was loose enough to move. Using my hand, I twisted and pulled. It was stuck.

"Can I help you?" a man's voice asked from behind.

My startle sent me airborne. Panic-stricken, I dropped the mallet into the gaping megapurse on the floor. Then stooped to pick up the bag off the floor as I plastered on the best smile I could. "Yes, I'm here for Mr. Digrokowski," I cooed, watching the man step closer.

His clothes were bland. His stance was nonthreatening. I sighed with relief when I surmised the probability he was one of Digger's henchmen was next to none. He said, "I'm afraid he's not in. Haven't seen him the last few days. I'm the building superintendent. Can I help you with something?"

Internally, I was having that moment in a movie when complicated algebraic equations appear in the air and someone adds and calculates using only finger dashes. And I solved it.

I reached into my purse and removed a paper. "I would love some help. I'm Mrs. Digrokowski." I flashed the marriage license. "Digger and I are just in the process of moving me in, and I came to take some measurements. He said he would leave the key for me, but I don't see it here."

His nervous smile made me wonder if this was what meeting Mr. Furley felt like for Janet and Chrissy in *Three's Company*. "Well, it's a good thing I was here today then, Mrs. D." He stepped to the door, jingling his collection of brass-colored keys. Selecting the right one, he clicked open the lock.

"I can't thank you enough," I gushed, getting the hang of the damsel in distress bit. I leaned toward him, aiming to make the most of my dress's sweetheart neckline, but deflating a bit over the realization that a thin woman's breasts didn't pack the same punch as the curvy set I left back home.

"My pleasure. You take your time now. I'll be sure to check that it's locked before I leave for the day."

I opened the door, still smiling in his direction. The door groaned. He inspected the loud hinges, but didn't say anything. "Thanks again," I blurted, slipping into the apartment.

The second the door closed behind me, I was hit with a rush of information. The stench of the apartment, the look of the dingy sofa, the dirty dishes in the sink, the clinking of the radiator...

But how could I remember things that didn't happen to me?

How could I hold memories that weren't mine?

Swallowing, I went straight to work. I rushed to the shallow, bedroom closet, where I had remembered seeing Digger go to each time he returned from his mysterious ventures.

Not wanting to spend another minute in the apartment that throbbed with danger, I dug through the boxes and clothing in the closet. Nothing seemed out of the ordinary. Nothing stood out.

I checked the pockets of the trench coats hung in a row on metal hangers. Beyond some cigarettes, a lighter and some change, there was nothing. I kicked a few of the shoes and boots on the floor of the closet.

Bingo!

One of the boots had barely moved. I crouched down and reached into the dank unknown. My hand met cold metal. I jerked back. The last thing I needed was my fingerprints on Digger's gun!

Checking the next boot, my hand felt paper. Pulling it out of the toe of the boot, I gasped. Alone, huddled next to a murderer's footwear, I flared my nostrils at what was in my hand.

A small stack of money.

Okay, so it wasn't drugs. But it could *buy* drugs…

Standing, my eyes surveyed the unkempt bed. I'd learned my first morning fitted sheets did not yet exist. And it was a woman's duty to make a bed with perfect corners. Every single day. The idea struck me as idiotic and purposeless. Thinking of the lady on the bus, I realized perhaps I had cared too little what kind of wife I had been. But it was a two-way street. And I hadn't seen Doug jumping up to make our bed, either.

Shaking my head, I rushed back to the front door, ready to leave. With my hand on the doorknob, I took one more sweeping look around the apartment.

Unnerving was the word. It was unnerving how familiar this apartment felt. Was it connected to what I needed to see? Or connected to what Barbara had already seen?

Letting go of the knob, I scurried to the bathroom, my full skirt swishing in the silence of the space. Placing a hand on either side of the bathroom sink, I stared into the mirror.

Glaring at Barbara, I saw panic. Hers or mine, I wasn't sure. But we knew what I was stealing from Digger would mean consequences. Likely, deadly ones.

My life as Liza Anderson was a meek one. Never making waves, never pushing, trying not to offend as I went about my business. Even though on the inside I was always ready to argue a point, I had never been in a situation with such high odds of bodily harm and true danger. Yet here I was on a naughty Nancy Drew adventure—breaking and entering, stealing money, taking drugs and witnessing a murder. Was I stuck in some elaborate *What Would You Do* game show? Or were the fates trying to show me just what kind of person I was on the inside?

Is this the kind of life I would live if I feared nothing?

Groaning, I abandoned the mirror in a flurry and left the bathroom. As I passed a small writing desk near the door, I stopped short. A flash of an image. A memory?

I closed my eyes, trying to focus. The desk. What about the desk?

Popping my eyes open, I yanked out the top drawer. Sifting through papers, I saw some sort of bank ledger. Barbara's name appeared over and over, going back several months. And judging by the numbers in the *deposits* and *withdrawals* categories, ol' Babsie should not have been late in paying her back rent. Removing the ledger had exposed a small booklet, similar to a checkbook. Embossed over the cover were the words *Bank of America*.

And as I read those three words, my brain reacted as if I *was* recovering from amnesia. I was now the proud owner of the memory of searching for a forward-thinking bank that would allow a woman to open a savings account without a man's name on the account.

Digger was depositing his drug money in Barbara's accounts. That's why she'd married him.

The new memory was a mere island. No bridges existed to link it to any other pieces of information. I could not remember if Barbara was forced into marriage. I could only speculate Digger was making her carry the cash into the bank for him, but it seemed like Barbara would have had to, it all being in her maiden name.

I read it over again.

Barbara's name. With his name nowhere to be found. Appearing innocent and disconnected from it all. Because why, in 1947, would a woman have a bank account in her maiden name if she was married? Barbara would look shady. And from the little understanding I had of the politics of marriage at this time, I bet just by being her husband, he would be able to cash it out at any time, even without his name on the account.

I crammed everything back into the messy drawer, slammed it shut and charged out of the apartment.

HIKING MEGAPURSE UP further on my bony shoulder, I knocked on Doc's semi-transparent office door. My fingers tapped the side of the purse like a growing tally. I wasn't sure whether the taps were tallying the dollars stashed in my purse, or the minutes I had left until Digger and New Yorker played a game of rock, paper, scissors to be the first to strangle me.

Old Red Face opened the door. "I was wondering if I would see you today."

I shoved past him, eager to get out of the hallway. "It's been four days. I said I'd be here."

In his usual sluggish and calm manner, he clicked the door latched, and turned to face me. My back was to his desk, purse yanked as high as it could be perched, hand clutching the straps.

"You look nervous."

"I am," I announced.

"You should be."

I sucked in a breath as he stepped closer, leering in that molester sort of way he did. "What do you mean by that?" I asked, sitting to avoid his closeness.

"This book of yours." He took the leather volume from his desktop and fanned the pages in my face. "I went most of the way through thinking this was an unbearable waste of my time. Silly, trivial inner thoughts of a prepubescent boy. That is, until the end." He watched my reaction. "A few pages before the end, this book went from Yiddish rambling to a valuable message in Russian."

My eyes widened, but I said nothing. Russian! Valentina really had written it. Looking back to Doc, I felt panic clawing up the inside of my throat. How much did he know? What would he ask?

Slapping the book closed against his thigh, I jumped at the loud sound. He looked into my eyes. "This story of yours makes some very impossible claims."

"It's just fiction!" I blurted.

Skepticism was smeared all over his face. He rounded his desk and sat as well, leaving me with some precious breathing room. "A girl like you, walking around with a book written in Russian, making claims about famous men from history could easily be...misconstrued. In the wrong hands, this could be proof for hefty accusations against you."

"I didn't write it!" My words echoed my sentiments of being on trial.

"That, my dear, is obvious. The first half is written in Yiddish. I think it was meant as a decoy to anyone who may have found this top-secret treasure." His cloudy eyes held a new gleam. "I can't imagine Barbara Jane Miller of Milwaukee would know how to write in Yiddish or in Russian."

I shook my head, confirming I did not know how to write in either language.

"So then who wrote it? And why do you have it?"

"I don't know." Fiddling with the straps of my purse, I declared. "I brought money."

My words caused him to laugh. "Good. Because I just may need to be persuaded to keep this our little secret." He thrust a handwritten paper at me. "Page one."

I raced my eyes over the words.

December 1898

Dear Diary,
The spider web was still there. Woven into the doorway just as it was yesterday. And the day before that. And every day when I pass. It is my disgusting reminder that nothing has changed. Why doesn't it blow away in the wind? The bitter wind that catches my tattered overcoat and rips it open. I often hold it closed as I clear a path through manure for the people around me. This is the life of a Crossing Sweeper. I stand on the corner and wait for someone with money, and the need for me to sweep for them. All day in the stench. All day in the cold. Meanwhile, the spider is tucked into his doorway. Not affected by the cold wind, the terrible stench or the crossing sweeper who temporarily huddles in its doorway. I am thankful tomorrow is the Shabbat. I need rest. –Yacob Zeyer

I looked up to see him watching me read. He held out a hand.

Lowering the paper, I nibbled my bottom lip before asking, "You want it back?"

He sneered and shook his head. "I want to be paid, sugar. I held up my end of this deal, now where's yours?"

I shifted. "This just seems like an old diary entry."

"Ah, but that is the writer wants you to assume."

Swallowing, I opened the large purse, momentarily wondering if I could smack him with the enormous bag, and run away with the papers. "I...don't know how much is fair."

His eyebrow lifted. "You say this as though you have more than enough?"

"No, as though I don't have much," I lied.

Anger flared through his eyes. "I do not like my time being exploited."

Wishing yet again I had a way to calculate inflation or type *value of the dollar in 1947* into a search engine, I tried to figure a number based on my rent rate. "Would twenty dollars be fair?"

His features eased. "You have twenty dollars with you?"

I nodded, fingering the wad of bills inside the purse. In reality, I had counted the stack on the way over and it was nearly a hundred dollars. I had almost offered him the whole thing, knowing how little a Benjamin would get you in 2011. The bus ride to this side of town had provided some time for my less-than-stellar math abilities to work.

He stood. "Let me have it."

Pulling the right number of five dollar bills from megapurse, I offered it across the desk. Shoving it into his suit pocket, he walked over to his coatrack near the office door.

I twisted around in the armchair. "Where's the rest of the translation?"

Cramming a hat over his fat head, he pointed to the wooden file cabinet. "I've left the rest on top there. It will take you some time to read it." He shrugged into a plaid suit jacket. "I have an appointment now. But I will be back. And I expect we'll have a conversation."

I bounced out of the chair and snatched the papers from the top of the cabinet. Power surged through me as if I were holding the Declaration of Independence. "I need to go," I told him, bending the papers and sandwiching them in next to the mallet.

"No," he commanded. His tone was stern. "You will stay here until I return."

I stepped toward him. "I have to get back to Heritage House. This is not mine. It belongs to someone else. Someone who is expecting these papers today!" I shrieked.

"I won't be long." He was still calm and composed. "It will take you time to read them anyway. Wait here."

In a burst of defiance, I taunted, "I could start making my own accusations, you know. Such as why does a psychiatrist know how to read and write Russian?"

Unfazed by my words, he jingled his keys. "I'm locking you in until I get back."

"You can't!" I shouted, rushing to the door.

He closed it in my face and turned the key. "And I'm a psychotherapist," he called through the door.

"Psycho is right!" I yelled back. I gave his door a good slam with my fist.

Looking around, I comforted myself with the fact this was a quiet place, safer than Heritage House. Safer than the station. A place no one would look for me.

The mantel clock chimed six. It was getting late. If New Yorker had come back for the translation, he would have been to the House by now.

Seeing Doc's telephone on his desk, I skirted around to sit in his chair. The phone was not as modern as those at HBC, which was a laugh to even think. Lifting the mouthpiece and the receiver, I waited for a dial tone. It was a rotary, an old one I had never used before. I spun the rotary wheel by placing my finger in the "o" and rotating. Was dialing zero the universal code for speaking with a human? One could hope!

There was a clicking sound followed by a voice. "Pacific Bell. How may I connect your call?"

"Yes, I need to be connected with Heritage House Hotel for Women on Sunset Boulevard, please."

"Just one moment while I make your connection." The operator's voice was so automated and robotic, she could have been a computer.

After a prominent *click,* there was ringing. Staring at the papers sticking out from the top of the purse, I waited. Ring after ring. Just as I was wondering when answering machines had become widely used, someone picked up. "Heritage House," the girl answered.

"Hi, this is Babs Miller. I'm calling for Elaine Glass. Can you please get her for me? It's urgent."

Like a younger sister taking a call for her annoying older sibling, she sighed and dropped the phone without a word.

I waited an eternity. Wishing I didn't have to hold both portions of the phone. Wishing I had started reading first instead of checking in on Elaine. Wishing I'd left the purse just a little closer.

"Babs?" a voice finally answered.

"Elaine!"

"No… Sis." She was upset with me. Calling for Elaine probably didn't help that.

"Sis, have you seen Elaine today? At the house? I spoke with her at the station, but do you know if she got home all right?"

Sis sniffed. I knew her well enough to know she was probably puffing her hair or checking her nails. Feigning indifference to my request. "I'm not her keeper."

I sighed at her answer. "Sis, I'm sorry. I'm so sorry for shutting you out, and for keeping secrets from you."

"So you admit you're keeping more things from me!"

"Yes, but they are not my secrets to share. And Elaine may be in trouble. Now, have you seen her at the house?"

"No. I came back at the usual time, but I didn't see her leave the station or come home. She's not here. Connie was just banging on her door telling her you were on the phone. So I thought I would make sure you were okay. You didn't walk home with me after our shift."

"I know. I had to rush to an appointment."

"What kind of an appointment?" she whined. "You used to tell me absolutely everything, Babs! Now you don't even tell me when you marry a lowlife."

I opened my mouth, but words didn't fall out. Breathing in, I tried to explain part of the real truth. "Right now, I'm at Doc's office. I'm avoiding a man who is looking for me and Elaine. Hiding from him."

"At Doc's? What man? Why is he looking for you?"

I shook my head without meaning to. "I don't want to get you involved, Sis. It's for your own good. But this man knows what Elaine looks like. He said he would be back to the house tonight to get something from us. She might be in trouble already." I glanced out the window. It was dusk, and getting darker by the minute.

"Oh no!" Her voice hushed. "You're not selling again, are you?" she reprimanded in a harsh whisper.

"Please. Just try not to get involved in the details. Ask Henry if he's seen Elaine. Or if he's seen a man hanging around the front doors. And consider this man dangerous and stay out of his way."

"You're not on your way back?"

I looked at the locked office door. "I will be back tonight, but I don't know what time. I'll be here at Doc's office for a while yet. Please say you'll do this, Sis? For old time's sake?"

"Old time sake…" she mumbled. "You have a lot of nerve, Barbara Miller. But okay. I'll ask around about Elaine. And I expect you to stop in my room the minute you're back. I don't appreciate being used. Or being left out."

"Thank you. I'll see you tonight." My words were more confident than I was feeling. Hanging up both ends of the old phone, I hurried to the papers.

My stomach was jittery. My palms were clammy. Desperate for water, my mouth felt like I had just eaten warm yogurt. But none of that mattered. I was about to put the pieces together. I was about to know everything Valentina had intended me to know. All that she had forgotten. The details of her other life.

Snatching the papers, I flopped onto the chaise lounge. Tucking my feet up under my skirt, I unfolded the papers and started reading.

CHAPTER 9

HISTORY'S HIDDEN FOOTNOTE

MY NAME IS Valentina Ivanov, and I am from the year nineteen hundred seventy-seven. I arrived here through the mirror twenty-nine years ago. What follows is impossible.

On my first day, I only knew that I was a boy. A very sick boy, who was surrounded by his loving family. The family did not act as though Yacob was different. They did not act as though it was strange for me to have no comprehension of the words they were speaking. They never acted as though they knew I was not Yacob. But they always knew I was not him.

Months later, after recovering from Typhoid, I found similarities in Yiddish to Russian, and started to make sense of the story. Yacob's mother was Elisheva, father was Aharon, older brother was Abram, younger sister was Shoshanah.

The Zeyer family treated me just like a member of the family. But outside papa's shop, life was terrible.

The street was crowded with people and push carts, horses and carriages. Women yelled across streets, babies cried for mamas and boys fought with boys until bloody. Men with bowler hats and black beards looked down on the others. Women with handkerchiefs around their heads and woven baskets in their arms hurried to places unknown to me. Signs, repainted over the weeks, announced how many rooms were available to let.

My job was to sweep horse manure out of the way for the respectables. Every day I would leave the crammed confines of Papa's Orchard Street shop, and walk to Ridley's Department Store on Grand. There, near the five-story building, I would take my post as Crossing Sweeper—waiting for a carriage to arrive carrying New Yorkers with money. Watching as people tumbled out of the trolley cars, and headed to the department store with purses on their wrists.

By winter, I learned there was no such thing as white snow. It was always brown from manure, mud and garbage. People living in the tenements still hung their laundry out of windows and fire escapes above me, the icy water dripping onto my hat as I walked. My job was much more difficult in the winter months, but my family needed the money all the more.

Still, I made big plans for Yacob. Once he had his bar mitzvah and was a man, I would have papa's trust. Perhaps I could man the pushcart. Or set up the outdoor table to peddle our wares. Or even get a job at Ridley's.

It took me some time to realize the Zeyer's knew I was not Yacob. At first, I was angry at them for not telling me. But it was better this way. They wanted their son back, and I yearned to belong to a family. They were kind to me. We had a pleasant life together. After a few years, I did not miss being a lonely spinster woman anymore.

On Yacob's eighteenth birthday, I was told the family secret…They were a family of prophets. Zeyer, literally translated, is "Seers." They had believed me to be one of them through the past eight years leading to my birthday, but I was not.

My gift from Elisheva and Aharon was the truth: to see what you have to see, look past yourself. They allowed me to overturn a beautiful, grand mirror in order to return home. I had always wondered why the mirror hung backwards in Papa's store. He had said it was due to the cracking, that he planned to have it fixed. But that day, I wondered if it had always been backwards to keep me from returning.

Though the Zeyers felt sure I must have seen what I needed to see, I had not realized it. A seer must both witness the scene or information as well as comprehend its importance before a mirror will send you back. So when I overturned this seer's mirror of time, I stared at Yacob's reflection, but I did not leave.

As I stood staring at the overturned mirror, Mama noticed something. A corner piece was missing from the mirror. She and Papa whipped themselves up into a fury with accusations and theories, but our family had always been one of strict secrecy so few, if any, knew of its powers.

They settled themselves by believing the mirror's piece had been missing since the day it had first cracked and broken, while being unloaded from their docked ship as they immigrated to America. They hoped and prayed the missing piece of the mirror had fallen into the bay among the other shattered shards.

We began to do research to help me learn how to go back. I started gathering stories of seers who transported before me. The family recounted amazing tales. They only knew of seers who had gone before our current year of 1889. Papa told me the first story he heard was about Sir Francis Beaufort creating modern weather forecasting in the 1840s after seeing processes by the Babylonians! It made me happy my fate was not found in ancient times.

Being from the future, two stories stood out to me.

First, was Louis Pasteur, the man who discovered germs. He changed our lives—especially mine, since I dealt with the unseen dangers of working with feces each day. But before he started his experiments on germs and diseases, he was in a coma. Once he woke, he wrote of seeing life in the 1660s. Of living it as a young boy. He told others it was a gifted dream that inspired him, but the Zeyers thought otherwise. Papa visited Pasteur when he spoke at a congress in New York. Intrigued or intimidated, I do not know, but Papa got him to talk. Pasteur told Papa his dream was real. And in this dream, he lived next to a man with three jars in the window. After passing the jars each day on his way to school, he knocked on the door to ask the neighbor what was in them. The man who opened the door was named Francesco. And he showed Pasteur his jars containing egg and meat. One jar was open, one was covered with gauze, the last was sealed. Pasteur recounted his curiosity at the maggots on the gauze and in the open jar. He said Francesco was interested in things that they could not see with the naked eye. Seeing this experiment of his next door neighbor was what Pasteur was supposed to see. He recounted it galvanized new ideas into his mind. In particular, regarding the process he eventually named after himself: pasteurization. He told Papa the discovery shocked him awake. He suffered a brain stroke and became paralyzed, but that didn't stop him. He went on to advance human society. And Papa went on to learn this neighbor was a famous Italian physician named Dr. Francesco Redi.

Second, one of the famous Wright Brothers. Long before their first flight in 1903, Wilbur was preparing to attend college at Yale when he was struck in the head during a hockey game. He fell into a coma and when he awoke, he had a story to tell. The doctors passed it off as an elaborate dream or a near death experience, but the story made its way into the papers. Wilbur Wright dreamt of being in Spain in 1709 where he befriended an elderly man named Bartolomeu. Papa was always curious how Wilbur and Bartolomeu came to meet, since a seer is never directly related to what the mirror shows. But the paper did not go into details. It simply stated this man was writing a paper that, when translated from Portuguese, was entitled: *Short Manifesto for Those who are Unaware it is Possible to Sail Through the Element Air.* And when Wilbur awoke, he had newfound ideas that led him to change the world as well.

These stories forever changed me. Changed my thinking. When I would hear about people coming up with new evidence for a long-cold murder, or ranting about a conspiracy theory, I would take pause. I searched the eyes in the black and white newspaper photograph. Were they a seer? Did they see proof in real life by going back in time?

The stories also sent my mind in a new direction. What did it mean to look past yourself? I believe it means the answer cannot truly involve you. Has nothing to do with your actions or words. For Pasteur and Wright, they witnessed information. A neighbor's activities. An acquaintance whose meeting seemed like pure chance.

What had I seen that could change the direction of the world? Mama and Papa couldn't guess what it could be, but they had never heard of someone living in the mirror as long as I had. So I tried to learn more about the mirror itself. It belonged to the Zeyer family and had always been in their possession, although the family believed it should be used by anyone who was able to see past themselves. And then, like a hit to the head, it was obvious. It *was* the mirror.

When I had first fallen into Yacob's body, I tried to tell the Zeyers about the locket from Zizi. But they had not known of any such locket or of anyone by the name Zizi who would have their most cherished family heirloom. And on the wall in Papa's shop it had hung. I had passed it every day. Any one of those days, I could have asked about it. Looked at it. But I hadn't.

Though I suspected I had the answer, I tried not to think it. And I never, ever dared to look into a mirror. Not even a reflective window.

I made it to that job at Ridley's and out of the streets. I watched my older brother, Abram, shame the family by marrying outside the Jewish faith. Watched my parents struggle as he left home and started his new life elsewhere. I watched Shoshanah grow into a beautiful young lady, marry and bless my parents with four grandchildren—the only girl acting as her namesake. I watched Mama and Papa pass into the beyond.

And on Yacob's fortieth birthday, I decided it was time to leave.

For me, I needed to see the piece missing from the seer mirror. To realize someone had taken it for their own. And placed it into a locket that was far more inconspicuous and transportable than the grand wall mirror. That there were now two ways to transport through time—from the Zeyer's mirror in New York, and through the locket, that was, through some great mystery, sitting in my pocket in Minnesota.

And with Shoshanah's husband manning Papa's shop and only she and him with me, we plan to overturn the cracked mirror a second time. I'm placing this diary in the vent now. No one knows of it but me.

If this is the last page of the diary, it worked. I will become Valentina once more.

CHAPTER 10

THREE MEN AND A BABY

"ELAINE!" I CRIED, bolting off the chaise. If her grandmother was named Shoshanah...

My feet began walking to keep up with my racing thoughts. I could *feel* the pieces coming together.

If a man had followed her from New York from the shop Valentina spoke of, that meant he was related to Elaine! That meant he and Elaine were members of the Zeyer family! That would also explain why this book was so important to him.

I looked at the leather diary. I suddenly didn't feel afraid. I *wanted* him to read Valentina's diary. Wanted him to know more. He deserved it, somehow.

Pacing and spinning for nearly twenty excruciating minutes, at last I heard approaching footsteps and the tinkling of keys. I tucked the book and the translation into megapurse. "Doc?" I called through the glass, too impatient for his fat old hands to wrangle the lock.

"Yes," he huffed, struggling to open the door.

Irritated, I yanked the door open the moment it was unlocked. "I really need to go!"

"Just a minute there," he said, grabbing my wrist. "I was serious about that talk." His furry, gray eyebrow arched at me.

"I already told you, it's just a story." I looked down. His hand was still clamped around my skin and bones.

With the release of my wrist, he pointed to the chaise. "So you read it. And now you're acting even stranger. I have a theory, you know."

I stopped trying to leave and looked at him. He was settling into the chair beside the chaise lounge, looking smug and sure I would listen to him. Obey his suggestion to sit beside him. It made defiance creep and tingle up my insides and turn my face red.

"My experience and scientific background," he started, "is pointing to signs that this has something to do with the unconscious mind."

I felt my head nod in agreement, annoyed I was intrigued. I didn't want him to be right. But I wanted answers.

"Sit," he invited with actual words.

I did as he said. I don't know why, considering the temper tantrum taking place within me.

He smiled. "You used to enjoy visiting me. Used to hang around all the time. My little pet."

Barf. I was tired of hearing about Barbara's daddy issues in this unprofessional doctor-patient relationship. "I'm here. I'm sitting. Explain this theory about being unconscious."

He leaned back. It reminded me of Gramps just before he launched into a ten-minute oral presentation on the cosmos. "Let's just say, for the sake of conversation, that this little story of yours is real. Partially, anyway. Let's say these people did in fact believe they were transporting back in time. But that's not taking in account a more obvious and simple explanation." He paused.

"Go on." I rolled my hand in impatience. "I'm obviously interested."

He chuckled. "That is just what I mean. You are not yourself, Barbara. That's how this theory came to me." He eyed the glass bottle of brown liquid on his desk. "A drink?"

"I really don't have time for this." I motioned to stand.

"All right, all right. No need to be rude, Babs."

I crossed my arms, mirroring my three-year-old daughter. Growing a touch more empathetic to her plight against my parental tyranny. Submitting to authority sucked. "I'm sorry. I do trust your credentials and opinion. I would like to hear why you think these people did not time travel." Because I think I'm living proof you're full of shit, I completed the thought to myself.

His red cheeks twitched in substitute for a chuckle. "Well, time travel is, by all accounts, completely impossible. And I'm not going to go into all the reasons it can never—will never—happen. I will only explain why it's far more likely these occurrences all take place in the unconscious."

Sitting in that chair in 1947, listening to a man who creeped me out explain how I was *not* a time traveler from 2011 was almost my limit. Was Elaine being a Zeyer what I needed to see? Had I realized it? Perhaps I could go home the second I glanced in a mirror?

Of course, there were none in Bernie's office.

"So for you to understand, let's start by pretending every human has been assigned a chest of drawers," he started, pointing over to the drawers in his wood cabinet. "Let's say this chest is always yours. It never belongs to someone else. Each *drawer* contains the sum of a person's life." He motioned to the three drawers of his file cabinet for further visual aide. "Louis Pasteur was mentioned in this *fiction* of yours. Perhaps the middle drawer is Pasteur's life. But the bottom drawer could then be the young boy from the 1660s. Why couldn't they be housed in the same file cabinet? Why couldn't they be the same unconscious?"

I furrowed my brow. "Are you talking about a soul? They had the same soul?"

He tossed his head from side to side. "Sort of. You must think broader than *soul*."

Staring at the cabinet's three drawers, I wondered if I was the middle drawer and Barbara Miller was the bottom drawer.

I turned back to Doc. "Keep explaining. I'm having a hard time understanding."

"Okay, you said soul. We can use that. What if one soul is on a track. It has lived lives in the past, and it will live lives in the future. It is an energy that continues. Reincarnation, if you will. If that is true, why couldn't a state of unconsciousness send this soul down to the lower drawer, considering it lived there once before."

My hand flung to my forehead. Was Doc saying I had lived this life before? Did he know I was not Barbara? "But how could one soul be in two people—drawers—at the same time?" I asked, eager for his reply.

"Hmm." His fat fingers tapped his lips. "It seems you've exposed a hole in my theory. How, indeed." He licked his lip, eyeing up the bottle once more.

"But you might be onto something," I pushed. "What if Pasteur really had been the neighbor of the physician doing the weird meat and maggot experiment. What if the ideas it prompted resided in his soul and moved on with it? Like when the next life began, it steered his next life's passion?"

Doc nodded. "Yes, yes... Like leaving some sort of residue that would continue into the next life."

Excited, I sat up straighter. With wild hands gesticulating, I concluded, "So it's not time travel, it's revisiting past lives!" My thoughts shot to this morning as I was first waking, I felt sure I had heard my children talking. I tried so hard to tune in, wondering if I could somehow hear them around my forgotten body, but was unable to. Occurrences such as that would be completely accounted for if I was floating between two host bodies while asleep. My energy trapped between the drawers.

Doc's mouth pulled tight. "Well, I wouldn't say that."

"Why not? That's what you're saying, isn't it? All the drawers share the same cabinet? The same soul and unconscious?"

"Yes and no. The accounts in this diary, if they hold any truth, reveal the past life visitor being able to make choices and changes that can affect the future. That could not be true if one was simply visiting a past life through a state of unconsciousness and reliving a memory."

I stood to pace. "But it would be true if it were *a form* of time travel," I stated. "It must be. Then time travel *is* possible, but not in the sense we understand. Perhaps it's not through a time machine or a portal. Maybe it's through an unconscious state and on one straight, restricted path." I pointed to the file cabinet, running my pointer finger from the floor to the top drawer. "Louis Pasteur could only travel to his previous life…and maybe even to a future one. But he could never do this *as* Louis Pasteur. He could never climb into a DeLorean and visit any time he picked. It would only work as this energy you mentioned re-inhabiting a body it had lived in before. That would eliminate the mind-breaking possibility of ever being able to go back in time and meet yourself or fix a mistake you made."

Doc was nodding, in a state of deep thought. "I don't know what a DeLorean is, but that, my dear, is genius." He stood and gave in to the bottle's temptation. A smile crept over his red face. "We must drink to this! This could open so many doors! Time travel…Examples of true time travel. Why, if we could tie this to grey matter or perhaps even the thalamus directly, this could be worthy of a Nobel Prize!" He poured his drink. "Although we would need proof."

If this was just visiting a past life, I was ready for my energy to go back to its current life. My hand was on the doorknob. I was prepared to flee from the room, bursting to conclude this outrageous adventure once and for all.

"You!" he accused. "You are my proof, aren't you?"

I ran.

Full on, as fast as I could carry myself, ran. Down the hall, down the staircase, out into the street. I heard him call after me, and I just kept running. With my chest burning and feet taking a beating from the high heeled Mary Janes, I ran all the way to the bus stop, megapurse ricocheting off of my body with repeated thuds the whole way.

Out of breath, I handed over my bus pass, looking behind me as the bus driver punched it in slow motion.

Unsure if Doc would have the desire or ability to chase me, I sat right at the front of the bus, ready to hop off as soon as it neared Heritage House.

As the bus heaved forward, my breaths slowed pace. I stared down at my hand, red from grasping the purse.

My mind was reeling together a frantic movie. I had once been Barbara. I had once lived in this world, in this exact life! I had made the choice to marry Digger. To sell drugs. The memories Doc had knocked loose were real. And they were mine. My unconscious was holding memories from Liza Anderson and from Barbara Miller. Oh, and maybe others!

My fingers surged with nervous energy, wiggling and tapping. I glanced around the bus. No one seemed to notice me or care that I was there. I was just an anonymous time traveler.

So the mirror must be a way to, what, knock people unconscious? Throw them into a different drawer? And what about Valentina saying only certain people could look past themselves. I was somehow different?

I shook my head.

So I really *was* special.

I had given up on the unfounded feeling I was somehow special long ago. In fact, I could recall the exact instant I forced the idea out of my mind forever. I was standing on a gravel driveway, attempting to say goodbye to a boy. United by our young age of seventeen and our keychains proclaiming, "Not all who wander are lost," it was one of those dreamy situations straight out of an episode of Dawson's Creek. The bright September moon overhead, surrounded by chirping crickets and fields of corn, standing close enough to touch, but not. And while I was intently watching the moonlight bounce off of his sad lips (emo before his time), he uttered the words, "I've just always felt like I was different. Meant for more than this. Special or something." And just like a slap to the face, I was startled out of my enchanted moment by one loud thought, "But that's how I feel!" I was smart enough to know two kids from a small Midwestern town could not *both* be so unique and special.

Yet now I was living proof that my feeling had been correct. It was not just some millennial, entitled way of thinking. It was true. Because I sure as hell couldn't name many people who were able to transport back in time via their unconscious.

Though once I got back, I might need to start some sort of catalogue of those who could. Maybe an online directory. Or a support group...

"Sunset and Vine," the bus driver stated, snapping me out of my thoughts.

When I hopped up to exit the bus, I caught my reflection in the driver's rearview mirror. I yelped! Hurrying to look away from its reflection, the bus driver glared at my outburst.

"Sorry," I mumbled, climbing down the steps to the sidewalk, wondering why I was still Barbara.

Why hadn't I gone back? Hadn't I seen what I needed to see? Doc and I had pieced together a theory that could change the world forever. Learned secrets that could change the course of lives. Maybe it just took longer than a quick glance?

Pushing past my disappointment at not transporting back to my awaiting babies, I became overzealous to find out about the day's visitors at Heritage House.

"Henry!" I called, trotting to stand next to him on the side-walk. "Have you seen Elaine Glass come back from her shift to-day?"

"Funny, Sis asked me that earlier," he answered, standing straighter. "What's going on?"

"So she hasn't?"

"No and I haven't seen Sis since she left either."

"She left?" I stared down the street. "How long ago?"

"Maybe half an hour?"

"Where did she go?"

I saw his face turn to concern. "Now just what are you ladies up to? I'm going to get Mrs. Mahoney out here. She needs to be informed if you ladies are in trouble."

"Henry, please tell me!" I grabbed his uniformed forearm. "Do you know where Sis went? At least which way?"

He sighed. "I saw her walk across to the bus stop, but she didn't get on a bus. She got into a black Packard."

My eyes opened so wide I felt as though they'd fall out of my head. "That bench way up there?" I pointed up the hill. "Who was driving it? Was it a man in a gray suit?" I was frantic, searching the scene near the paper stand. Not being able to see it well, I looked back to Henry.

"I didn't see." Henry turned toward the entrance. "I'm going in to report this to Mrs. Mahoney right now. I don't know what you girls are mixed up in, but it seems serious."

I didn't respond. I couldn't. My hand was on my head, my body was on tippy toes—craning to see, grasping at theories of my own.

Had she been picked up by New Yorker? The man in the gray suit? Had Digger already found out his money was missing?

As I stood frozen in place in a form of shock, ready to barf at the thought of something terrible happening to Sis because of stupid old me, Henry disappeared.

"Babs," Marjorie called, pushing through the glass door, "what the hell is going on around here?"

"Do you know where Sis went?" I yelled in her face.

"No, but she told me to sit here at the door and wait for Elaine to get back."

"Arg!" My hands flew into the air. "I asked her to stay here. I didn't ask her to go find Elaine."

"Well, it seems no one can find Elaine."

"What do you mean?" I asked.

Marjorie lit the end of her cigarette before answering. "Sonny from HBC was here earlier asking for her. He was being vague with Henry, but once I popped out to chat, he told me to tell Elaine all HBC transfers were put on hold. Ain't that a bite?

Lainey actually gets the big break to move to New York, and now it's on hold because of the commies. Sonny said it might take months for this to blow over." She took a drag. "And get a load of this, he's engaged!"

"Miss Miller!" Londa shouted from behind us.

"Uh oh. That's my cue to duck and cover," Marjorie mumbled, dabbing out the end of her cigarette on the side of the building. "I'll keep an eye out for Elaine and Sis."

With Marjorie gone, I came face-to-face with Londa's agitation. "Londa, I have your money. I have all of it." I rummaged through megapurse as I continued speaking, "Please, please tell me you know where Sis went?" I reached out, grabbed three tens and slapped them into her hand. "Here's what I owe you—seventeen for back rent, twelve for October, a dollar extra for the trouble I caused. Take it. And please help me."

Londa's expression reminded me of a cocker spaniel who couldn't understand which command you'd just given her. She stared at the money in her hand. "Thank you for paying your debt. Though I'm curious how you've suddenly come into money, I fear I don't want to know."

My nervous eyes continued to scan the sidewalk, scan the road for black cars, scan the bus stop for men wearing gray suits. What the hell was a Packard and what did it look like?

Londa put the money in a pocket of her cardigan. "And while I do take an interest in what you girls are up to, I am not privy to the details of your private lives."

"So you don't know? Then I have to go." I staggered forward.

"Babs, you should know I asked Henry to turn a gentleman out today."

I stopped short. "What did he look like?"

"Heavy accent, dark hair," she described. "He said he had an appointment with one of the ladies of the house but couldn't tell us her name. So we asked him to leave."

"He was an ornery bloke," Henry interjected. "Gave me the impression he'd be back, though I haven't seen him since."

"That was for me. He was here for me. And now I'm worried he may have taken Elaine. Or Sis. Or both of them!"

Londa was wringing her hands. "I'm going to call the police."

"And tell them what?" I retorted, tossing my hands into the warm California sky, wishing it *was* possible to time travel back to fix mistakes. "I don't know his name or where he's from or anything about him!"

"But then why was he meeting you here? I don't like any of this, not any of this."

Henry lunged toward me. "I think I know where he is. I don't like playing sleuth, but when I asked who he was here to visit, he pulled a few things out of his coat pocket before telling me he couldn't remember. One of the things in his hand was a motel key. I'd know that gold keyring anywhere. It's from the Starfire just up the road. Used to work there before Mrs. Mahoney hired me here."

"Up the road? On Sunset Boulevard?"

"Right next to the Brown Derby." Henry pointed.

Overwhelmed, I hugged him. Squeezed him so tight I made both him and Londa uncomfortable. "I have to go."

"Oh, no you don't," Londa ordered. She grabbed my upper arm. "I'm not having another one of my girls wander off into the night with no explanation!"

"Londa, this is so important. You have to let me go. You said yourself you weren't our keeper."

"Well, I am to some degree," she argued. "I'm responsible. And I'm still calling the police!" She jerked me toward the entrance, and Henry acted as bouncer to be sure I went in. Marjorie was seated near the door, watching everything with a mouth full of chewing gum. Chawing away like this life or death situation was the best form of entertainment she'd ever witnessed.

"Now, are you going to tell me what's going on, Miss Miller? Or will you be speaking with an officer of the law?"

Never had I been forced against my will to stay somewhere. Lucky, I suppose. But my mother had never been strict about curfews or sleepovers. Never demanded I stay home.

I turned away from her face without answering, and marched toward the staircase, damning the Mary Janes still digging into my feet.

Instead of heading to my own room, I went straight to Sis's. Maybe there was a clue. Something she had left out or written down.

I stumbled through the dark room and clicked on the lamp. I searched, but everything was neat and clean.

I needed to get over to the motel. Maybe New Yorker had Elaine and Sis with him.

How I longed to see the look on New Yorker's face when I told him he was a Zeyer and so was Elaine.

And how overjoyed Elaine would be to hear about the delay in her transfer. She would be able to have the baby just as she planned.

Oh, but if I completed my mission and headed home, I wouldn't be here to provide her with my advice. To prepare her for a home birth.

My brow furrowed.

I was a bad person.

Another thought hit me. Had my messing up Elaine's birth been the subconscious residue that pushed me into becoming a birthing assistant in the first place?

Shaking my head, I powered myself by summoning the mantra of Dorothy: *There's no place like home. There's no place like home.*

Looking at Sis's empty, perfectly made bed, I turned to leave.

"You really need to tell me what's going on," Marjorie said, leaning in the doorway to Sis's room. "You girls have been a *traaain* of mystery tonight," she sang, thrusting her hand toward me like a train through a tunnel. "First Elaine missing, then Sis dashing out with only a cryptic message. And now you, throwing an absolute fit because you can't go chasing into the night. Seriously. What is going on?"

I sighed and dropped to sit on the end of Sis's bed. "Elaine is probably with a man from New York who is expecting me to bring him something tonight. That's why I'm so upset I can't leave. He may be keeping her against her will until I can deliver it."

"Mm-hmm, so that's your fault." She smacked her gum. "And Sis?"

I dragged my hand down my face. "Sis was seen getting into a black Packard, and I don't know–"

"Your beau drives a black Packard," Marjorie interjected, jolting up from her relaxed position. A frightened look came over her face. "What have you done, Babs?"

My head was shaking. I stood. "You're sure that's what Digger drives?"

"Yeah, I'm sure. The last time you snuck out to meet him, we were all in the middle of game night. We called out the window to you as you drove away with him, remember?" She stepped into the room, anger replacing the fear on her face. "That was the night we were all playing *Who Here Is* and everyone picked Sis, remember?" She crossed her arms.

I grabbed my purse and clicked the light off. "I don't remember that game. And it doesn't matter right now. I need to get out of here. Sis is in trouble."

"And that's your fault, too." Marjorie stood blocking the doorway so I couldn't leave. "The question was, 'Who Here Is the best friend?' We all chose Sis. All twenty of us girls wrote the same person in secret, and when we flipped our papers, it revealed the largest consensus we'd ever had. And what had our dear Sissy Rose written?" She stepped toward me like she might shove me. "You. You, Babs. For whatever reason, she picked you as the best friend in the room. And look where that's gotten her!"

It was me who shoved first. I nudged her out of my way, and headed into the hall with hot tears stinging my eyes.

"You better make this right, Babs!" Marjorie yelled after me.

Rushing through the hall and around the corner, I froze on the mezzanine. Below, Henry and Londa were interrogating a woman I didn't know.

"Who told you to come here tonight?" Londa asked in her Mother Superior tone.

"I already told you. Elaine asked me to come here tonight. I spoke with her earlier today at work."

I skittered down the grand staircase as fast as my aching feet would take me. "Judy?" I asked once I'd gotten close enough to speak.

The woman turned. "Yes?"

"*You* know her. Why am I not surprised?" Londa grumbled.

"Judy, when did Elaine talk with you last?"

"That's just what they were asking me. Had I known it would be this difficult to visit, I would have just invited Elaine to meet at my place."

"Was it recently?"

She shook her head. "No, it was while we were at work. I work at the station with her."

"I work at the station, too," I muttered.

"Oh, and you are?" she asked with formal sweetness.

Londa shoved in. "This is Barbara Miller. You don't know her?"

"Oh, well that's just who Elaine said we would be meeting up with tonight! Surely, you can clear up this misunderstanding then, Barbara?"

Londa was shaking her head in disappointment. "Who haven't you gotten messed up in your personal affairs?" Like the mama bear we Millennial Moms bragged about being, Londa became a real one. She expanded her chest, lifted her head and raised her arm to point. "I will not tolerate this nonsense at

Heritage House. Rent payment or no, I want you out of here, Barbara Miller. Out of here, tonight!"

Judy's mouth was agape, and Henry wouldn't make eye contact with any of us. Everyone was uncomfortable watching Londa's thick bosom rise and fall with deep, angry breaths.

"But I–" I tried to argue.

"Right now!" Londa shouted. "Consider yourself evicted due to poor behavior—behavior that is anything but what we expect from our girls. Your sneaking out, your late rent payments, your seedy friends, and your secretive demeanor... And don't think I didn't know you fainted in the hallway because of..." Her face dove in so close to mine I felt her hot breath. "... *drugs*."

"What about the police officer?" Henry dared to mutter. "He said not to let anyone leave until they arrived."

"Then she will have time to pack her things!" Londa fumed. She glared at megapurse. "She already has her luggage out. Now she can fill it!"

Judy looked terrified. She turned to tiptoe out and away from this scene, but I wasn't going to let her. I turned to Londa. "Give me five minutes to speak with Judy outside."

Judy gasped, making it clear how little she wanted to be alone with me.

Londa's scowl deepened. "The nerve..."

"Five minutes seems fair to allow me." In my mind, I was screaming blackmail, trusting she was catching my drift. Hoping she would acquiesce so I didn't have to use her sexual orientation against her.

She threw her hands into the air. "It's as if the monkeys have taken over the zoo!" She stomped toward her precious bay window solarium, signaling her surrender to my request.

I grabbed Judy's arm and glared a warning look to Henry not to follow us out. He didn't even move.

"Please tell me what's going on? Where is Elaine?" poor Judy protested all the way out into the early night's darkness. Made me drag her by the arm all the way around the building to my smoking alley. "Please!"

I let go. "Judy, I *know*. And I know *you* know. So let's just talk openly. Do you think there's a possibility Elaine is hiding out somewhere, having a premature baby right now?"

I saw Judy take a gulp even through the shadows. "Gee, I sure hope not."

"Do you know what her actual plan is now? She said she wasn't going to go to the maternity home anymore."

Judy shook her head. "No, I know. I told her how terrible it is. How terrible it was!"

"So did she have a new plan?"

Judy's expression made her look so young. Like an innocent child being scolded. It saddened me to know she had already grown a baby in her womb, and then given it away. I shook the thought out of my head.

"We were going to talk things over tonight," Judy explained. "I was going to try to convince her to tell the father. He's established. Has money. Might do the right thing."

"So you know who the father is?" My shock was apparent.

"Yes," Judy replied slowly. "But he doesn't know about any of this. Elaine hasn't told him a thing. You and I are the only people on God's green earth who know about Elaine's baby."

"Oh, I hope she's okay," I muttered, staggering back toward the sidewalk. Feeling unsure if it was worse to imagine her having a premature baby alone, or being trapped with a very persistent, pissed off New Yorker. "I'm guessing she's barely in her third trimester. If she really is holed up somewhere having a baby..." I trailed off.

Judy shook her head. "How do you know about this stuff? I don't know what that word means."

"Premature?" I asked.

"No, you said she's in her third of something. What does that mean?"

My eyes widened. "Trimester? Counting the weeks of pregnancy?"

Judy was still staring at me, waiting for a connection with my words.

"Well, I just mean she is close to the end, but the baby is not ready yet. It would be very worrisome if she was born today."

Judy looked to the ground. "I'm frightened to think what might happen. I do know Elaine was adamant about giving the baby away. She wants it to live."

"The baby could be okay," I reassured myself more than Judy. "Let's just hope she's with the guy I think she's with, so we know just where she is." Though that could mean she was in danger.

"Sonny Greensburg?" Judy asked.

A physical startle shot through my body. "What? What did you just say?"

"Is the guy you think she's with Sonny Greensburg from the station?"

"No..." I was tipping back, feeling faint. Overwhelmed with information. "It just couldn't be," I stammered to myself.

"Oh, no. He wasn't your beau, too, was he? I know the girls at HBC call him a wolf and all, but he just got engaged. I tried to tell Elaine, but she's insistent on putting his name on the birth certificate anyway. I just think that's..."

Judy was still talking, but I was no longer listening.

Was Sonny Greensburg actually Joseph Greensburg? Was the wolf at the station Gramps?

Wait, if Elaine was a Zeyer and Gramps was the father of her baby...

My head was swimming. Taunting me.

And I was too lost in thought to see the police motorcycle pull up.

"MA'AM, I'M GOING to ask you once again to calm down," the officer ordered from behind me, precious hours after my conversation with Judy had concluded.

"Just please tell me how much longer you will keep me here?" I begged, scanning the lobby.

"We have your official statement, and are taking this threat seriously, Mrs. Digrokowski," another officer said, walking back to the table where I was seated.

I dropped my head. In a desperate attempt to leave Heritage House, I had told the officers about Sis being in danger. Who knew saying the word "murder" to two cops riding a motorcycle would land you in house arrest. Seriously, though. Two male cops per one motorcycle. I was tiring of the bizarreries of 1947.

Sitting on the wooden chair in Londa's solarium was the most painful waiting game I had ever played. Thankfully, the police arriving had stalled Londa's immediate eviction notice. She had even taken megapurse up to my room for me—probably just as an excuse to leave the tense situation unfolding as they interrogated me in her precious sun room. But I was more comfortable with the stolen money and secret translation out of the room.

Officer Wright of the L.A.P.D. paced, causing his shiny handcuffs to dangle and clink. Thanks to the echo in the lobby, I could hear his conversation with the other cop.

"The marriage certificate was just confirmed," the short cop said to Officer Wright, walking in from outside.

Londa shot me a look. Huh. Barbara hadn't told anyone about her holy matrimony.

"And her story checks out with the death at the Palindrome. That's the Vincent Venticini case," he explained. "Still could have been anti-communist like we figured. Got a name to check up on now."

They walked back to the front of the expansive lobby, leaving me alone with my guilt-ridden thoughts. The short one went back outside, while Officer Wright spoke with Londa.

A while ago, the officers sent backup to Digger's address to look for Sis. Oh, and to arrest my husband for murder.

Knowing the officers would get Sis out of Digger's apartment brought sweet relief. And knowing there were no mirrors in the lobby also brought a sense of relief. I felt sure if I glanced in a mirror now, I would go back. But how could I do that knowing Sis was in trouble, Elaine was still missing and New Yorker was searching for me and the translation?

During my time seated at the table, I had done the math. My mother was sixty-four-years-old in 2011. Backing that up to 1947, this *was* the year she was born. But Elaine was not the name of Gramps' wife. Though I had never met her, I knew her name was Loretta. I had never heard a peep about anyone named Elaine Glass before arriving in 1947. My mother was born in December, so it was possible Elaine was carrying my own mother...

Judy claimed Sonny knew nothing of this baby. Assuming Sonny was indeed Gramps, I had to wonder if he had *another* woman named Loretta pregnant with my mother right now? Was that why everyone kept calling him a wolf? Because getting two women pregnant at the same time was not only wolfy, it was downright douchey.

"Just got a call in from the radio," the outside officer announced, entering the building with Henry. "No one was found at the apartment."

Both men turned to me. "Do you have any other ideas where the perpetrator may have taken this alleged hostage?"

My head was shaking. "I don't. I mean, Sis works at the Palindrome, and Digger hangs out there. Someone could check there?"

The officers exchanged a look. Then Officer Wright nodded. "Considering the circumstances, we are going to call off the search for Miss Rose at this time."

"But she's with a murderer!"

"Allegedly, Mrs. Digrokowski. We will continue our search for *Mr. Digrokowski* in connection with murder." Officer Wright's face said it all. He couldn't fathom a wife turning in her husband.

"Once we locate him, we will bring him in for questioning. And as for you, I expect to see you at the station tomorrow morning at nine. I'm not sure how your statement was missed during our earlier questioning, but since you were present at the Palindrome the night of the murder, we will need it on file." He tipped his hat at me.

I stood. "Am I free to go?"

He sent me a disapproving look. "Ma'am, it's the middle of the night. I suggest you get some sleep."

"Of course," I said, running my eyes over Londa's sagging, sleepy face.

"And I've sent in the call for a patrol car to monitor all guests coming in and out," he added. "Security detail for the evening."

Once he was out of earshot, Londa looked back to me. "I've taken the liberty of packing your things. I will allow you to sleep here tonight, but after that, consider yourself evicted." She grabbed my limp hand and slapped a ten-dollar bill in it. "I've turned down your bed." She crossed her arms, making it more than clear I was to go to my room.

I wanted to argue. I wondered where Sis was sleeping. Where Elaine was sleeping. If they were in places they would be allowed to sleep! Feeling like the world's worst person, I dragged myself to the staircase.

If I snuck out, the patrol car would likely follow me. What would happen if the police interrogated the New Yorker and myself about the translated documents I was carrying? At the very least, Doc had been right about the diary containing Russian and making me look like a communist. And at the worst, I could be detained or arrested. Kept against my will. Unable to go back. Unable to see my babies.

Before opening the door to my bedroom, I made a promise to myself.

I would not look in a mirror until I knew Elaine and Sis were safe.

CHAPTER 11

TICK-TOCK, CHOP-CHOP

THE SHARP KNOCKING on my door startled me awake. In my half-asleep state, I almost glanced in the mirror. It was becoming more apparent why the Zeyers kept their mirrors flipped over.

Hopping out of bed, I saw it was eight in the morning. I opened the door, shocked to see Ruth, the rude buxom beauty I'd had words with in the powder room on my first day.

"He said you have two hours," she said with a tremble.

"What? Who?" I peeked out the doorway to look down the hall. It was empty. Just a mile of oriental carpeting, like always.

"He said you would know what that meant. You have two hours to get the money," she whimpered.

I grabbed her shoulders. "Where did he talk to you? When?"

"Just now. I took my rubbish out to the tins in the alley, and he grabbed me!"

"Is that where I should meet him in two hours? The alley?"

"I don't know, and I hope I never see him, or you, again!" Off she ran, down the hallway, leaving me to drown in fear and guilt.

Rushing back into the room, I dressed as quickly as I could, buttoning up the over-the-belly-button slacks, and forcing the shirt over my head. Sis was already the voice in my head. I heard her scolding me for wearing slacks two days in a row and leaving my hair so wild.

Next, I went to the bedside table. Yanking open the drawer, I retrieved the stack of notes, photos, postcards and ads I had collected throughout my twenty-two days in 1947. I shuffled through my theories and thoughts, my handwritten math figuring out 2011 was sixty-four years in the future. A whole page of my real name and Barbara's, rearranged a hundred ways to search for a clue or hidden anagram, *Da Vinci Code* style. None of them hinted at Gramps being Sonny. Scribbles about reincarnation, a soul residing on earth around seventy years, twin souls, being trapped between drawers...but none about my grandfather. None about the possibility my grandmother wasn't actually Loretta.

Though my notes had done nothing but appease my daily desire to return home by making me feel productive, I didn't want to leave them. I wished there was a way I could take them with me.

With a sigh, I began ripping up the incriminating evidence of my out-of-body experience, and scattering the scraps into the woven waste basket.

Me and this basket—we'd come full circle.

Giving a quick glance around the room at the packed megapurse and bags, I took in a deep breath. This would be the last time I ever looked at any of this. I didn't need to take the bags with me. Once I returned through the mirror, Barbara would drop dead.

Would Londa let the girls keep any of Barbara's things? Would she sell them?

Reminding myself to hurry, I stuffed the diary, the translated papers and what was left of Digger's stolen money into a white handbag. Careful to avoid checking my reflection, I popped open my brown bottle and took three pep pills. Fuck it. This was it.

Gulping the little white pills down with two-day-old water from the bedside table, I grabbed the half-empty pack of Pall

Malls, and left the pale green wallpaper of my room at Heritage House forever.

Woman on a mission.

Feeling akin to a superhero, I propelled myself through the hallway, around the corner and down the grand staircase. Noting it was all for the very last time.

In the lobby, I bypassed Old Jackie Kennedy at the front desk, ignoring her queries about where my things were, or if I had informed Mrs. Mahoney about my departure.

Shoving the doors open and stepping out into the sunlight, I stopped at Henry's side. "Goodbye, Henry. Thank you for telling me about the Starfire Motel. Take care of the girls."

He opened his mouth to reply, but I spotted the patrol car, and kept moving.

Marching across the street, I walked right up to the parked police car with the bubble bumper. The officer on duty rolled down his window, sensing I was coming straight for him.

"The suspect wanted for murder will be right there in that alley in less than two hours. Call for backup. He has a hostage."

"Wait, Miss," he ordered when I turned to leave.

"I am on my way to the police station right now," I shouted. "Call Officer Wright. He can confirm I'm due there."

He held up a finger and radioed in. I tried to slow my breathing. Forced myself to avoid looking into his driver side window and just ending it all.

"Officer Wright is expecting you," he confirmed, looking up at me. "As for your tip, are you sure he will be there? I've been here all night and—other than the doorman—haven't seen a single male approach."

I bent down and pointed. "You can't see the alley from here. He must be coming up from the back of the building. He was here this morning, and told a girl he'd be back in two hours."

"Why?" the officer asked, his voice full of skepticism.

"Because he wants his money back."

The officer's eyes widened at my admission.

I pulled the corner of a twenty out of my little white handbag. "I'm turning it in to Officer Wright."

The officer moved to open his door.

"No, please stay here. Call for backup. Please, you have to catch him!"

He glared. "I can't just trust you will turn the money in."

"Fine! Take it, then." I thrust the money through the open window. Wondering if anyone, besides Digger, would know I'd spent nearly half of it already.

He took the money from me. Reluctant and disbelieving, he nodded.

The streetcar rolled down the center of the street, blowing my hair over my face. It was still odd to see blonde hair streak past my eyes. "I have to catch that streetcar, or I will miss my appointment with Officer Wright."

I thought I was home-free, but then he grabbed my wrist. "That streetcar doesn't go to the station."

Shit.

Think.

"Ah, but that bus does!" I exclaimed, pointing down the road.

He released my bony wrist. "Fine. But I will be watching you board that bus."

"Two hours!" I called back, racing to get on a bus I didn't need.

True to his word, the officer stepped out of his car, door ajar in the midst of morning traffic, and watched me climb the damn stairs of the bus.

"Final destination?" I asked the driver.

He rattled off several locations, one near HBC.

Determined to get to the Starfire, I sat. Moments later, I watched as the bus drove right past the one-story motel, wondering if I was being too careful. Would the officer have seen the bus make a forced stop this far away? Perhaps I should have chanced it.

As the bus rambled its way through Hollywood, I stared down at a discarded, crumpled paper map. It confirmed I was nowhere near the ocean.

No matter. Perhaps when I was back to real life, I could return. Even come back with the kids! Oh, how it would be remarkable to see old Hollywood again. See how it changed…or stayed the same. Being so unfamiliar with the area, I wasn't sure if major buildings would still be standing in 2011. But bringing the kids here to show them the sights meant I would tell them about this. Would I? Being children, they would have no trouble believing it. But should I put this burden on them?

Oh! Since they were my children, would they too be able to look past themselves? Hugging the purse to me, I sent out a prayer that someone removed the locket from my possession before one of the kids looked into it.

As the bus neared HBC, the other passengers started muttering to one another, and craning to see out the windows.

I tugged on the bus pull cord to signal my stop, and everyone turned to look at me.

"Are you one of them?" an elderly man asked me.

"One of what?" I looked out the window. There were a dozen or so people in front of HBC, picketing.

I darted down the bus's steps. From my vantage point on the street across from the station, I read some of the picketers' signs. *Stop Violating My Civil Rights. First Amendment Rights = Political Rights. Hollywood Won't Oppress Me.*

Since a quick scan of the crowd didn't reveal Gramps, Elaine or Sis as one of the political activists, I ran back the way the bus had come. Wearing the lowest heeled shoes Barbara owned on my tiny feet, the clicking against the pavement kept time with the racing clock in my mind. I rushed back toward the pink motel.

Out of breath, I entered the Starfire's parking lot. Walking along the iron fence surrounding an inground pool, I looked up at the browning leaves of an aging, unkempt palm tree. Once at the painted stucco building, I entered the door marked OFFICE. The place gave me the heebie-jeebies. Minus the pink exterior, the motel was straight out of *Psycho*. And if the office manager looked anything like Norman Bates, I wasn't sure I'd have the guts to continue this daring mission.

Pushing through the glass door prompted a bell to clang overhead. I stepped up to the front desk, trying not to pant, and trying not to think about what could be lurking behind the motel door once I got there.

"May I help you?" a handsome man in a bowling shirt asked.

"Yes, a friend of mine asked me to meet her here. Mrs. Zeyer? Silly thing didn't tell me which room," I said, based on the hunch New Yorker's last name was Zeyer.

He checked his handwritten log of guests. "I got a Jonathan by that name."

"Yes! That's her husband," I lied. "That must be the right room." I tried not to climb over the desk and take a copy of every key behind him.

"Room nine," he said.

"Thanks!" I barely managed to reply, pushing past the chiming bell once again.

I followed the gold-colored doors. Room one, two cars parked in front. Room two, curtains were open wide revealing nothing of note. Rooms three, four and five all appeared vacant. Door six opened as I passed, prompting me to look back at the person exiting. A middle-aged woman. Rooms seven, and eight, and...

Knock, knock, knock!

My rapping on door number nine was met with silence. A breeze blew by. It was a beautiful, sunny day outside the door.

I waited just a moment more before trying the handle.

The door opened! "Elaine?" I called, walking into the deserted room. Of all of the scenarios I had played in my mind, an empty room was not one of them. "Elaine, are you in here?" I asked again, approaching the bathroom.

The door shut behind me. The sound was soft, but it caused my back teeth to hum as if someone had scraped a blackboard.

I yelped and swung around to face the person responsible. "You!" I screamed.

The man in the gray suit ran at me and closed his hand over my mouth. I protested, fought, kicked. Wished I had taken Sis up on her offer to join Judo Gymnastics. "Please stop," the man managed to say through my wild wriggling. "Jules sent me."

I went limp. He nodded to my wide eyes and slowly uncovered my mouth. "What did you say?" My voice sounded as shaky as I felt.

"Jules sent me," he repeated, a kind look overtaking his face.

I shook my head and staggered away from him. "No, that can't be true," I snapped at him. "Jules who?"

"Jules Anderson. Your daughter. I met you here to explain." He raised his palms in surrender. "I'll explain it all, Grandma."

I could hear my heartbeat in my ears as I comprehended his words. "You're my…grandson? Jules is only three years old."

His face relaxed and he let out a breath. "She's not in 2058."

"No." I stated, my head shaking. "No, no, no, wait a minute…" I swallowed the stale taste in my mouth, and sat down on the sofa.

He sat next to me, comfortable and calm. "This is all okay, Grandma. It's all happening just like your story. That's how I knew where to find you."

"Because I told you the story of…what's happening to me right now?" My hand massaged my forehead, willing it to keep up with the words presented to me.

"Yes." He pulled at the tie around his neck. "And it's every bit as uncomfortable as you described."

I snapped my gaze to his face. "Where is Elaine?"

"Easy…"

"What is your name?" I continued. "How do I know you're really my grandson?"

A half-grin appeared on his face. "Ever the skeptic, Grams. My name is Gianluca. I was born in 2040."

My eyebrows raised. "Gianluca?"

He shook his head. "The less you know the better. But just know I've been well-versed. I know exactly what I'm here to accomplish." He smiled. "It's not like the old days."

"Ha!" I was incredulous. "This is astonishing." I stood and walked to the window, then paced back. "Okay, so what are you here to accomplish?"

"I'm here to fill in the gap," he stated with ease. "To close the hole in your story. It was your last...you always wanted to know what happened to those you cared for after you went back. There was no way for you to know. So, we devised a plan for me to meet you here, then leave you a message. Mom prepared me for this. She even made me practice using a pen."

I was nodding. "Because you're from 2058..."

"It took a long time to figure out which one was you." He looked over Barbara's body. "It wasn't until I saw you stumbling back to the house in the middle of the night I figured it out. I remembered the part about the murder night. But then I didn't know which one was you and which one was Sis."

Mouth gaping, I was too stunned to speak.

"Took quite a bit of surveillance," he continued. "You two were always together—like you said you'd be—so I had to figure out which one of you was ornerier." He chuckled.

"How long have you been here? In the past?" My fingers were glued to my lips, head stuck in a shake that wouldn't end.

He looked down and double-tapped his temple. "Oops, old habits," he mumbled. "It's been somewhere around four weeks—just before you arrived. That's as close as we could get me."

I rushed to his side and grabbed his lapels. "You've been here for a month! Jules must be so scared for you. Your body is just lying there in a coma!"

Using a light touch, he removed my hands. "Mom helped me plan all of this. It's fine, Grams. We waited until I turned eighteen and all." He looked down at his host body, which appeared to be around forty-five years old. "And I look forward to returning to being eighteen again."

The sound of footsteps caused us both to freeze and look at the door.

He stiffened and whispered, "That must be him coming back. I'm not going to talk to him. And I'm not going to interfere with you again. Don't worry about Faulty Actions of Future. I already know everything that's going to happen to you. Because you told me."

"Faulty actions?"

"Uh, yes, when your actions in the past negatively affect the future outcome?" he explained in a way that questioned if I knew what he was talking about. I didn't.

"The butterfly affect is real?" I blurted.

The footsteps continued, passing the door.

He let out a breath. "I really need to go."

I couldn't break my stare. "If you are who you say you are, I wish I could see you. The real you. Not the you in this host body."

He let out a small snicker. "It's so good to talk with you."

"Yes," I agreed, contemplative. "Tell me, do we still drive cars? Watch TV? Eat crappy, fake food?"

Smiling, he raised his hands in surrender. "I'm not telling you any of that, Grams."

"Because of this faulty actions thing?" I asked. He nodded. "Please. Just tell me one thing. Something that will have no effect on me."

He thought a moment. "Maybe...just that you shouldn't worry so much about the future."

"What?" I felt like I could listen to him talk forever. Fascinated, incredulous and stupefied, I waited for his words.

"It will take a few generations, but the things you worry about..." His fingers splayed in the space in between us. "...just slowly become nonissues."

"That's vague."

He chuckled, and tugged at the neck of his collared shirt again. "Well, I just wanted to let you know your grandkids are a very collective, inclusive group. And though the movies you guys made and watched like to paint a dark picture of the future, it's just not like that."

"I don't understand what you're trying to say. And I want to. It's not every day I talk to someone from the future."

He smiled again, causing me to wonder how I had ever feared him. "Okay. Maybe an example." After a moment, he exclaimed, "Oh! Do you still hate cats?"

I let out an exasperated grunt. "I never said I *hated* cats. I'm just not the kind of person to own animals. But, yeah, what does that have to do with anything?"

"Just that there are younger generations of us who will agree with you in the future. Not about the hating part, but it's rare for someone to keep an animal in their home."

"Are you saying it's illegal to have a pet?"

He chuckled. "No, not illegal. We just..." He spun his hands. "...collectively decided it was harming animals and the earth for humans to own other living creatures." He shrugged. "So we gradually stopped buying them, which stopped the breeding of them. A communal agreement of sorts." He looked thoughtful. "Much like you spoke about the end of cigarettes."

"Gah! Everyone smokes so much here."

"I know! Disgusting," he agreed. "But not illegal."

I was engaged in a reflective slow nod when we heard footsteps approaching again.

"This is it, Grandma." He pecked my cheek with a kiss. "I'll see you in 2040. Be brave!" Ducking out the door, I heard him greet someone along the way back toward the office.

I stood in a state of shock, listening to footsteps step closer and closer until the person making them stopped in the open doorway.

"Who are *you*?" New Yorker asked, staring at me standing in his motel room, uninvited.

I blinked, snapping back into my current matter at hand. "Where's Elaine?" I accused.

New Yorker was large, tall. Didn't strike me as scary or dangerous, though. "The girl from the train?" he asked. He stepped into the motel room, but didn't shut the door. With a warm breeze blowing his dark hair from behind, he looked over at the mirror on the wall, almost prompting me to look as well. "She has something for me."

"Yes, I know," I started, yanking out the translation from my white handbag. "I have it right here."

"You?" he yelled, grabbing the papers from my hand. He started reading the instant they were in his possession.

"It's all there," I told him. "The impossible, true story of the mirror and its abilities. It's about your family."

His eyes jumped from the papers to my face. He scowled. "Who translated this? And where is the book?" I handed him the leather diary as well. "How did you know about this? How did she know it was in our shop's basement? No one ever goes down there. That's how I knew to follow the girl. Only people familiar with the shop ever go to the basement."

"Elaine, the woman from the train, is a Zeyer. Her grandmother is Shoshanah." I pointed toward the translation in his hand.

"*My* grandmother was Shoshanah," he whispered. He looked back at the papers.

"Where is she? Do you have Elaine? I thought you took her." I lifted my head up in defiance, bracing myself for his answer.

He shook his head. "I do not know. I went to the house, but they would not let me see her."

"But what about your threat? That we had to translate the book or you would harm us. About sneaking into Elaine's sleeper car and stealing the book?"

His bushy, black eyebrows were creased together in the center of his forehead. He shook his head. "It was not a threat. It was a statement. I wanted to know what the book said, yes. So I followed her here. But I did not know this Elaine was a cousin or a Zeyer."

"She doesn't even know it herself. That's part of the reason I need to find her. But she was so frightened of you. I thought there was reason to fear you. To fear you'd do something terrible if you didn't get the translation."

He was still shaking his head. "I took the book while on the train to try and read it. But I could not read the most important part. The part that explains how seers are transporting without using our mirror. That's all I wanted to accomplish. I wished no one any harm. Wait, do you have part of our mirror?"

"The mirror in the locket?"

"In a locket? How clever!"

"I was told the locket came from a woman named Zizi."

"Zizi!" he cried. "Uncle Abram's daughter…Abram stole it? He took it on purpose?" He turned away from me, concerned and concentrating.

"If Elaine isn't here with you…" I said, backing to the door.

He was reading again. "Does it explain more about the locket in here?"

"I'm sorry, but I have to go." I walked around his tall frame, and out the open door.

"Wait!" he called. "Who are you? Are you a seer, too?"

"Read the translation," I called over my shoulder. I took a sweeping glance around the motel grounds and parking lot, looking for my grandson, the stalker from the future.

And when I didn't see him, I broke into a run, headed for the only place Sis could be.

THE DAY JAKEY was born was the scariest day of my life. Just one hour into my labor, I barely survived the car ride to the birthing center. He was so low, I physically couldn't sit. I rode kneeling on the car floor, hunched over the seat, screeching and wailing in the most immense pain of my life. I had warned everyone he would be born early. Sensed it somehow. And with Jules' birth only lasting five hours from beginning to baby, I also warned the midwives it might be fast. But no one was ready for two-hours fast.

Upon arrival at the birthing center, I had to crawl up the handicapped ramp. It was April, and in the midst of a freak Minnesota snowstorm. Doug had managed to throw a robe and slippers on me before we left the house. Drowning in back labor, I was uncontrollably screaming, and cursing myself for ever thinking I was tough enough to birth a baby with no drugs. For a second stupid time.

The midwives weren't ready for me. Two other women had come in before me. They believed the change in barometric pressure was causing women to go into labor. I didn't give a shit. That meant I didn't have a midwife to myself.

They put me in room two (there were only three birthing rooms altogether) to labor alone with Doug, while they checked on the other women.

Screaming inhuman sounds that hung in my mind for weeks afterward, I forced Doug to walk me to the toilet. Unable to fully stand, I hobbled there. Straight out of an episode of *I Didn't Know I Was Pregnant*, I fell to the floor before making it to the porcelain seat.

He was coming!

Doug raced out to get the attending midwife, a woman I would work for six months later. By the time they were back, I was on all fours on the bathroom floor. Clawing at the tiles, screaming at them to pull him out.

He was coming too fast, the midwife said. I needed to breathe, she coached.

Ignoring her wisdom, I harnessed the power of the instinct to live. At that moment, fingernails scratching at the bathroom floor tiles, throat hoarse from shrieking in pain—I pushed him out. I wasn't supposed to yet. But I did.

And he landed on the lone white towel the midwife had prepared. To be forever remembered as the boy born on the bathroom floor.

Panting and crying, I started to shake uncontrollably. Without my glasses on, I couldn't see. I was lost in the sea of the strange hormones and emotions that fill a woman right after she gives birth. But even with all of that, I could see he wasn't breathing. I could see he was purple, bruised from his dramatic exit, and blue from lack of air.

Doug was shaking along with me. He called to our baby, shouted at the midwife.

Minutes passed.

Half-naked and bloody, and completely vulnerable, I sat on the cold bathroom floor with Doug. Waiting. Praying. Wondering if our baby would be alive when the next minute ticked on the overhead clock.

That was the feeling.

The terrified feeling of watching a scene unfold with a life hanging in the balance. Being completely helpless and defenseless to powers beyond your control. That was the feeling inside me as I walked through the alley behind the Palindrome. I was as scared as I had ever been. At least that I could consciously remember. Because Sis had spent the night with a killer. And the thought she might be dead was hanging in the back of my throat like bad acid reflux after too much coffee.

Pulling on the metal handle, the big black door squeaked open. I stepped inside, hating my association with the place.

My eyes dashed right to the spot we had last seen Vinny.

The floor was shiny and clean. Not a hint of a stain. All of my coins were gone. Where, I didn't know. Had the cops taken them as evidence? Washed them off and used them?

I shook my head and stepped in further. In front of me was the door to the basement. The moment New Yorker had talked about his shop's basement, a flash from Barbara's memory had surfaced. The Palindrome's basement. Only those familiar with the location ever used the basement. Part utility room, part storage, there had been times waitresses were asked to fetch extra chairs.

With no weapon other than my peppy adrenaline rush, I opened the heavy basement door, wondering if I was already too late. Hating myself for spending so much time getting to this point.

When I didn't hear anything coming from below, I opened the door wider. Its metal echoed in the empty hallway.

"Hiya, cookie," Digger growled from behind me.

Startled and screaming, I ran down the wood stairs with feet slamming against each step. Only, at the bottom I realized I had trapped myself. Even as I found myself in a near-death situation, my pop culture brain couldn't resist a reference. This time, I heard the characters from the movie *Scream* taunting me saying, *victims always run for the stairs instead of out the front door.*

Digger was on his way down after me.

Thud. Thud. Thud.

At the bottom of the stairs, darkness concealed most of the room. A small bit of light peeked through a rectangular window at ground level. "Sis?" I cried. "Are you down here?"

I heard a muffled sound, and ran in the direction it had come from.

"You better have my money!" Digger was down the stairs, mere feet away from me.

I dropped to my knees, my face on Sis's lap. She was wiggling in the chair. The laughter and joy that usually filled her eyes were gone. Her eyes were red and puffy. She was struggling to talk through her gag, and writhing in an attempt to stand, despite the rope around her. Her purse was overturned, the contents strewn around her feet. "I'm so sorry!" I sobbed. "I'm so, so sorry! Oh, God!"

Digger was next to us. He grabbed my hair and pulled me to a standing position. "I know you took my money. Now, tell me where it is, or you're both joining that spic in the ground."

"Okay!" I screamed.

My mind was giving my life a once-over. I lived through this. I went back, and Jules grew up and had a son. The ending was all there. I just had to figure out how the hell I got out of this.

Digger was still yanking me by the hair. He ransacked my little white handbag, and chucked it over beside Sis's when it offered nothing of use. My heart pounded as I watched him slide a huge-ass knife out of his side pocket.

Apparently, he had gotten himself that new knife.

Twisting my arm behind my back, I felt the hot tears pouring down my face, mixing with the sweat that now dampened Barbara's pale skin. "Help!" I screamed. "Somebody help us!"

Digger laughed. Actually laughed. "No one's gonna hear you down here, cookie. Now, tell me where you hid my money, or you lose a finger."

Sobbing, I looked to Sis. Pleading with her to forgive me for ever putting her in this situation. Hating that this was not just some random person's circumstance, but my own. Barbara Jane Miller's. This had been my fate in this lifetime.

Impatient with my nonresponse, Digger pulled my arm tighter behind my back. "I had the other one. Thought you'd come looking for her. But when you never showed, I went and got me the only person you give a shit about sittin' right there." He pointed at Sis with the knife.

"Let her go! She didn't do anything!"

"Did you really think you could steal from me and live?"

In slow motion, I saw him slice the sharp, shiny knife blade through the air. It gleamed before disappearing behind my back. I felt like I could hear the sound of it slicing through space before it connected with my finger.

Sis was screaming into the bandana stuffed into her mouth and hopping in the chair.

I felt the most intense cold I had ever known. Colder than squeezing an ice cube in your fist. Colder than the cruelest winter white wash.

Then came the pain.

Sputtering and gasping, I fell to the ground sans one finger-tip. I grabbed my maimed hand with the good one, and scooted back toward Sis, who was still hollering through her gag.

Digger took a step closer. I cowered into Sis's leg, crying from the pain and panic.

The three of us froze for a hair of a second, as we heard slamming doors and voices above us.

Digger looked up at the ceiling, deciphering the sounds.

I looked up at Sis, down at my bleeding hand. I shoved myself back up onto my knees, and pulled the gag out of Sis's mouth.

"He traded me for Elaine! He let her go!" she cried. "She must have brought the police!"

Digger stooped and pointed the knife at me. "No way she brought the police. I made sure she knew better than ta do somethin' like that."

I was shaking my head at the horror of it all. How badly had he roughed up pregnant Elaine?

He was back in my face. "Now, where the fuck is my money? Tell me now, or I'll kill you dead."

My knee was on something hard. Ripping it out from under me, I was holding the key to my escape—Sis's hair-puffing hand mirror.

There were definite footsteps above us. Digger growled. "Don't test me! It's going to take them longer to find us than it will for me to kill you." His eyes narrowed to evil slits, and he backhanded me.

Face stinging, I fell backward into the darkness. I opened my mouth before I'd fully landed. *"WE'RE IN THE BASEMENT!"* I hollered at the top of my lungs, as loud as I'd ever been. As loud as I'd been pushing that eight-pound baby out of my body.

I cowered away from him, and looked into the mirror.

It was dark, shadowy, shady. I stared in at Barbara's reflection, even as I felt Digger's hand on my shoulder, trying to force my face away from the mirror.

"Miss Rose, are you down there?" a commanding voice bellowed.

I couldn't look away. "I'm sorry, Sis! I love you!" I yelled to the mirror, afraid to peel my eyes away from the swaying over my shoulder, even to check the massive amount of blood drenching the small hand mirror.

My mind raced through all the things I had learned, as I lost my breath.

Time travel was possible through past lives. Elaine Glass was a Zeyer. Gramps had a baby somewhere who was a true seer.

I was being suffocated. From transporting through the mirror or Digger's giant, tightening hand around my neck, I wasn't sure.

Just as I felt the mirror pulled from my grasp, the darkness came back. Feeling the same as it had on my way in. I tried to remain calm as I drifted through the cave-like darkness. I don't think I screamed this time.

And then, though my eyes were still closed, I sensed the darkness being replaced by light.

CHAPTER 12

ROSES ARE RED, IVANOVS ARE BLUE

WITH A GASP, I was back. The steady beep-beep-beep of the machines around me signaled it was real. I was back in 2011. I looked down. I was me! Chubby, boring Liza.

I felt my body, desperate to see if I was still alright.

I had my fingertip!

In all its splendor, it was still there. There was no pain. No sign of a cut. Nothing to indicate anything had happened, other than uncontrollable shaking. Trauma or shock? Real or imagined?

Taking an enormous breath, I was hit with a vague recollection of someone saying, "I'll be right back." Like I had been here while I was also there.

Looking over, I saw a pad of sketch paper and a graphite pencil. Doug.

Doug was always doodling. Oh, my stupid, nonviolent, namby-pamby Doug!

Desperate to collect all the pieces as my senses came back to life, I snatched the pencil and started writing as fast as my cramping, limp hand would go. I couldn't let Valentina's warning go unheeded. I had to empty everything from my short-term memory. As quickly as possible. I wouldn't lose these memories.

Elaine Glass is a Zeyer, a true seer of the mirror.

Sis Rose is the best woman I've ever known.

Forcing my tired, locked muscles to work was painful, but I wrote faster and faster until I flipped to the next page. And then, the next, and the next until I had depleted my memory of all of its contents. Wondering, as I wrote, if it was the draft I used to tell Gianluca my story.

As I was scribbling the final note, the hospital room door opened in a flurry. "There, there, I thought I saw your vitals jumping," a nurse said, rushing to the machines at my side.

She looked down at my notepad, and I covered it in a rush, and glared at her for trying to see.

"Easy. I'm a friend," she said to my scowl. "Do you know where you are?"

I nodded, wanting nothing more than for her to leave. With tears stinging my eyes as my emotions came into focus, I cried, "I need to see my children! Where are they?"

She was already looking on an iPad of sorts. Oh, sweet technology! She looked up. "I see your emergency contact here. I'll have the desk make the call right now." She continued looking at monitors and numbers. "The doctor will want to come in and check on you. Your EEG readings for brain activity have been unlike anything we've seen."

"I'm fine. Just please go find my children. They're most likely with my ex-husband. His name is Doug Anderson. He lives on..."

I was cut off by my room's door opening. "Liza!" Doug called.

"Doug!" Relief hit me like a hammer to the face. The moment I saw his blue eyes, I started to sob. This was real. I was back.

I cried because the terror in the Palindrome basement was over. Cried because I had left Sis there alone. Cried because I was a coward in both of the lives I knew about.

He wrapped his arms around me. I think I heard him choking back tears as well. I pulled back to look at him. "I need your phone."

"What? Why?"

"Please!" I demanded.

He pulled the blessed hunk of plastic out of his pocket. Tapping the screen, I typed into the search bar: *Sis Rose Hollywood CA*. In an instant, it was there.

LA Times, October 1947. Sis Rose testifies against double murder suspect.

"What are you looking at?"

I let out a breath. A long, thankful breath. Sis had lived. Thank God above, she had lived.

Switching gears, I pushed Doug's phone back to him. "Where are they? I need to see them."

"Liza, it's ten o'clock at night. They're at my mom's, sleeping. They're fine. I promise." He hugged me again. "God, we missed you."

Then I knew he was crying.

Our embrace meant so much. His concern meant so much. When our hug didn't end, he sat on the bed, crushing the sketchpad. "Sorry, I didn't think I left this on the..." His eyes skimmed the page.

I watched him as he read, so curious what his expression would be. His eyes went over each word with greed, growing furrowed. "What...?"

I looked at the nurse. She was watching our exchange. "Later," I told him, eyes still on the nurse.

"Where are my glasses?" I asked, frustrated with the filmy, blurry look of everyone.

"Ah," Doug said, jumping up to dig in a duffle bag, "I have them right here. And have, every day, so they would be ready for you when you woke up."

Replacing them on my face, I looked at him with sincere intent. "You've been here every day?"

He looked at the nurse. She was becoming quite the obstacle to our private moments. "More or less." He put his arm around my shoulders, sitting next to me on the hard hospital bed again. "I'm so relieved, Liza. You have no idea."

"No, *you* have no idea." I took in a deep breath. He looked older. More tired.

The nurse interjected to ask various questions about any pains, allergies, history of heart attacks and the rest. Checked my vitals. Rattled off the history of comas, and all that would happen to me medically moving forward. Told us the doctor would be in soon. And just when I was thinking she was in my room for the night, she left.

"How are they, Doug? Have they forgotten me?"

He scoffed. "Forgotten you? How could they?"

Tears stung my eyes, threatening to fall once more. "They're so little. I've been gone so long. How can you know if Jakey doesn't remember me anymore?"

"It hasn't been that long. One month isn't that long."

"Twenty two days," I corrected.

"How did you know...?"

I shook my head.

He went back to his thought. "Well, I'm sure he would always know his mother. Somewhere deep inside, he would just know."

I let out a grunt at his assumption, knowing first-hand just how much time you could spend with a person without knowing you were related. But I had more pressing questions. "How much have they grown? What are they up to?"

His smile was genuine. As genuine as I had seen in years. "Jules spelled her name."

"She did?" I sat up straighter.

"And Jakey, the little weirdo, has taken to licking the sliding glass door. Can't get him to stop!"

Smiling felt good. To revel in the small delights. To get back to silly inside jokes, instead of stalkers and time travelers. Micro over macro.

His face turned. He took my hand in his. "This has been so...bizarre. I feel like I finally understand all that crap—*stuff*—you talked about at our sessions, about how tough it is to be home with them, every day, alone."

I could not believe my ears. Two months of thera-py—painstaking to even get to—hadn't ever cracked this nut.

"So, thank you," he continued. "Thank you for being a good mom. And taking care of all the little things I didn't even know existed. Because running out of wipes and diapers sucks! And it never happened when you were around." He shook his head.

Tears stung my eyes again. I cleared my throat and removed my hand. "So how did Jules handle seeing me here?" I looked around my sterile environment.

He turned away. When he swung back around, his eyes were red. "It hasn't been easy for her. Especially that first day."

"Oh, God! Yes, I was in Valentina's room!"

"Yes. And that disturbing old woman didn't even call anyone. We don't know how long you were laying there before the nurse came in and found you."

"What happened to the locket?" I blurted.

He made a face. "She said you would ask that. Why? She wouldn't tell me."

"I need to know where it is."

"It's at home," he said. "She insisted I take it because it was yours."

I heard the beeping of my machine pick up pace. "Where at home? Not where the kids can get to it—Oh! You didn't open it, did you?"

"Shh," he coaxed, rubbing my shoulder. His eyes were on the machine next to the bed. "Calm down, please. I left it on my dresser. The kids can't reach it. And I'm not sure why it matters, but I did open it. It's just a mirror."

My head was shaking no. No, no, no. "It most certainly is *not* just a mirror, Doug. But I'm insanely glad you think it is."

He tucked loose hair behind my ear.

"I need to talk to her right away," I said.

"Who?" he asked, looking over my face with a mixture of pity and relief.

"Valentina."

He shook his head. "Let's not talk about her right now. Right now, let's talk about you. How do you feel? How are you? Can you feel everything?"

I shrugged, looking myself over. Not as excited to be back in my almost thirty-five-year-old body as I had hoped. Maybe I just needed a pep pill.

I almost laughed at my own joke.

"What?" he asked. "What could have possibly made you smile like that?"

I shook my head. "You should go get the kids. Please. Please just let me hold them."

Now he shook his head at me. "Are you crazy? You know what they're like in the middle of the night. No matter how much they've missed you, you can't possibly want your first moment with them to be a whining, slobbering mess all over you because they're tired."

"It doesn't matter how they are. It just matters that they are here with me."

He sighed, standing and rubbing his palms on his hips—something he did when anxious. "If you're really sure. Are you sure? I mean, a few more minutes of peace might be just what you need?"

"No, Doug. My babies are just what I need."

"Okay…" he conceded, bending to grab his wallet out of the duffel bag. With jingling keys, he bent to kiss my forehead.

"Leave me your phone, will you?"

"What?" he asked. "Why?"

"Please. I just want to read some of the things I missed out on while I was gone."

He looked down on his prized possession. "I guess." He handed it over. "Welcome back, Liza. Just wasn't the same without you."

I looked next to the bed. "Doug," I called. "Who left these roses?"

"Oh, yeah." He shrugged his head at the vase and envelope. "Gramps brought those by today. He hadn't been in to visit you one time since you got here, weird old man."

I reached over to the envelope under the roses.

"I'll be back with the little monsters as soon as I can."

Doug left me alone with the beeping monitors. As I read the first sentence of the letter, the beeping sped up. Strange to have an audible indication of fear of the unknown.

> Liza,
> Valentina said to give this letter to you. I refrained from read-
> ing it, but I hope you'll decide to share it with me since it may
> be the last thing she wrote before she passed away.
> Gramps

Frowning from the sad but somehow expected news of Valentina's passing, I opened the next envelope. It was small. Notecard size. It was aged around the edges and crumpled. The envelope was no longer sealed. It had the current date written on the envelope.

Pulling the frail paper from the small envelope, once again the beeping on the machine next to me picked up pace. This was not a note from Valentina.

> Today you left. Barbara died, just as you guessed. Elaine re-
> ally had gone for help, and came back with Officer Wright
> and other members of the LAPD. Digger was found guilty of
> both the bartender's murder as well as Barbara Miller's. Sis
> was devastated at the loss of Barbara. She held a beautiful
> funeral service. Doc was there acting peculiar, and insisting
> he help gather Barbara's things right after the service. Elaine
> attended, safe and healthy. Girls from the house spoke, but
> none as beautiful as the words Sis said. She called you her
> soulmate. If your hunch was correct, and you could never
> find Sis or Elaine because they changed their names after
> marriage, I have the name you asked me to find. The trumpet

*player's last name is Lenicci. But if you still can't find Sis,
look for Elaine again. I have a hunch perhaps you should try
searching for Elaine Wright.*

Eternally with you,
-G

My shaky hands let the note drop. I looked up to see Gramps
peeking in the doorway. "So it *was* for you," he said as our
eyes met.

I outstretched my arms to him, "Gramps! How much do you
know? I'm dying for a confidant!"

He waltzed over to my side with the usual hitch in his step.
He dropped a kiss on my forehead. Pulling the chair as close as
he could get it, he sat. "I know you weren't just in a coma, Liza."

I lifted my hand. "How did you get this note?"

He looked at the faded paper. "Valentina."

My brow furrowed. "But how could she have gotten it?"

"It was given to her by the same woman who gave her the
locket." He reached into his pocket and pulled out a faded envelope. Written on it was my everything—my name, my location,
today's date. Gramps spoke in a solemn tone, "Valentina did a
lot of searching for you, young lady."

I reached out and touched his hand. "Did you ever…look
into the locket?"

"I did." He nodded. "I saw nothing but an old man."

"I met you, Gramps," I said to his defeated expression. "I
actually met you when you were still Sonny and working in Hollywood!"

A smile crossed his face. "What a wonder…"

The nurse came in to take my vitals again, this time with
a doctor.

Gramps scooted away from the bed. "We have much to discuss." He stood. "I'll visit again tomorrow. I'd love to hear more
about that dream you had." He winked.

I allowed myself a smile.

If only I'd seen him wink. Or eat a sandwich. Then I would have known Sonny was Gramps. Would have known right away.

THE PALM TREES held hands over the road as we drove under their brief shade, escaping the reflecting gleam of the California sun off of the traffic surrounding us. It had been almost two months since I had lived in 1947. Two months since I laid eyes on Elaine. Over sixty years since she had seen me as Barbara.

"Mom! Jakey keeps touching me," Jules whined from her car seat in the back of the rented van.

"He can't even reach you!" I argued from behind the wheel.

"This is it," Gramps said from the passenger seat. "Turn here, Liza."

A nervous excitement crept over me as the van thumped over a speed bump, and we entered the parking lot of an assisted living building.

"Are you going to tell her about the mirror?" Gramps asked, knowing all too well what he was asking.

"I haven't decided yet."

"Is this it, Mom? Are we getting out?" Jules asked, tearing at her three-point harness buckle.

"This is really it!" I sang.

Gramps opened his door before I had the van in park. He was as eager as I was. Traveling all the way from Minnesota with two young kids, he deserved this moment as much as I did.

By the time I wrangled Jakey free from his backward-facing seat, Jules and Gramps were already at the front of the building, ready to go in.

I tossed Jakey onto my hip, yanked down the back of his shirt and moved forward. Forward went my feet. Forward went my mind.

Entering the front, we were met by a friendly face seated behind the front desk.

"We're here to visit Elaine Wright," Gramps announced, slapping his palm on the desk. His grin pulled his saggy lips from one side of his face to the other. "She is expecting us."

Jules had her arm around his pale, knobby leg—bare, since he insisted on wearing Bermuda shorts.

"Sure," the lady replied. "Mrs. Wright is in room sixteen. Right down the hall."

"We're going to meet Grandma Elaine," I said, more for myself than for Jules.

She dashed down the hall, sending her tutu flouncing in her self-propelled breeze. Gramps kept up with her somehow. Powered by the optimism that came from understanding a sixty-year-old secret, I supposed.

He knocked on the door.

"Come in," Elaine's warm voice answered.

"Lainey!" Gramps announced. "It's me—Sonny!"

"Sonny!" She crooned. "I cannot believe it's you." Her eyes sparkled.

"And I brought our family, just like I said I would," he explained, pointing to me and my gaggle.

Elaine's smile was just the same. At age 88, her charming glow was still there. She was still present. Still Elaine. I longed to hug her. To tell her who I was. To apologize.

But Gramps had his own agenda. "Like I said on the phone, we traveled all this way to have a serious conversation. I just can't believe you were going to make me take this terrible unknown with me to the grave!"

She bowed her head.

"Why didn't you tell me you fell pregnant?" He dropped to the bed next to her wheelchair, getting right to the point. "Why did you just leave her at my doorstep, with only a scribbled birth certificate and a Techinot?"

After confronting Gramps with my newfound information about Elaine, he had broken down and showed me the same items that had sent my mother into a seventeen-year silence. Her birth certificate was from California, not Minnesota, with the mother's name blacked out. And a handwritten prayer for new mothers in Hebrew, which Gramps explained was a Techinot. A special prayer that had been the mind-changing reason he hadn't taken my infant mother straight to the orphanage, as he had first wanted.

Tears glimmered in Elaine's eyes. "It still haunts me. It was the decision any girl would have had to make back then. It's not like it is now." She shook her head.

"Where did you have the baby?" I jumped in, letting Jakey squiggle out of my arms to toddle around the small bedroom.

She swallowed. "At a friend's home with her help. I had planned to go to a maternity home and leave her in their care, but…"

"But you thought it would be better to leave her with me? When I didn't even know you were in the family way?" Gramps accused, his voice bitter and hurt. "It didn't leave me in a much better place than you. I was lucky to marry Loretta on accounta she was the kind of girl willing to raise another woman's baby. And then when Suzy found out! She hasn't spoken to me in seventeen years, Elaine!"

"You named her Suzy?" Elaine asked.

"Suzanne," Gramps muttered.

Now it was me who bowed my head. "I tried to talk her into coming with us to California. She wouldn't."

Elaine's face saddened.

"But maybe once we head home and tell her all about you, she'll come around."

"I thought it might have been you," Gramps said, staring out the window. "The Techinot and all. But when I looked for you, you were gone. Gone to New York. And I never found you again."

"Funny thing," Elaine stated, sadness seeping through her words. "I only stayed there the one winter. Chuck and I were pen pals until I came back to California for him." She sniffed.

"And he might have been the kind of man to raise her—Suzy. But it was too late for all of that."

Jules sensed the tension and stuck her face an inch from mine. "Mama, watch how big my twirl is!" She spun, sending her purple tutu unfolding into a circle. She tipped and laughed at herself.

"That's great, sweetie." I smiled, petting her shiny hair and leaning back into the adult conversation.

"Thank you." Elaine's tone was humble. She was looking right at Gramps. "For raising her. For continuing a family."

Gramps cleared his throat and looked away.

I looked away as well, fascinated at the sum of Elaine's life around me. The wedding photo of her and Officer Wright. Photos of children. Grandchildren. An entire branch of the family who didn't know they, too, were seers. "You had other children?" I asked, pointing to the photos.

She nodded and looked down at Jakey tugging on her skirt. "Hello," she said to his little face. "I'm your great-grandmother."

"Mom, what's this?" Jules lifted a music box from Elaine's dresser.

"Don't break that, honey!" I squealed, diving in to take it from her hands.

"It's okay," Elaine cooed, wheeling herself closer. When the wheelchair stuck a little, I pushed her free. "This was from my knight in shining armor. My husband, Chuck."

"Oooh," Jules gasped.

"He saved me in my darkest hour." Elaine got a far-off look. She lifted a photo from the back of her row of memories. "The space of time when my best friend was too busy grieving to be there for me while I gave away my baby." She wheeled back over to Gramps and handed him the photo.

Tears prickled my eyes as I prepared to ask her the most pressing question on my mind. "Gramps told me all about Sis. We searched for her as well. Finding you was a miracle, but finding her too would just be..." I trailed off because Elaine's face was the answer to my question.

"I'm afraid you've missed her."

My bottom lip quivered. The tears stinging my eyes filled in, blurring my sight. I felt sickened that the last time I ever saw her was in a dank basement. "Can you please tell me how? When?"

"Not that long ago. Four years back, maybe? We kept in touch until the end." Elaine took the photo from Gramps, and handed it to me. "She had quite the happy life."

"Oh my God!" I cried. In the frame sat the picture from the Palindrome. There we were—Sis, Elaine and Babs—in our tulle and carnations.

"What is it, my dear?" Elaine asked.

I was overcome. Bending, I hugged her. Hugged her bony, frail frame. I didn't want to let her go, but felt as though I might have been smothering her. Pulling back, I wiped away a tear. "Well, bless your heart." She was staring at me. Then she looked back to the black and white photograph. "That there is Babs. She was killed right in front of Sis. Took Sis a long, long time to get right again."

The guilt and pain stung my heart, and my sinuses. "I read about Sis testifying at the trial. That was the only article I could ever find under the name Sis Rose."

Elaine nodded. "She married not long after Barbara's funeral. Why, I think I still have Sis's funeral program here." She wheeled over to her dresser.

"Mom, Jakey's acting funny," Jules said, snapping me out of my moment.

I turned in time to see my little man squat and scrunch his face. I rushed to him, just as vomit heaved from his small body.

"The little tyke must have gotten car sick. I told you not to slam on the brakes so hard," Gramps scolded me.

I bent down to him. "It's okay, honey. It's just a little–"

"Serendipity," Elaine and I said in unison.

She gave me a bewildered smile. "Sis was the only person I ever knew to call it that." She went back to the drawer.

"I'll take him to the bathroom and wipe him up," Gramps offered. I kissed the top of Jakey's head as Gramps pulled him by the hand.

"Oh, Mama!" Jules said. "Isn't this *so* beautiful?" She held up a double-row pearl necklace, causing her to squeal in delight.

"Here it is," Elaine sang in triumph.

She handed me the folded paper. I glanced over the prayer, program, schedule. But when I read the last page, I was taken aback. On the back were the words to *Have I Not Commanded You*, the silly church song Jules had been singing for the past three months.

"Is something wrong?" Elaine asked, tilting her head to read my expression.

I swallowed and looked over to my daughter. She was humming, and trying to click the pearl necklace around her neck. "Did Sis have any connection to this song?" I asked Elaine without removing my eyes from Jules.

Elaine peeked at the back of the program. "Oh, yes! Asked for that song specifically. Very special to her."

I crouched to be face-to-face with my happy three-year-old. My pleasant girl with the easy, natural laugh. Taking both of her hands in mine, I looked deep into her eyes. Searching.

"Will you please put this pretty, pretty necklace on for me, Mama?" she asked with a smile.

"Sure, honey." Staring into her twinkling blue eyes, I clicked the pearls behind her neck.

"Doesn't she look lovely?" Elaine cooed, clasping her hands together. "Perhaps it's time for those to belong to a new beautiful lady." She touched the necklace with her knobby finger. "They used to belong to Sissy Rose."

Jules laughed in glee, twirling again.

"I think they still do," I whispered.

EPILOGUE

"WELCOME TO STARBUCKS," the young barista greeted. "Would you like to try our limited-edition Unicorn Frappuccino, new as of April 2017? It's very popular."

I shook my head, staring up at the menu. "I'll just take a large coffee."

"Dark or light roast? Grande or Venti?" she asked, poised at the cash register.

My eyes glued to the door behind us, I mumbled out inconsequential answers and paid. Shuffling down to the waiting area, I watched out the window as a group of children marched down the street with a caretaker. The teacher led them in a line down Madison's East Main Street, headed straight for the Wisconsin Capitol Building. They looked to be around Jules age, somewhere around fourth grade. From the Starbucks, I had an amazing view of the capitol.

As my Grande light roast appeared at the counter, I snagged it and situated myself at a high top table next to the window. The coffeehouse was busy for a Monday afternoon, but then, Madison was a college town, and Spring meant finals were around the corner.

I saw a woman with an anxious look on her face heading for the door. She was wearing flowing pants and a breezy, sleeveless blouse.

I held a breath as she entered. Our eyes met. I tilted my head to see if she, too, was searching for a stranger.

The woman stepped toward me. "Liza?" she asked, unsure.

"Yes. Amalia?"

She let out a breath. "Azalea, but yes." With a nod, she sat at the empty seat of the high top. "That unique name is brought to you by Woodstock," she explained, flopping an oversized purse on the stool next to her. "It gets better. My middle name is Zappa." She grinned. "But anyway, I really can't thank you enough for driving all this way to meet with me in person."

"Well, Azalea, I've never received a call like yours," I replied. Leaning in, I added, "I'm just dying to know the rest of the story. Please." I outstretched a hand, gesturing for her to talk.

After a quick glance around the room, she rested her arms on the table and took a breath. Her curly hair fell around her slender, forty-something face. "Well, this all started with the passing of my mother," she started. "As I said in my initial email, when we were going through her will, we came across a peculiar message."

"With my name on it," I finished, knowing this portion of the story. "But what was it? And why did it have my name on it?"

She swallowed. "It's paperwork that was included as a caveat of an inheritance my mother received in 1959 from a man named Bernard Gillinghardt."

Doc? But how? My brow furrowed. "What was the inheritance? Can I ask?"

Her head started shaking. "I'm not entirely sure. That was before I was born. But the letter from the attorney, and the pages of information from Mr. Gillinghardt, were all in a safe in my mother's basement. And when I read what it said..."

I adjusted on my wooden stool. "Please. What did it say?"

She looked down. "You'll think I'm crazy."

I reached across the table. "I assure you, I will not."

"Well," she started, making eye contact. "It seems to be research on transporting back in time through the unconscious."

A grin stretched across the span of my face without my consent. Doc had continued his research. He had followed through—even without my details. "What year did you say the inheritance arrived?"

"1959," she replied.

Old Doc hadn't made it much past age 50. I sighed. "So, at the risk of *me* sounding crazy, that makes perfect sense to me."

Azalea smiled. "Well that's a relief." Her finger started tapping on the shiny table. Then she reached into her floppy bag and pulled out a manila envelope. "I guess this belongs to you then, Liza Anderson of 2011."

"What?"

She handed over the envelope. "That's how it's addressed."

I ran my fingers across the penned letters. "So it is." I looked up at her thin face. With a flip, the folder was open. And inside, what treasures! A copy of the translation, rejected scientific articles, even notes and journal entries about Barbara Miller's hypnotherapy. I snapped back to Azalea. "What was your mother's name?"

"Cecilia Miller. Grew up over in Milwaukee."

With bugged eyes, I dared to ask. "Was she related to Barbara Jane Miller?" I clenched my teeth waiting for her to reply.

Azalea shoved herself back a bit. "Yes. That was her older sister's name, but she died when Mom was only six or so. How could you possibly have known that?"

I took a sip of my coffee. Slow and deliberate, both marveling at the cunning persistence of ol' red face as well as deciding whether or not to include Miss Woodstock in my elite circle or not. "Well, Azalea Zappa, how would you like to hear a story about a locket?"

ABOUT THE AUTHOR

Gina Dewink was born and raised in Minnesota's heartland. Since 2001, her career has been in nonprofit communications. In addition to her communications career, Gina Dewink is a contributing writer for mediums such as *Thrive Global*, *The Line Media*, *507 Magazine* and *Rochester Women Magazine*. She lives in Minnesota with her husband and two children. *Time in My Pocket* is her first novel.

REVIEWS ARE PRICELESS

If you enjoyed *Time in My Pocket*, please consider leaving a review on Amazon.

Learn more at ginadewink.com or follow Gina on Twitter and Facebook.

Time in My Pocket is also available in ebook and audiobook.

www.ingramcontent.com/pod-product-compliance
Lightning Source LLC
Chambersburg PA
CBHW021010120726
47905CB00009B/2949